SECRETS OF THE BRIDGES

GARRY NADLER

PublishAmerica
Baltimore

© 2011 by Garry Nadler.
All rights reserved. No part of this book may be reproduced, stored in a retrieval system or transmitted in any form or by any means without the prior written permission of the publishers, except by a reviewer who may quote brief passages in a review to be printed in a newspaper, magazine or journal.

First printing

All characters in this book are fictitious, and any resemblance to real persons, living or dead, is coincidental.

PublishAmerica has allowed this work to remain exactly as the author intended, verbatim, without editorial input.

Photo used in cover art provided by Miranda Prather.

Softcover 9781462643844
PUBLISHED BY PUBLISHAMERICA, LLLP
www.publishamerica.com
Baltimore

Printed in the United States of America

Dedication

To my loving family who supported me throughout my life, instilled in me the importance of love and family, taught me lifelong lessons about right and wrong, honesty and integrity, and encouraged me to always challenge myself, work hard, do my best, and to follow my dreams.

Acknowledgements

I want to recognize and thank my family and a few good friends for all their support and encouragement, and for the help they provided by editing manuscripts and offering suggestions about the storyline. I acknowledge and thank the many readers of my first book, **Secret Wars**, who told me how much they enjoyed my first book, and repeatedly asked about my next book and when it would be available to read.

Above all, I recognize and honor all the men and women who dedicate themselves to keeping all of us safe and protect the American way of life, namely: those in law enforcement who put their lives on the line every time they go on duty, the US Military service men and women who fight and die for the freedoms we enjoy, and the prosecutors, judges, and defense lawyers who use the law to put criminals behind bars.

Chapter One

Saturday, Last Week in September
Sunshine Skyway Bridge Rest Area
South St. Petersburg, FL
10:39 p.m.

Two teenagers were doing what lots of teenage lovebirds do in the back seat of a car. The light chop of southern Tampa Bay lapped against the pilings of the old Sunshine Skyway Bridge when the hormone driven activity was unexpectedly and abruptly interrupted. Randy's girlfriend, Randi bolted upright at the banging sound on the side window. Then Randi screamed, drowning out the, "Help me. Help me," cries from outside the car.

Randy turned to look. Two small dark handprints could be seen on the side window, and something dark was slowly dribbling down from each. Just as suddenly, they heard a dull thud and the form in the window disappeared. Randy gingerly opened the rear door.

The body of a young girl was crumpled on the ground. The light was poor, but they could both make out some dark stains splotched haphazardly on parts of the girl's body. The only sound was from the endless waves sloshing underneath the pier and Randi's labored breathing.

Randi was visibly shaken and scared. Randy just gawked and couldn't think clearly as he stared at the seemingly lifeless body on the ground. After a few moments Randi blurted, "Randy, we've got to help her. Do something. Call the police."

"Yeah. Right," Randy agreed as he jammed his hand into his pant pocket to fish out his cell phone.

"Hello, you've reached the 911 operator. What is your emergency?" was the immediate response from the pleasant and calm female voice on the other end.

"There's a young girl here who's been hurt." Panic was evident in the teenage male voice making the call.

"Where are you? Can I get your name, please?" The GPS locator in the cell phone and the Caller ID system at the 911 Center confirmed what Randy told the operator. All 911 operators get prank calls, so she was trained to verify that calls were real. A caller giving a name and location that corresponds to what the 911 system told her was a good indication that it was.

"How badly is she hurt?"

"There's some blood and she's lying motionless on the ground." Randy spoke rapidly.

"Did you hurt the girl?"

"No. No, of course not." The 911 operator wasn't completely convinced.

Randy provided additional information to the 911 operator as requested. The sound of sirens could be heard in the distance as Randy told her about the position of the girl's body. Within a few moments the familiar red and blue flashing emergency lights of an emergency vehicle were visible racing towards them.

◻ ◻ ◻

Earlier, Randy Swanson had smoothly guided his late model Ford Taurus to the rest-stop on the Pinellas County side of the Sunshine Skyway. The dark colored SUV coming towards them in the long exit lane was the only vehicle Randy could see in the parking area. Randy's pretty passenger was Randi Kingston, his girlfriend. The 16 year-old teens were juniors in high school, but had known each other since the 4th grade. Over the years they laughed and joked about the similarity of their names, but were just casual friends. That changed about six months ago when each became more interested in the other as boyfriend and girlfriend. They started dating regularly two months ago.

ASAP." He stood and holstered his gun. The kids were not dangerous, and the 911 call was not a hoax as many had been these past few months. Vicki breathed easier, rushed around the Taurus, and turned her attention away from the teens.

Bright flashlights illuminated a small oasis surrounding the girl's body. After a quick glance, Vicki checked for a pulse in the girl's neck. "She's alive. Get that blanket out of the trunk." Randi and Randy craned their necks to watch, but stayed put on the driver's side—eyes wide as saucers.

The EMS driver, the senior Emergency Medical Technician, flipped off the lights and siren a few hundred yards away once they saw the flashing lights of the FHP cruiser. Officer Freemont began motioning frantically. Kelly Tinsley, the driver, skidded to a stop behind the cruiser, jumped out, and rushed around her vehicle snatching up equipment. Monte Greene joined the controlled chaos by grabbing the items his training taught him were necessary as tools of the paramedic trade. Monte reached the limp body first, now carefully covered by a tan blanket. He reached under the blanket to check the girl's pulse as Kelly opened bulky metal cases and began arranging her medical equipment. There were hushed whispers between the paramedics, then into a cell phone, "Pulse strong. Slow, but shallow breathing. No conscious response. Okay Doc, we'll transport immediately. Got it."

Monte rushed back to the EMS vehicle and returned with a portable gurney. Kelly had started an IV drip, and was holding the fluid-filled plastic bag at arm's length above the girl's chest. The injured girl was carefully lifted onto the gurney. Kelly attached the bag to a rod inserted vertically near where the girl's head was resting. Temporary first-aid bandages were carefully wrapped around what looked like cuts on her left arm and hip. The blanket was smoothed and pulled up gingerly under the girl's chin. The gurney was quickly wheeled towards the rear of the EMS vehicle and efficiently loaded into the back. Vicki, a veteran of dozens of crashes, leaped into action by closing the metal cases, snatched both up, and hurried over to the emergency vehicle. Kelly quickly took the cases, stowed each in its place, and thanked Vicki with a nod and a wave. The engine fired up with a roar, siren and emergency lights were switched on, and the EMS truck rushed up the long exit ramp and was quickly out of sight.

Vicki turned to the teens, "Okay, now let's get some information from both of you."

Randi was still shaken and scared, and needed to sit down. Vicki looked around and spotted a bench. "Over there," she pointed.

All four walked the 50 or so feet together. Randi and Randy held hands as they settled onto the bench which was conveniently located a few feet from an overhead pier light. The officers remained standing. The teens held hands and sat rigidly on the bench. Randy was clearly trying to protect and comfort his girlfriend.

Vicki had her clipboard out and started filling out the incident report with such items as location, date, and time. No one spoke as they waited for Vicki to start the questioning.

Vicki checked the teen's driver's license information, and neatly wrote down each of the teen's name, address, phone number, and other personal information. Randy kept protesting that they knew nothing about the girl, or what had happened to her. Officer Vicki Freemont nodded knowingly, but just kept plodding along with seemingly unnecessary details.

It was past 11:30 p.m. and Randy was worried, "Uh, Officer. Can we call our parents so they won't worry that we're late getting home? Randi's curfew is midnight."

"You're sure you don't know what happened here?"

"No, ma'am. We swear we don't," as they looked at each other then back to the officers.

"Sure, make your calls. If you want I'll speak to your parents."

"Thanks." Randy flipped open his phone and punched in numbers.

By midnight the report was completed and the teens were released to go home, but not without a stern lecture from Trooper Freemont about the dangers of being alone in places they shouldn't be. Randy nodded obediently. Randi wiped tears from her cheeks.

The troopers watched the teens drive slowly up the ramp and out of sight. "Let's get back on patrol," sighed Vicki as she walked to the cruiser. Her partner followed.

Back in the cruiser they reported in over the radio, "Cruiser 1423 preparing to leave our last reported location. We'll be heading north on I-275 from the north end of the Skyway. Over."

"Roger, Cruiser 1423."

"I'll file the written report when our shift's over," said Vicki while turning the key.

"Shouldn't St. Pete Police follow up?" her partner asked.

"Probably. They have joint jurisdiction, and it should be easier for them to find out who the poor girl is and what happened. We'll send a copy of the report over to them after we brief the Captain and get his approval."

CHAPTER TWO

Monday, First Week in October
Police Department
St. Petersburg, FL
8:07 a.m.

Lucas Brasch, his friends call him Luke, sauntered into the detective's area for the first time in over three months. The last time he was on the job it nearly cost him his life.

Prior to this job, Luke had spent almost twelve years with the military serving honorably and with distinction as a criminal investigator. Such a career isn't necessarily unusual for a Jewish kid from St. Petersburg, FL. Service to God and country is a common theme in Judaism. Many young Jewish men and women go into the Peace Corp, enter politics, or simply take a variety of local, state, or federal government jobs. A few go into the voluntary ranks of the US military, as did Luke. Luke's personal sense of right and wrong, his need to reach out and help others, and the way he leads his everyday life is driven by the values stressed during his childhood.

After many personally fulfilling years in the military, serving mostly in Europe and the Middle East, Luke grew a little restless and very homesick. Luke had impressive credentials as a military investigator. He received some college level education from the military when he studied for the advanced training required of investigative officers, but hadn't earned a four year college degree. When Luke left the military he needed only another 36 credit-hours for his BA in Law Enforcement. Study and education is very important to Luke, so when he returned home for good it made sense to find work as a civilian cop, and continue pursuing his degree. His hard work and dedication to his education will finally pay off in May when he joins his classmates at the graduation ceremony.

The St. Petersburg police department snapped Luke up immediately, and assigned him to the detective squad after several months of general on-the-job orientation. He had to familiarize himself with police operations before earning his detective badge.

In mid July of this year, Luke was assigned to a five member team investigating a string of murders and other vicious crimes connected to a violent gang with most members living in a two square mile area of south St. Petersburg. Several gang members had been spotted in a rundown shack located in a largely deserted neighborhood. The five member team surrounded the shack and closed in for the arrest. Five police officers arresting two street thugs were usually favorable odds for the good guys. But, not this time. The nastiness and firepower of the gang was badly underestimated. Without warning, rapid bursts from assault weapons slammed into the approaching officers. SWAT was immediately called for additional backup but it was too late. Three of the team members were hit before the SWAT team arrived to retake control of the situation.

One detective was hit squarely in the chest. His Kevlar vest did its job, but the impact knocked him backwards. He smashed his head onto the car fender, and was rendered momentarily unconscious. The detective's headache subsided in two days, but the discomfort from the bruises to his ribs remained for a week. He was cleared for duty the following Monday. Another officer was shot in the arm. Luckily it passed clear through completely missing bone. A quick trip to the Emergency Room and a few stitches fixed him up good as new. He was released from the hospital the next day and back at work in two weeks.

Luke received the most serious injury. His Kevlar vest took one round in the lower right section causing him to flinch, bend over slightly, and stumble backwards. The second shot slammed into him a split second later catching him in the upper left part of his already compromised vest. The second bullet crashed through the vest with enough energy to penetrate his chest and cause serious damage.

Emergency surgery removed the bullet. It was only two inches from his heart. It also missed his lung. Luke was lucky. Only two ribs were cracked from the impacts to his vest. Another rib sustained a hairline fracture from the force of the impacts. Unfortunately, one cracked rib did smash into his heart. It was touch and go for about a week.

The doctors, family, and friends were all relieved when Luke started to recover. Over the next three weeks, the medical team monitored his progress, evaluated his mental abilities, tested his physical strength and coordination, searched for any damage to his heart, and conducted other medical tests. Last week he was cleared by the medical team to return to work, but only on a limited basis.

His chief doctor signed the release. It read,

"Detective Lucas Brasch is medically released for restricted duty with the St. Petersburg Police Department on a limited basis. Detective Brasch's work-load should be limited to mostly inside office and desk work, with minimal, non-physical field work. A follow-up evaluation of Detective Brasch's ability to resume unrestricted work is scheduled for late December of this year."

Several detectives paused from whatever they were doing and went over to welcome Luke back. There were smiles and handshakes all around. Each of these detectives was his friend and a visitor at the hospital and at his home during Luke's long recovery. It's a big deal though, when a previously injured officer returns to work. This same ritual occurred when the other two detectives had returned to work months earlier.

After about ten minutes of pleasantries and chit-chat, a fellow detective, Rocky Kowalski, asked, "Have you checked in with Loo yet?" **Loo** was the moniker used for Lieutenant Nick Thompson, the leader of this team of detectives.

"Heading there right now."

"It's really good to have you back, Luke," repeated Rocky as he grabbed and gently shook his friend's shoulder. Luke thanked him again and went down the hall to his Lieutenant's office. Luke stuck his head around the open doorway as he rapped twice on the door jam. Loo looked up from the notes he was taking with one hand while holding a phone to his ear with the other. A quick motion to Luke with his pen indicated that he should come in. Loo returned his attention to the phone and his note-taking. A few moments later Loo motioned to a chair opposite his cluttered desk. Luke complied and waited patiently with his hands resting loosely on the arms of the chair.

Luke wore a perfectly fitting navy sport coat, light blue dress shirt, colorful coordinated tie, and khaki slacks. Brown loafers on his feet. All very preppy, as was Luke's style. Luke hated "casual dress" and didn't own a single pair of jeans. Luke knew that almost everyone wore jeans at some time. But, for some unspoken, probably unrealistic, reason he felt that jeans were for cowboys and folks that didn't much care how they looked. No shorts either, at least not until he was eighty years old, living in a nursing home, and wearing socks with sandals. Some friends thought he was obsessed with his clothes. Luke paid no attention. He liked the way he looked and dressed.

Luke's Lieutenant made more of a splash with his appearance. Today he wore a purple shirt with a stark white tie, and black pants. A gaudy pink sport coat was draped around the back of his chair. His black shoes sported their usual shine. His bushy mustache and slicked-back dark hair completed the unique package.

The phone conversation was finally over, but Loo continued to make notes for a few more seconds after he hung up. Smiling broadly at Luke, the lieutenant finaly rose from his seat and extended a hand across the desk. Luke rose and leaned forward to take his hand. Two quick hand pumps and then a release before both men again took their seats.

"You look good. Resting works for you," said Loo with a grin.

"Maybe, but it got real old about two and a half months ago."

"You know, some guys would almost die for that much time off." The twinkle in Loo's eye gave the joke away.

Both men respected the other professionally and as casual friends. The two chatted for a few more minutes before Luke decided to bring up the subject of work. "I'm ready to get back in the trenches. What've you got for me?"

Loo's mood and tone changed immediately, "Luke, I've read the report from your doctors. You know you're allowed to work only on a limited basis."

"I do know that, but there must be something I can work on that won't strain my delicate heart." Luke placed both hands over his heart for emphasis.

Loo made a face. "How is your heart anyway?"

"Getting stronger every day. Doc said the last EKG and Echocardiogram were both normal. The cracked ribs have healed nicely, and I don't get winded just walking five steps to the bathroom anymore."

"That's good news. Tell you what," said Loo as he pushed files around until he found what he was looking for and passed the folder across the desk. Luke took the file and started inspecting its meager contents.

"Not much here," commented Luke as he scanned the three pages.

"That's all there is. The paramedics took her to St. Petersburg Regional Hospital. The emergency doctors felt it was better to take her there, even if it was farther away, because her vital signs were so good when the EMTs checked her out at the Skyway. The doctors thought St. Pete Regional could provide better care. But she's just a kid. Maybe 12, 13 years old. No ID. Nothing."

"Well, maybe I can try to track down some leads and ID her. Hopefully locate parents or a relative. Look into forensics." Luke contemplated the new assignment and continued, "Shouldn't be too hard. Who's partnering with me?"

Loo hesitated and made another face. "You're on your own with this one, Luke. You know how short-handed we are. All the other detectives are overloaded already. Anyway, you shouldn't need any help with this case."

Luke rose. "Thanks for the vote of confidence, Loo. You're probably right. This should be a quick close, and no strain on my poor heart."

"Just remember what your doctors said. Take it easy. No over exertion."

"I'll go slowly. I promise. A quick computer search. Go see the girl. Maybe an interview or two. Piece of cake." Luke patted the file with his hand for emphasis.

"Oh, by the way, Luke, the trial of those scumbags who shot you guys starts today. Jury selection may take most of the day." Loo thought it was important to keep all his detectives up-to-date on matters that affected them personally.

"Thanks, maybe I'll stop by and check out the progress. Perhaps the prosecutor can use my testimony."

"Sure, you do that. Glad to have you back," repeated Loo as he made a shooing motion with his hand. Luke gave him a fake salute, turned, and left the office with the file.

10:17 a.m.

The computer search for missing young girls that might be in the Tampa Bay area resulted in three hits: a seventeen year old Hispanic girl from Sarasota, a three year old toddler from Tarpon Springs—probably a domestic problem—and a ten year old African American girl from South St. Pete. No help since the file indicated that the victim is a Caucasian girl about 12 or 13 years old.

Luke was placing the computer printout in the file when his phone rang for the first time that morning. It was his mother. "Hello, Lucas. How does it feel to be back at work?" His mother was the only person that called him *Lucas*. He adopted *Luke* when he started Middle School because he thought *Lucas* was too formal. His mother refused to change what she'd called him since his birth.

"Hi, Mom," cheerfully ignoring the question.

Lucas' mom persisted. "How are you feeling? Does anything hurt?"

"Mom, I'm fine. Remember I told you my doctors cleared me to go back to work. They wouldn't have done that if there was anything wrong with me, would they?"

"I remember. I'm just worried about you."

"I know you are, Mom, but you don't have to worry so much."

"My job is to worry about you, Lucas. That's what mothers do."

Exasperated, "Mom, you already worry too much."

She changed the subject and her tone quickly, "Lucas, have you talked to that nice young lady, Lacey Hirsch?"

"Mom, I am working," Luke said with emphasis.

Ignoring her son's firm response, "I know you are, Lucas, but you need to spend time with your friends."

"I'll get around to all of my friends when I get the time."

Another quick change of tone and subject. "You're a good son. I love you."

"Love you too, Mom."

Luke realized immediately that urging Luke to call Lacey was the real reason for this ruse.

Luke changed the subject back, "I'll call Lacey first, Mom."

"Good. You should ask her out. Take her to a nice restaurant."

Ignoring the obvious match making, "I promise to call her, Mom. Gotta go. I'll see you when I come by for Sabbath dinner on Friday."

"Okay, Lucas. Be careful out there."

"I will, Mom. Thanks for calling. Bye."

"Good bye, Lucas." Both hung up just as Rocky Kowalski passed Luke's desk on his way out the door. "What kind of case did Loo throw you?"

"A young girl was badly hurt over the weekend. No ID. Two teenagers called it in between smooches on the Skyway. FHP tossed it to us."

"Did she show up on a missing person report?"

"Nope. That's the first thing I checked."

"Why is this a police matter? Shouldn't Child Services be involved?"

"They probably will be once we get an ID and determine the extent of any criminal activity—if any."

"Have you interviewed the vic yet?"

"She's not a **vic**, Rocky. She's a young girl who was *victimized*, and she has a name. I just don't know it yet."

Rocky's arms flew up in a sign of submission. "Hey, no offense, man. Just making conversation."

"Don't sweat it, Rocky. These kid-cases just get to me."

"Me, too. I apologize. If you need any help, maybe I can shake some time loose from some of my eight cases." All the detectives juggled multiple cases at any single moment. Handling ten active cases was not unheard of. Dealing with less than five cases usually meant those cases were particularly difficult and complex, or the detective wasn't physically or mentally capable of handling more. Luke found himself in the latter category.

"It should be an easy one to solve once I see the girl and the teenage lovebirds. But, thanks. I'll keep it in mind."

"Good luck. I'm off to interview the pastor of one of my suspects. Don't expect much, but I gotta do it anyway. See ya," and Rocky was gone.

Luke returned to his notes and tried to decide his next move. It was after 11:00. so a trip to the courthouse to track down the prosecutor seemed like a good idea. A quick mental time check told him he could get there before noon with time to spare.

Maybe he would call Lacey this afternoon and invite her to lunch sometime this week. Why not? They were friends. It would be his way of thanking her for stopping by the hospital three times, and almost weekly at his home while he was recuperating from the gunshot wounds. In fact, Lacey was the only person, other than his mom, Rabbi Alan Bloomberg, and one other detective that checked in on him more than twice in three months. Luke convinced himself that he really did owe Lacey a nice lunch.

In fact, Rabbi Bloomberg visited Luke once a week while he was in the hospital, and continued the visits after Luke was released to recuperate at home. Rabbi Bloomberg was in his late 40's, quite modern in the way he leads his congregation, and was so popular that his contract has run for over 20 years. Luke was one of five students in the first Bar Mitzvah class Rabbi Bloomberg taught at the synagogue, and Rabbi Bloomberg officiated at Luke's father's funeral. Luke has enormous respect for the man, and Luke's spirits were always lifted when the Rabbi visited.

CHAPTER THREE

Monday, First Week in October
Court Complex
Pinellas County, FL
11:49 a.m.

Detectives often use their own personal vehicles on the job as Luke was now doing. His late model SUV was inconspicuous and had the roominess needed for his equipment. It was fitted with the largest possible engine, special suspension, and other goodies needed on police vehicles.

After parking in one of the few open spaces Luke walked leisurely toward the main entrance. He breezed through security and headed for the elevators where he waited patiently for one of the three to come down. An older couple was standing in front of him.

Luke was suddenly startled by the light tap on his left shoulder. He turned and was pleasantly surprised to see the friendly face of a stunning women smiling up at him.

"Lacey, hi. I didn't expect to see you here."

"And I didn't expect to see you either, but I'm glad I did," she said with fake annoyance.

Luke laughed, "I'm glad too. You know what I mean." Luke was flustered, and a tell-tale blush crossed his checks.

Lacey held up a stylish briefcase, "I'm just turning in a report on one of my teenage clients. Her parents are going through a mean divorce and the poor girl is a mess. Nasty custody battle. The judge ordered the evaluation." Lacey made a face and continued, "What's your excuse for being here?"

"Nothing official. The trial for the gang-bangers we were trying to arrest when we got shot started this morning. I just wanted to talk to the prosecutor and offer whatever help I can."

"Then you're free for lunch in a half hour or so?" Lacey eyed him expectantly. She had no inhibitions about making the first move to get something she wanted.

"Uh, sure." Luke preferred to ask women out but didn't protest. At least this way she saved him from what he considered to be a potentially difficult phone call. He honestly hadn't known how Lacey would respond. Now he knew that his concerns were groundless.

Lacey glanced at her watch and offered, "Meet me down here at 12:30. We can decide where to go then. You do want to go to lunch with me, don't you?"

"Yes, of course I do." He looked into her sparkling eyes and continued, "I should be finished by then. I'll be waiting right here for you."

The elevator doors opened and the small crowd piled in. Lacey got out on the second floor and waved at Luke as the doors slid shut.

▫ ▫ ▫

Lacey Hirsch was the only child of Sidney and Bess Hirsch. Her dad was the founding partner at Hirsch and Gottlieb, one of the most prominent law firms in the Tampa Bay area. The firm mostly represents large corporate real estate development clients willing, and able to pay their huge fees. Occasionally, they would take other types of cases—even some pro bono work, for free, on worthy issues or for deserving clients.

Lacey's family belonged to the same Jewish synagogue as Luke's, and Luke and Lacey were friends during the Sunday and Hebrew school years. Lacey's Bat Mitzvah was four months after Luke's. Lacey has remained proud of her Jewish heritage and upbringing.

Lacey is well educated with a BA in sociology, and a PhD in psychology from the University of Florida, and was in the top ten percent of both classes. After graduation, Lacey opened a private practice where she gravitated towards child psychology almost exclusively. After seven years experience in a thriving practice, she now sees patients only on referral so she can slow down and enjoy life a little. About a year ago she reduced her patient load from eight or nine client sessions a day to five or six.

Dozens of lawyers, doctors, and other professionals are on lists that the Rabbi or administrative staff at the synagogue hand out, but Lacey is one of the few professionals that Rabbi Bloomberg specifically refers congregants to when they are in need of her services.

Sidney Hirsch set up a trust fund for Lacey when she was a small child. It now has almost tripled in value and provides a significant source of income allowing Lacey to work and earn a living at her own pace. Daddy's multi-million dollar trust fund made Lacey a very wealthy young woman—but that came at a cost. Even though she was a psychologist and should have known better, Lacey's last two "boyfriends" turned out to be disasters. Lacey was a very desirable single woman, but both guys were interested in her only for her money. She just didn't see it until it was too late.

Daddy was always suspicious of the men Lacey dated. The first guy tried to get Lacey to invest $100,000 in a shadowy scheme to buy a failing manufacturing company that was clearly worth much less. Sidney asked a young new lawyer in his firm to check out the details. The muscle-bound idiot boyfriend wanted the $100,000 to first go into his own bank account, claiming he then would use those funds to leverage up to some unspecified balance. He wasn't even smart enough to set up a dummy corporation to even try and look legitimate. Pure stupidity. A stern lecture from Daddy, and a veiled threat to surgically turn him into a girl chased the now ex-boyfriend out of Lacey's life forever, and all the way to Atlanta. The whole experience unfolded in just four months. Lacey wasn't even a little heartbroken after Daddy explained everything to her.

About a year later Lacey started dating a man she first had met in college. Their budding relationship went smoothly for over six months until the young man claimed he lost his job as a warehouse manager and was in jeopardy of being thrown out on the street by his landlord.

His tale of woe ended with a plea for Lacey to loan him $50,000 to get back on his feet. This time Lacey was more cautious, and told her boyfriend she'd think about it and let him know in a few days. That didn't sit too well with the boyfriend.

Her monthly bank statement, phone bill, and credit card bills arrived while she was wrestling with her decision. Lacey could only stare at the statements in her trembling hands. The many charges to the "900" numbers amounted to $1,378. She hadn't called any of those smut lines. The bank statement listed eight ATM cash withdrawals, each for the bank limit of $400. She never withdraws cash from bank ATMs. The Visa and MasterCard statements showed charges of $587, $1,193, and another for $3,647, all to internet "Dot Com" sites. There was no indication of what was purchased. Lacey hadn't bought anything from an on-line store in months, and never anything that expensive. If she wanted something, she just went to a local store and bought it.

There was no evidence that her boyfriend was responsible for any of this, but she just knew he was, and was livid about being used again. Lacey flew out of her condo and sped over to her soon-to-be ex-boyfriend's apartment. She had a key, and bolting through the front door shouting for him. The ruckus resulted in a well-tanned young woman, clad only in pink bikini panties, scurrying out of his bedroom with her head down as she—unsuccessfully—tried to hide enormous bare breasts with her hands. Lacey was momentarily startled as the half naked brunette dashed out the front door.

"You goddamn son of a bitch," screeched Lacey in the direction of the open bedroom door. The cowardly creep said nothing and didn't even come out of the bedroom. Lacey flung the key at the wall across the room, clinched her fists, set her jaw, and stomped out of the apartment. Lacey felt intense anger and betrayal. How could she have let someone exploit her again?

She called her dad on the way back to her condo. Her credit cards were quickly canceled, the police notified, and appropriate fraud teams alerted. About a week later Lacey's dad told her that an arrest had been made, and she might be expected to testify if the case went to trial. "It will be my pleasure," she sneered at the news, and promptly swore to never again allow any other men into her life romantically. She had faithfully kept that promise to herself since that terrible scene.

◻ ◻ ◻

Seeing Luke now, and the other times since he left the military brought back old high school memories. Their casual childhood friendship eventually turned romantic. Luke and Lacey started dating each other exclusively in the last half of their junior year, and continued through most of their senior year in high school. The flame smoldered and seemed to die out when Luke confided to her that he was joining the Marines after graduation. Lacey wanted a boyfriend in St. Pete, not someone hip-hopping around the world at the whim of generals she never met. Luke was crushed, but understood. They promised each other to stay in touch and remain friends. They did, but only wrote or called each other occasionally over the years. In reality, they saw more of each other these last few months while Luke recovered than all the years since high school.

She wasn't involved with anyone else, so why not try to rekindle the old spark. Her personal promise to swear off men seemed childish and silly now. Hopefully Luke wasn't seeing anyone steadily. She didn't think so since Luke never talked about another woman in his life. The few times she saw other women visiting Luke, she didn't pick up any signals of special feelings between them. Lacey decided to take the plunge and see what happens.

◻ ◻ ◻

Luke arrived downstairs before Lacey and leaned on a wall while he waited. One of the elevator doors opened and there she was. Luke could only stare. Lacey Hirsch was dressed in a smart looking fitted black skirt, white satin blouse, grey jacket, and designer black sandals on her feet. Her halo of shiny, billowing raven hair and makeup were perfect. A silver necklace with three tasteful dangling charms encircled her neck. She wore diamond studs in her earlobes. A red ruby surrounded by a dozen or so small diamonds set on a silver pin adorned her right lapel. A dramatic black, white, and grey silk scarf was draped around her neck with one end slung down her back and the other over her left chest. She loved combining black, white, and grey garments into unique outfits to which she added brightly colored pins, necklaces, bracelets, and scarves as the mood struck her.

Luke thought of how Marie Osmond—of Donnie and Marie fame—looked when Marie was in her early 30's, but Lacey had a little less billowing hair style with softer waves. Both women were attractive and bubbly, had a big smile, and were very friendly. Even now after all those children Marie Osmond still looks pretty hot. So does Lacey.

Lacey wasn't drop-dead gorgeous like a few of the other young single women Luke knew, but he recalled that Lacey always looked glamorous and sophisticated. Lacey obviously took pride in her appearance, and was an expert at showing off her best features.

Lacey took both of Luke's hands in hers, stretched her five feet four inch height up on her toes, and kissed him on the cheek. Luke stood six foot two inches, so he bent over slightly at the gesture. She slipped her free arm under his and they made small talk for a few minutes before Luke brought up the subject of lunch.

"Any favorite restaurants?" he asked nonchalantly.

"I haven't been to Spaghetti Grill in a while. You know, the place over by Tyrone Square Mall. Let's go there if you don't mind."

"Sounds good. I haven't been there in a year or so either." Luke wondered if Lacey remembered that he took her there twice on dates in high school. She remembered too, but said nothing about that.

Luke needed his car handy if a call came in, so Lacey left her year-old black Jaguar XK convertible on the courthouse complex lot. They made casual conversation about nothing and everything on the drive to the restaurant. It wasn't until the waiter came by to take their orders did the friendly banter stop. They both quickly ordered so they could return to focusing on each other. Lacey kept up the conversation, punctuated by occasionally brushing and touching Luke's hand. Luke purposely kept his hand on the table between them so Lacey could keep doing it. It had been over a decade since these two flirted with each other, and both easily fell back into the once familiar habit.

The food arrived and their hands became otherwise occupied with manipulating silverware, but the chatter continued between mouthfuls of food. Lacey eventually got around to asking Luke about his police work. "So, what kind of murder and intrigue are you working on now that you're back from the…uh, injury?"

"Actually, I'm only allowed limited duty. No murder or intrigue. The doctors are still evaluating my heart."

Lacey paused in the middle of cutting off a strip of her lunch to stare wide-eyed at Luke. "Your heart! What's wrong with your heart?"

"Nothing. They're just being careful. I told you that before, didn't I?"

"Yes, you did. I know you don't have to tell me anything. But, as your friend I would like to know. Maybe I can help you." Lacey was more concerned than Luke thought she should have been.

"That's very gracious of you, Lacey, but I'm not hiding anything. Really, there's nothing wrong with my heart. Initially, the doctors were concerned that a rib may have been pushed into my heart so they're just being careful. That's it—everything." Luke held his hands palms up and shrugged for emphasis. This subject had come up during several of Lacey's earlier visits at Luke's home. Luke had always maintained that his heart was fine, but didn't go into any detail. Now Lacey wanted details because her feelings for Luke were becoming more intense.

Lacey persisted. "Did they run tests?"

"You sound like my mother," joked Luke, but his annoyance was obvious. "Of course they ran tests. That's how they know I'm fine. Plus, I feel as good as I did before the injury."

"I'm sorry if you think I'm prying. I just care about my friends," she repeated in a huff.

"Well, I'm pleased to be one of your friends. In fact, I'm proud that you're my friend," Luke countered trying to nip a potential misunderstanding in the bud. It didn't work immediately. Lacey was offended by Luke's seeming refusal to confide in her, a long-time friend.

The awkward silence that followed drove them back to their meals. What seemed like an eternity of silence was agony for both of them. As a professional trained psychologist Lacey knew she needed to thaw the chill that engulfed them.

"Luke, so what are you working on?" Lacey cocked her head inquisitively and a forced grin appeared across her face when Luke looked up.

Luke was relieved. Deep down he still had feelings for Lacey, but was annoyed by her refusal to believe him. He decided to start anew with a different subject.

"Okay. My lieutenant assigned me to a case that happened over the weekend. A young girl, not sure of her age—probably 12 or 13—was badly injured on the Sunshine Skyway. We don't have any ID, nor do we know how she was injured. I have to do the ***detecting*** because I'm the detective here, and find out who she is, where she came from, get her back to her family, and, of course, figure out what happened. If a crime has been committed, we need to do something about that."

"How do you do all that if there's so little information?"

Luke returned his fork to his plate and pushed it away. "Well, I'll interview the girl, the kids that found her, maybe the officers that were the first on the scene, and the paramedics who took her to the emergency room. I'll then follow whatever leads develop. Mostly drudgery and leg-work. You know, pick and shovel grunt stuff. A little luck usually helps." They both laughed, further thawing the chill.

"Which hospital, if you don't mind my asking?"

"Of course I don't mind. St. Pete Regional."

"A good facility. That's one of the hospitals Daddy donates to every year. In fact, so do I, but not nearly as much. If you need help getting cooperation at the hospital, I'm your gal." Lacey was proud of her status as a benefactor, and sat up straighter and taller. Then she realized what she had done. "Luke, please don't tell anyone else. We donate to charities anonymously. Please keep this to yourself."

Luke covered her hand with his and made a zipping motion across his mouth with his other. "My lips are sealed." His smile was genuine.

"Thank you, Luke." Lacey hesitated before continuing. "On a more serious note, you know I work with kids in my practice. I get referrals from the courts, and some lawyers send me the children that don't handle their parents' divorce very well. I understand what the kids that age are going through. I also know how hard it can be trying to communicate with young girls. I'd like to help if you don't mind."

"Really! That would be great. I don't deal with teens too often, except street-gang types trying to act tough. Probably not the kind of kids you deal with."

Luke looked at his watch. "Gotta get to the hospital. If you're done, I'll get the check and take you back to your car. This is my treat. No arguments," as he waved in the general direction of the busy waiter.

"I invited you, but I'll make you a deal. You can pay for lunch if you let me go with you to see the girl."

"And if I won't take you with me?"

"Then I'll pay the check and forever keep reminding you that you're not a true gentleman."

Luke chuckled. "Okay. I surrender. You can tag along."

With that settled Lacey whipped out her cell phone, punched in some numbers, and spoke softly to whoever was on the other end. Luke signed the receipt and offered a hand to Lacey as they left the table.

Chapter Four

Monday, First Week in October
St. Petersburg Regional Hospital
St. Petersburg, FL
2:16 p.m.

Luke found an open parking space near the back of the lot and pulled in. Luke and Lacey walked the several hundred feet to the spacious entrance and approached the Information Desk. Luke introduced himself to the woman behind the counter, showed his badge, and asked for the room number of the unidentified girl admitted over the weekend. The woman looked at the badge, nodded, and turned to her computer. A few swift keystrokes, a momentary look at the screen, and she jotted the information on a note pad. Handing the slip of paper to Luke, she pointed to her left saying, "The elevators are over there, Detective. She's on the third floor, but you should check with the nurses' station first."

Luke took the piece of paper, glanced at it, and thanked her with a smile. Lacey followed Luke to the elevators in silence. They waited in more silence for an elevator to come down and the doors to open. Two women wearing hospital scrubs stepped out. Luke motioned for Lacey to go in first. Luke followed Lacey and pushed the button for the third floor.

Inside the elevator Luke made a snap decision. "Lacey, I think it's best if I do the questioning. After all, this is an official police investigation. Please, don't take this personally."

"I would never dream of interfering and I don't take it personally. I'll just stand in the background and watch you work. I can be as quiet as a mouse." Lacey smiled at him.

Luke and Lacey followed the signs to the nurse's station about half way down the hall. After showing his badge and introducing himself, Luke inquired about the unidentified young girl. The nurse on duty knew exactly who Luke was asking about. "She's in that room," pointing to the second door across the hall. "But, she hasn't regained consciousness yet."

"What? You mean she's been unconscious since she arrived?" Luke was stupefied. "Why wasn't that in the file?"

"I don't know anything about your file, Detective, but I can tell you that she's remained in an unconscious state since she arrived here."

Luke glanced at the nurse's hospital name tag, "Ms. Hopkins, I don't think you understand. This is a criminal investigation. I need your help to identify the girl and find out what happened to her. I also need to know her medical condition to determine if any crimes have been committed."

"Oh, I understand. But, I don't think I can help you. All I know is what's in her medical chart, but HIPAA laws prevent me from discussing her medical condition with you, or anyone else, without permission from a parent, a guardian, or a court order."

"Fine. Can I at least collect her clothes? Maybe forensics can find something."

"I'm sorry, Detective. There aren't any clothes."

"What do you mean **there aren't any clothes**? Why don't you have them?"

"She was naked. She wasn't wearing any clothes when she arrived here. They brought her here in a blanket. No clothes." The nurse stared at Luke with a blank expression on her face.

Luke turned around to glare at Lacey as if it was her fault. "I can't believe this. Why isn't any of this in the police reports?" he barked at the nurse when he turned back around. Lacey ignored his outburst.

"I can't speak to that, Detective. We only know about her medical situation here."

Luke's annoyance ratcheted up. Lacey noticed and took a step closer. She touched his sleeve and tried to whisper in his ear. Luke turned around and bent over slightly. Lacey spoke calmly, "Maybe you can talk to her doctor."

Luke took a calming deep breath, straightened up, and turned to face Nurse Hopkins, "Can you please give me the name of her doctor?"

Nurse Hopkins consulted her file. "Doctor Brett Williams. I can page him if you want."

"That would be great. Thank you." Luke was settling down somewhat.

Six minutes later a young man in a white hospital coat with a stethoscope draped around his neck approached the nurse's station. The man looked really young and Luke immediately thought of Doogie Howser, the teenage genius doctor on TV in the early 1990's.

Doctor Williams approached Luke with an outstretched hand. "I'm Doctor Brett Williams. I assume you're the detective inquiring about my mystery patient." His up and down stare at Lacey verified her status as someone people took notice of.

"Thanks for meeting with me, Dr. Williams." Luke flashed his badge and identification for the third time in fifteen minutes. Dr. Williams returned his gaze to Lacey. "Uh, this is Lacey Hirsch," said Luke ignoring the PhD that entitled her to be called **Doctor**. Lacey didn't correct him. The doctor shook Lacey's hand longer than was necessary for a formal introduction.

Luke broke the spell. "I don't want to take up too much of your time, Doctor, but what can you tell me about the girl and her condition?" Dr. Williams reluctantly shifted his attention away from Lacey, let go of her hand, and turned towards Luke.

"I thought this was just an accident. Dumb kids doing stupid things on the Skyway Pier. Why are the police involved?"

"For one thing, Doctor, we don't know who she is. Also, we think there may have been some criminal activity involved. She did have stab wounds, didn't she?"

Dr. Williams studied Luke for a few moments before answering, "I suppose you could get a court order for this information, so I'll cooperate and save both of us some time and effort."

"Thank you. Please go on."

"You're welcome. The girl had jagged cuts on her upper left arm and left hip." Dr. Williams indicated both positions on his own body as he spoke. "Neither was serious and no indication of how she got them, nor do we know what made them. It could have been a knife, or maybe just a sharp object. We cleaned the wounds, gave her a tetanus shot, and a hefty dose of antibiotics to ward off any nasty infections. We used butterfly stitches on both. Minimal blood loss. There might be small scars, but nothing ugly."

Luke was trying to make sense of all this. "All right. What about all the blood splotches on her body?"

"I didn't see any splotches. I only saw her after she was cleaned up. If she had them, I suspect she just rubbed or touched the cuts and transferred the blood to other places on her body. Those were the only wounds."

"The nurse said she was naked when she arrived. Is that correct, Doctor?"

"No clothes? Really? There's nothing about clothing or being naked in her chart. As I said, I only saw her after she was in a hospital gown, so I can't confirm either way."

"Any evidence of sexual assault?" Luke was taking notes and he wasn't happy about what he was hearing.

"I didn't check her for sexual assault. Let me recheck her chart." A few moments later Dr. Williams returned from behind the nurses' station flipping pages in her medical file. "Sorry, no one checked her for sexual assault. No order from the police or the admitting doctor to do one either. But, it's been less than 48 hours, so we can still check for physical bruising, but we won't find any live sperm—if there was any sperm at all. She is definitely a minor, so you know I can't conduct an invasive exam now without approval of a parent or legal guardian. I can only treat her for medical emergencies, which is what I did, and am doing. Checking her for sexual assault now is not a medical emergency, and whoever brought her here didn't indicate one needed to be conducted. Sorry."

Luke repeated himself "Doctor, we don't know who she is or where to find her parents. There's no temporary guardian yet, but I can get one appointed and obtain a court order for the examination. I'll call you when I get the paperwork signed by a judge."

"You do understand that I can't start until I get the court order or a signed release from the guardian."

"Yes, of course. But, you can be prepared to start as soon as the paperwork is in place?"

Dr. Williams entered the exam on her chart pending the paperwork, and tapped the page with his pen for emphasis. "Done. I'll conduct the exam myself as soon as possible. Fax the order to this number," as he scribbled a fax number on a prescription pad and handed it to Luke.

Luke glanced at the number and put the slip of paper in his pocket, "Will do. She's still unconscious, Doctor?"

"Yes, but I'm not sure why. Probably a psychological defense to whatever she experienced. We haven't found a medical reason, but I am planning additional tests if I don't see any improvements by tomorrow afternoon. She's young, in generally good health, and should come around on her own. That's the most desirable outcome."

Lacey completely understood what Dr. Williams was explaining, and agreed with his diagnosis and course of action. She decided to wait until she and Luke were alone to tell him she concurred with Dr. Williams.

Luke asked, "Anything else you can tell me about her?"

"Nothing significant I'm afraid. She appears to be a healthy, normal young girl in her early teens. She has reached puberty, probably eighteen months, maybe two years ago. She's a little too thin, but lots of young girls are too thin." Dr. Williams looked at Luke, then Lacey, but neither said anything, so he continued, "If there's nothing else, I'll start on the exam as soon as you fax over the order and then I'll send you the results about an hour afterwards."

The doctor took the business card from Luke and pushed it into a breast pocket. The men shook hands and Doctor Williams turned to Lacey, "Nice to meet you. I hope to see you again soon."

Doctor Williams went over to the nurses' station to make preparations and order a sexual assault exam kit. Luke and Lacey retraced their steps to the elevator. Luke was fuming, "A naked unconscious teenage girl with blood on her body in some dark, out-of-the-way location! How the hell can this not be a criminal investigation? What were those idiots thinking?"

"Maybe it's just a mix-up or a misunderstanding." Lacey tried to be sympathetic because she didn't know how the police operated, and couldn't think of anything else to say.

"We call it a f—k-up. Pardon my French."

"What are you going to do now?"

"Well, after I get the court order for the sexual assault exam, the only thing I can do is try and interview the officers and the paramedics that were on the scene and find out what went wrong." Luke's earlier frustrations returned like a torrential downpour.

"If you want me to come with you, I'd love to," offered Lacey in an attempt to calm Luke down. Luke stared down at her as he decided what to do. They approached the elevator just as the doors opened and three hospital workers stepped out. Lacey stepped in first, followed by Luke and another nurse who had just rushed up. Lacey pushed the button and looked at the nurse for confirmation. The nurse smiled and nodded. All three rode down in silence.

Luke seemed to calm down while walking to the car, "Lacey, I've got to make some calls and set up interviews. I can do it from the car. Can you wait while I see who's available?"

"Glad to. I don't need to be back in the office for a few hours. I find this very interesting. I'll wait right here with you." Lacey cocked her head provocatively and flashed bright white teeth.

Luke wasn't sure how far he should let this collaboration go. Lacey wasn't in any immediate danger, nor had he violated any departmental regulations regarding citizen involvement. Luke enjoyed being with her, but he was technically on the job. Luke started to rationalize. Since Lacey worked with the courts, it wasn't such a stretch for her to work with the police. He would have to think about that possibility some more.

Luke called the desk sergeant for the phone numbers he needed. Lacey offered to write them down as Luke repeated them out loud. Luke thanked the sergeant and flipped the cell phone closed.

"I'll try the FHP first." Lacey read him the number as he punched it in. "Hello. My name is Detective Lucas Brasch with St. Pete Police. Is Officer Freemont or her partner available?"…"Thanks, I'll hold."

After what seemed like an interminable delay, but was only four minutes, the voice on the other end returned with the answer, "Both officers ended their shift a few hours ago. If you give me your number I'll get it to them and they can call you back."

Another damn delay. "Sure." Luke repeated his name and recited his cell and office numbers. The voice read them back for confirmation. "Right. Thank you."

Lacey looked down at her phone numbers. "Want the EMT number?"

"Why not," as he flipped the phone open again and punched it in. Luke repeated the same story and waited while Kelly Tinsley and Monte Green were hunted down. Finally, "Kelly Tinsley is just starting her shift. I'll page her for you."

Three minutes passed as Luke got more and more annoyed until, "Hello, this is Kelly Tinsley. To whom am I speaking?"

Luke sat up straight and introduced himself. After a quick confirmation of the basic facts, Luke asked if he could meet Kelly somewhere to discuss the case further. "Certainly, I'll be here unless a call comes in and I'm sent out on a run. But, I can't add anything. And why are the police involved? We just transported an injured girl to St. Pete Regional?"

"That's what I need to talk to you about. Where are you now?" Luke repeated her location out loud and Lacey jotted it down. Luke didn't want to risk more delays if an emergency call sent Tinsley out, "I'll be there in about a half hour."

To Lacey as he started the engine, "Well, it looks like you'll get another dose of police work if you don't mind."

"I'm game. Now we're partners." Both laughed, but Lacey was serious.

Twenty five minutes later Luke turned into the small parking lot adjacent to the fire house that was home to the EMT Unit. Lacey was really enjoying the experience, and almost skipped alongside of Luke as they made their way inside.

Luke's badge, ID, and request to see Kelly Tinsley resulted in a powerful-looking woman in her late thirties approach from a far doorway.

Luke repeated the few facts he already knew and got an immediate confirmation from Kelly. Trying to expand his knowledge base, Luke continued, "What can you tell me about her physical condition when you arrived?"

"The girl was on the ground, lying on her back, crumpled, contorted, and covered by a blanket. We checked her vitals, did a quick visual exam, put emergency bandages on the two cuts we found, started the IV we always administer, and checked in for transport instructions."

"Any other physical injuries?"

"None were obvious at the scene, but my partner checked her out more thoroughly on the way to the hospital. No serious bumps or contusions on her head. No marks on her face. No other cuts or obvious broken bones. We think she took a tumble because he found a few small scrapes. He found blood splotches on other parts of her body, but nothing else."

"Where did the blood splotches come from?"

"Probably from the girl touching the open wounds and smearing her own blood around." Confirmation of Dr. Williams' conclusions, but Luke wanted to dig deeper.

"Did you check to see if she did smear her own blood?"

"No, didn't see any reason to, but there was some blood on her hands."

"Did anyone collect the blood to verify if it was hers or not?"

"We didn't, nor did we think it was someone else's blood."

"Okay. Did you try to revive her?"

"Yes, with traditional smelling salts, but she didn't come around. That's why we took her to St. Petersburg Regional rather than to a closer hospital. The on-call emergency doctor said St. Pete Regional was better able to take care of her, especially since all of her vitals were pretty good."

"Was she naked?"

"Yes, covered by a blanket, like I said."

There was no mention of the girl being naked in the report, but Luke let that go.

"Is there anything else you can tell me?"

"Don't you have our report?"

"Yes, I do. Thanks." The single page report was clearly identical to what Kelly just told him. Nothing different except for the girl being naked and having blood on her hands.

Luke extended his hand, "Thanks for seeing me. If you or your partner thinks of anything else, please call." Luke handed Kelly his card.

Luke was visibly annoyed. Back in Luke's car he turned to Lacey and said, "It's getting late, and I've got to check back in at the station. I'll drop you off on the way."

"That's fine. This has been fun, in a learning kind of way. An enjoyable new experience."

The engine purred to life and Luke headed out, "Glad you had a good time. It wasn't much fun for me—no offense."

"None taken." Lacey eyed him skeptically, "Is this case really going as badly as it seems?"

"Yes, it is. A whole day and I don't know a damn thing more about who she is than I did when I first got the case."

They rode in silence. Luke continued fuming. He was angry and frustrated. Lacey just sat primly, hands folded in her lap.

Lacey showed Luke where she had parked and he stopped behind her car, "Thanks for your help, Lacey."

She leaned over and gave him a quick peck on the cheek, "My offer still stands. If you need more help, just let me know."

"Thanks, but I hope I can handle the rest by myself."

"Remember that I'm just a phone call away. In fact, why don't you call me and we'll go out again?" More forwardness from Lacey; she knew what she wanted.

"Sure, I'd like that. I'll call if I'm free this weekend." Luke took the bait, but was still uncomfortable with her boldness.

"I'll be waiting." Both smiled. Lacey headed to her office and Luke went back to the station.

Chapter Five

Monday, First Week in October
Police Station
St. Petersburg, FL
5:52 p.m.

Luke was finishing up his notes and preparing to leave for the day. He'd skimmed the new file his lieutenant had left on his desk. It was an abandoned, possibly stolen, SUV found near the Pinellas County entrance to the Howard Frankland Bridge connecting St. Petersburg with Tampa across Tampa Bay. It was a rental from Avalon Car Rental at the Tampa International Airport in Hillsboro County. He'd run that down tomorrow.

It was too late to call the courthouse to check on the court order for the sexual assault exam on the unidentified girl, and no messages from Dr. Williams about any changes in the mystery girl's condition. The phone rang just as Luke was pushing his chair under his desk, "Detective Brasch. What can I do for you?"

"Ah. Detective Brasch. I didn't know if you'd still be there or not."

"I was just leaving. Can I get your name please?"

"Oh, sure. I'm sorry. I'm Detective Ronny Sinclair from the Tampa Police Department. Your lieutenant gave me your name."

"Okay. How can I help you, Detective?" Luke pulled out his chair and sat down.

"We've got a dead girl found on our side of the Howard Frankland bridge we're trying to identify. I think she was a runaway, and I've been checking the shelters here in Hillsborough County. No luck. Thought I'd check Pinellas."

"Makes sense to me. Did you fax a picture to the shelter over here?"

"No. Don't have a phone number or address. And anyway, that'd be too cruel if the dead girl is from your shelter. I prefer the personal touch. Know what I mean? If you've got the time, I'd appreciate it if you could stop by the shelter over by you and check it out."

"Sure, I can go over there tomorrow morning. Did you fax a photo to the station?"

"You should get it in about two minutes."

Luke was always thinking about his own cases, "Detective. Maybe you can help me out if you don't mind."

"If I can. What do you need?"

"I've got a rental car, possible stolen, dumped on my side of the Howard Frankland. I need to talk to the folks at Avalon Car Rental at the Tampa airport. Could you do the honors?"

"Not a problem. Fax the particulars to the number on the fax I just sent you. I'll drop in on Avalon in the morning, and we can trade reports tomorrow afternoon."

"Sounds like a plan. Thanks."

Luke hung up and trudged over to the fax machine, retrieved the photo from Detective Sinclair, and jotted down the number. He returned to his desk and set the photo aside. Next, he collected the stolen car papers, filled out his own fax cover page, and sent it all on its way to the Tampa Police Department addressed to Detective Ronny Sinclair.

With that done, Luke headed home for the second time feeling much more tired than he had expected.

<u>Luke's Condo</u>
<u>Seminole, FL</u>
<u>7:27 p.m.</u>

Luke absentmindedly watched TV as he picked at the leftovers he collected from his fridge. He sat leisurely in his living room as the 50" plasma HDTV worked its magic. A commercial featuring a teenage girl shopping for clothes with her mother yanked him back to his first case: identifying an unknown teenage girl. Without realizing it, his thoughts drifted to the favor he promised Detective Sinclair and thought to himself, "How do I approach the subject of identifying a dead teenager to the caretakers at a girl's shelter? They're supposed to protect those girls from just such tragedies. What should I expect? How will they react? Shock? Disbelief? Tears? Hysteria? What?"

Luke slumped back and watched a few more minutes of the TV show he wasn't really paying any attention to. Then it hit him. He now had a credible excuse to call Lacey—not that he really needed one.

When she picked up on the other end Luke tried to be cheerful, "Hi, Lacey. It's me, Luke."

"Oh, hi Luke. I didn't expect to hear from you so soon, but I'm glad you called."

"I just wanted to make sure you weren't mad at me for my sulky behavior this afternoon."

"No. No, Luke. I know how stressful your work can be at times."

"Well, that's comforting. I don't want my job to get between me and my friends, especially you."

Lacey's heart fluttered and her blood seemed to run hotter.

Luke let out an audible sigh as Lacey replied. "We're friends. We're partners, remember. You're stuck with me for the duration."

Luke chuckled causing Lacey to giggle. Luke loved her laugh.

"Okay, partner, I've got a job for you."

More seriously, "Great. What do you need me to do?"

Luke explained the situation with the dead teenage girl in Tampa, then, "So, how should I approach the ladies in charge of the shelter? I assume it's only ladies in a girls' shelter. Right?"

"Of course it's only ladies, and you approach them with sensitivity and compassion. Those ladies deal with tragedy every day, and they understand the reality of street life. Sometimes people get hurt or die, and they know it."

"Lacey, I'm a cop with a job to do, not a social worker. I'm looking for information which may very well be unpleasant. I don't know how to be sensitive and compassionate while I'm showing someone gruesome pictures of a dead girl."

"Don't sell yourself short," warned Lacey.

"I'm not so sure," protested Luke.

Out of the blue, "Would you like me to go with you to the shelter?"

"Could you? I hate doing these kinds of things alone."

"Glad to help—Partner. I just need to check on my appointments first."

Genuinely relieved, Luke steered the conversation away from police work. About fifteen minutes later, Lacey steered it back.

"Luke, what if your unidentified girl at St. Petersburg Regional is also a runaway and might be known at the shelter?"

Silence on Luke's end. Lacey became concerned, "Luke, are you there?"

Finally, "I'm here, Lacey. I hadn't thought of that. Sure, she could be a runaway."

"So far you don't know anything about her, so there's no reason to restrict the investigation to a girl living with her family. Right?"

"Yeah. You're right. Maybe the ladies at the shelter know who she is." More silence as Luke's mind raced. Then Luke continued, "I don't have a picture of her, but I can take one at the hospital before we go to the shelter. Good idea, Lacey. Thanks."

"I like to earn my keep."

Luke could almost see her smile through the phone.

Lacey checked her appointments. She could reschedule the first two. They coordinated their plans, which included Luke taking Lacey to meet his lieutenant just to cover all the bases and keep his own butt out of the fire.

Tuesday, First Week in October
Police Station
St. Petersburg, FL
9:13 a.m.

Lacey entered the station and asked for Detective Lucas Brasch. A few minutes later Luke approached the sergeant's desk beaming broadly. A quick, "Thank you," to the sergeant and Luke escorted

Lacey directly to Lieutenant Nick Thompson's office. Luke knocked on the open door and ushered her in. "Lieutenant Nick Thompson, this is Dr. Lacey Hirsch, the psychologist I told you about."

Lieutenant Thompson rose and graciously extended his hand. Lacey stepped forward, "The pleasure is all mine, Lieutenant."

Today, Lacey was dressed in a tailored white skirt and matching jacket. Her black scoop-neck top displayed a dramatic silver swirl design. Jewelry consisted of a silver pin in the shape of a butterfly, silver dangling earrings, and a triple strand silver necklace. A black and white scarf encircled her neck with both ends draped down her back. To Lacey, an outfit like this was necessary for her image as a successful psychologist.

Nick Thompson caught himself gawking at the striking women in front of him and let go of her hand, "Uh, Luke has told me about your background and the work you do with kids. He thinks you can help him with his unidentified teen girl case."

"I'll certainly do my best."

Luke broke in, "She's already helped point me in the right direction. Dr. Hirsch adds a fresh perspective."

"I'm sold. I checked with the chief judge over at the courthouse, and she had only praise for your work and professionalism, Dr. Hirsch."

"That's nice to hear, Lieutenant. Thank you, but please call me Lacey."

Loo pressed a button on his phone and summoned a rookie female police officer. "Please escort Dr. Hirsch…uh, Lacey to Human Resources and get her properly registered as a consultant. I'll call ahead and alert them. Stay with Lacey until everything is in order, then escort her to Detective Brasch."

The officer nodded that she understood, "Sure thing, Loo." The officer led Lacey out of the office and down the hall.

Luke thanked his lieutenant and returned to his desk for more computer searching. About a half hour later, the officer marched to his desk with Lacey in tow. "Thank you, Officer. I appreciate your help." Luke rose and nodded at the officer as Lacey repeated her thanks.

"No problem, Ma'am." They shook hands briefly, and the rookie returned to her other duties.

"Look, I'm legal," grinned Lacey holding her new ID Badge for Luke to see.

"Just a formality. At least now they know where to send your checks."

Lacey shot back in a huff, "Luke, I'm not looking for new work so I can earn more money."

"That was stupid of me. I'm sorry. I didn't mean it that way. I meant to say that you should be compensated for your time." Luke was genuinely apologetic for his verbal blunder.

Lacey glared at Luke as she found a place in her wallet for the ID card. Still staring, she sat down in the chair next to Luke's desk. Soon Lacey started to calm down, "Okay. I'm ready. Do we have an appointment at the shelter?"

"Actually, no. I can't find an address or phone number for a girl's shelter anywhere in Pinellas County."

"The shelter is in a secret location to keep unwanted **bad guys** from finding the girls." Lacey made a quote sign with her fingers as she said and emphasized "Bad Guys".

"Then how can they operate? How do girls needing the safety of the shelter find them?"

"It's all through an underground network. Trusted people who know about the shelter help find the girls on the streets. The exact location has been kept secret for decades."

"So how do *we* find it?" Luke pointed back and forth between himself and Lacey.

"I know where the shelter is located from my work with troubled teens stumbling through the courts."

"You do? Wow, you never cease to amaze me."

"Now, don't get all mushy on me." Luke thought he saw Lacey blush.

"So where is it, and just as importantly, how do we make an appointment?"

"I still need to be careful to protect the shelter and the girls."

"Of course. Their secret is safe with me." Luke held up his hand in a swearing motion.

"I know it is. So, I'll give you the information in the car. Do you have a GPS system?"

"Sure. It's got all the fancy stuff—as if I ever use it all."

Lacey made a face about Luke buying things he didn't need or use. "Well, okay. I'll put in the address, but you can't save it to your GPS address book."

"Oh, come on, Lacey. Don't you trust me?"

"It's not you, Luke. Someone might overhear us or steal your GPS. I'd rather be safe than sorry."

"You're being paranoid, Lacey." Luke paused, and then continued when Lacey just glared at him, "Okay, I'll go along with that."

"Good, I'll call for an appointment from the car. I'm ready to go. Are you?"

Luke just stared. He'd never seen this tough, hard-nosed side of Lacey, and wasn't sure if he liked it. "I need to put some files away and collect my notes. Give me a few minutes."

"No problem. I've got nowhere else to go. Take your time." Lacey sat back and rummaged through her purse for a mirror to check her still perfect hair and makeup.

Chapter Six

Tuesday, First Week in October
A Secret location
St. Petersburg, FL
11:19 a.m.

Luke had already stopped at the hospital and taken a picture of the mystery girl with his cell phone camera. Now the GPS announced, "You have arrived," as Lacey pointed at what appeared to be a dilapidated old house with a gray dirt parking area on its left. The dull blue paint was pealing in places, some of the white wood trim was cracked and rotten, and a few bricks were missing from the stoops on the porch. No identification signs of any type; not even numbers for an address. "I've been here twice before and the outside seems to get older and more run down each time," Lacey sighed as she surveyed the old house.

"It certainly is isolated and nondescript."

"That's how they keep the location secret. No one would suspect what this place really is."

Luke maneuvered around two cars and a windowless van. All were at least ten years old, dented, and scratched. The van had obvious rust spots on the doors and a fender; all probably part of the deception.

The single rap followed by three quick raps then another single rap on the blue door summoned a heavyset African American woman in her fifties. The secret code changed regularly and was relayed to Lacey when she called for the appointment, and only then because Lacey was known to the lady at the shelter. The overweight woman looked through the peephole and inquired about their identities. Luke held up his detective badge and Lacey produced her new ID. Satisfied they were who she was expecting, Yvonne Franklin opened the door and ushered them inside, but not before she poked her head outside to look around in all directions. She repeated the street search before shutting the heavy door behind them. There was no one else in sight.

Yvonne took both of Lacey's hands in hers, "It's been too long, Doctor Lacey." Yvonne's smile spread across her round face revealing coffee-stained teeth and twinkling eyes.

Lacey beamed back, "Yes, it has been too long. You look good. How've you been?"

"Oh, don't mind me, Doctor Lacey. I'm taking the medications and watching my diet."

"Good for you. Keep it up. These girls need and rely on you. We can't have you getting sick now, can we?"

Yvonne blushed, but her light brown complexion made it hard to detect.

The inside of the house was nothing like the outside. The rooms were nice-sized, freshly painted, and brightly lit. The furniture and furnishings were modest and well-used, but clean and in good repair. From what Luke could see, the entire place looked inviting and homey. Whoever lived there would feel comfortable, welcome, and safe.

Lacey introduced Luke to Yvonne and led up to the reason they had come. Yvonne suggested they all sit down. The chairs and sofa were arranged so they each faced the others and were surprisingly comfortable. Luke took over, "Ms. Franklin...." Yvonne cut him off immediately with a wave.

"Detective, all my friends call me Miss Frankie. You're a friend of Dr. Lacey, so you're a friend of mine. Call me Miss Frankie," as she smiled at Luke.

Luke shot a quick glance at Lacey, then back at the smiling Miss Frankie. "I'm proud to be your friend, Miss Frankie."

"That's better, young man. I'll call you Detective Lucas. Now what can I do for you two nice people?"

"Luke is fine, Miss Frankie."

Miss Frankie nodded and looked at Lacey for confirmation. Lacey nodded her agreement. When Miss Frankie turned back to Luke he continued with a forced smile. "This might be upsetting or unpleasant. I have some questions for you and I need you to look at a few pictures."

Ignoring Luke's comments, Miss Frankie struggled to stand up as she spoke, "Lordy me. Where are my manners? Can I get you nice folks some refreshments? Coffee? Iced tea?" Miss Frankie was a gracious host, but she was not eager to confront whatever might be coming.

"No thanks, Miss Frankie." Both Lacey and Luke answered almost in unison.

"All right then." Miss Frankie plopped back down, took a deep breath, and stared directly at Luke. Her pudgy hands clasped neatly in her ample lap. "Ask your questions, Luke."

Luke wanted to be easy on Miss Frankie, so he started by asking about the history of the shelter and Miss Frankie's involvement with it. Miss Frankie explained that the shelter started in the late 1950's as a place where battered women could find a safe haven from abusive spouses or boyfriends. In the 1960's the shelter started accepting abused women with their children. As the number of abused women and their children grew, mostly because of population increases, space became a problem, and a second shelter was created to handle the overflow. Miss Frankie started volunteering in 1983 and took over as the director in 1995. In the 1980's, runaway teenage girls started arriving in greater numbers. At about the same time, some of the abused women had teenage children—girls and boys. After a few unsettling incidences with the teenage boys *bothering* the young girls, the shelter directors decided to re-organize and change directions. This shelter became female-only in mid-1989. The other shelter accepts women and their children, boys and girls, as long as everyone behaves. The shelter is their second chance. They don't get a second, second chance. Serious rule infractions result in getting kicked out. In both shelters the women are offered clothes if they need any, group counseling, and private individualized sessions when necessary. Some women need help to learn about better hygiene and making themselves presentable. Some women are counseled on birth control choices. Others need help with things as simple as filling out an employment application or doing basic arithmetic because no one will hire a cashier who can't count change correctly. Bolstering self-esteem is also important and a primary focus. The shelter teaches these skills so the women can get a decent job and earn enough to take care of their families as a single mom. The shelters even provide leads to help the women find respectable work.

Young girls under 18 without children are helped here. They're all minors. Most of the young girls who come to this shelter stay a few weeks, some only a few days, while others stay for months. A few stayed almost a year. It all depends on the caseload at Social Services and the girl's situation at home. Usually the girls had run away from their families after some argument or conflict with natural or stepparents. A few were physically or sexually abused and refuse to return home. Miss Frankie concluded her history lesson with, "We connect those girls with Social Services and have them placed in foster homes when we can. Sadly, a few of the girls have stayed here more than once."

"How many people work here, Miss Frankie?" asked Luke.

"Two of us are paid but it's not much. Three, sometimes four volunteer regularly."

"And all five or six of you know all the girls?"

"Oh my, yes. We're all involved in helping the girls either return home or find foster homes. I'm here six or seven days a week. The others come in as scheduled or as needed."

"All right, Miss Frankie. I'd like to show you a picture and ask you if you recognize the girl. Is that okay?"

Hesitation, and then in an almost inaudible whisper, "Yes, show me the picture."

Luke produced a black and white picture. Miss Frankie's hand immediately flew to her mouth and tears welled up in her eyes. Lacey reached out to comfort her, "Do you recognize the girl?" Lacey was as gentle as possible.

Dabbing her eyes with a tissue offered by Lacey, Miss Frankie pointed with genuine sorrow, "That's Jasmine. Is she dead?" The sobbing intensified when Lacey nodded in the affirmative.

Luke and Lacey waited anxiously for Miss Frankie to compose herself. Lacey broke the silence, "Can I get you some water, Miss Frankie?"

"Thank you, Dr. Lacey, but I have to take care of myself. I'll be back in a minute." With that, Miss Frankie pushed herself up and lumbered to the kitchen. Luke and Lacey could hear cabinet doors and drawers open and close, running water, and other sounds of activity, none of which drowned out spurts of sobbing and low moaning. Miss Frankie returned, eyes still moist, carrying a plastic tray with three glasses and a pitcher of water. She filled all three glasses and offered two to Luke and Lacey. Once accepted, Miss Frankie picked up the last one and took a sip. Luke and Lacey followed suit. Another sip and Miss Frankie replaced her glass on the tray and slumped down in her chair.

Luke leaned closer, "Miss Frankie. What can you tell us about Jasmine? Do you know her last name? Where she's from? Anything?"

Miss Frankie struggled to speak. "Griswold. Jasmine Griswold. That's her name. She arrived here about a month ago. Poor girl was scared out of her mind when she arrived. She said she was 15, and her step-father tried to rape her one night when her mother was out cold in a drunken stupor. We get a lot of that here. Her step-dad beat her up and chased her around until she got away. She wouldn't say exactly where she lived because she didn't want to be sent back home. I didn't push it. One of our volunteers found Jasmine curled up inside a discarded cardboard refrigerator box in a vacant lot, so I guess she came from that part of St. Pete, but I can't be sure."

"Was Jasmine injured or sick when she arrived at your shelter?"

"She'd been smacked around. A few small bruises. Nothing serious. We don't conduct medical exams unless it's obvious we need to. Jasmine was just scared and confused. She needed a safe place, a mother, a friend. That's all."

"What can you tell me about her activities, her demeanor after she arrived?"

"After a few days when she realized we weren't going to send her back to that kind of abuse, she settled down, started eating better, and mixing with the other girls and volunteers. That's usually what happens. It takes time to earn trust when you never had anyone in your life you could trust."

Lacey added, "Some abused young girls take months, even years before they learn how to trust anyone, much less who to trust. It's a credit to Miss Frankie that she can earn their trust in a relatively short time."

"Now, Doctor Lacey, don't you start tootin' my horn. All I do is listen to them when they want to talk—and love them. That's all any of them needs once the abuse stops."

"I'd like to talk to the other girls who might have known Jasmine." Luke paused and then added, "And your staff if you don't mind?"

"Only myself and Miss Abigail are here now. Can't say that the girls will talk to you, with you being the police and all, but the staff will."

"I'd like to try, Miss Frankie. Maybe we can develop a lead or find Jasmine's family."

"Three girls are here now. The other seven are at school, four in middle school and three in high school. I'd appreciate it if you talked to them here, not at their schools. Only the principals know the girls are staying here."

Lacey chimed in, "I agree with Miss Frankie. Let's not add any additional stress if we can avoid it."

"Sure, we can do that. We'll talk to the girls and staff that are here today, and come back at a better time for the rest of the girls. Can you give me the names, addresses, and phone numbers of the staff and volunteers not working today?"

Miss Frankie trudged over to a small desk and flipped pages in an address book. Luke wrote down the first four names and their contact information. "Our last volunteer is Stanley Robbins, address…"

"What? A man volunteers here?" Luke was surprised. Lacey was appalled.

"Sure. Stanley's harmless. He's been hangin' around here for years."

Lacey countered, "Miss Frankie, I didn't know anything about this Stanley Robbins. Why is he allowed to come here regularly?"

"Stanley came with his mom over 15 years ago, before we were a girl's-only shelter. He was about 14 or 15 then, maybe even older. He had some learning disability, you know, a little slow in the head, but he functions pretty well now." Lacey was glaring at Miss Frankie, who continued, "Stanley's mom was beat up pretty bad. We got her patched up and let her stay here with the boy for about five months or so. After she was back on her feet, Stanley kept coming around offering to help out. He did some carpentry, painted some rooms, you know, odd jobs. We knew him pretty well by then and could use his help. He never asked us for a dime. Funding was just as tight back then, so we let him help out whenever he offered to do some work."

Lacey bored deeper, "Does he have any contact with the girls?"

"Of course he does. With so many girls here every day, one or more of them is always under foot when Stanley's working."

"Does he talk to the girls? Does he have any physical contact?"

"I don't watch him every minute, and I pay no attention to their idle chatter. No one has complained about him, if that's what you're worried about."

Lacey persisted, "Does Stanley ever see the girls when they're away from the shelter?"

"I think so. I overheard some of the girls talking about when Stanley took them out for a hamburger or they went for a drive. The girls think I don't know, and I pretend not to notice 'cause it's good for the girls to get out once in a while."

Lacey was standing menacingly over Miss Frankie now and Luke was getting nervous. "And none of the girls ever told you that Stanley acted inappropriately? No touching in private areas? No lewd remarks about body parts?"

"Dr. Lacey, Stanley is a gentle, kind man who helps us out around here when no one else does. The girls like to get out and act normal. Stanley gives them that chance once in a while. That's all."

Luke almost shoved Lacey aside to stand before Miss Frankie, "I need Stanley's address and phone number. I hope you're right about Stanley, Miss Frankie, but I need to talk to him."

Miss Frankie read off the address. There was no phone number.

"Let's sit down again," offered Luke hoping they hadn't lost Miss Frankie's trust. "When was the last time Stanley was here at the shelter?"

Miss Frankie looked at Lacey, then Luke, and back to Lacey. "It's best if you answer Detective Luke's questions," Lacey spoke sternly, but placed a sympathetic hand on Miss Frankie's knee.

More hesitation. Finally, "Last Thursday. He fixed some stuck door hinges upstairs."

"Did he talk to any of the girls?"

"Jasmine, Riana, and maybe a few others. They were all here then." Miss Frankie's eyes flew open wide. "Oh my." Both hands flew to her face.

"What is it, Miss Frankie?"

"We don't keep no records of the girls comings and goings, and we don't file Missing Persons reports when girls just leave here. Girls go without saying goodbye all the time, so I didn't think anything of it. Thursday was the last time I saw Jasmine, and Megan hasn't been around since Saturday. Oh God. What have I done?"

Miss Frankie was rational enough to identify the picture on Luke's cell phone. The unidentified girl from the Sunshine Skyway was Megan Fisher.

Miss Frankie called Miss Abigail and the three girls into the living room. Miss Abigail basically repeated what Miss Frankie had said. All three girls knew Stanley, but didn't say anything bad about him. No touching or improper language was admitted to. All three knew Jasmine and Megan but had no idea where they were. Lacey seemed to believe them, but Luke reserved judgment.

Chapter Seven

Tuesday, First Week in October
Luke's car
St. Petersburg, FL
12:43 p.m.

Luke punched Stanley Robbins address into his GPS and started following its directions. He drove fast but not recklessly. Lacey broke the chilly silence, "Luke, what do you really think about Stanley Robbins being involved in Jasmine's death and Megan's injuries?"

"Just a feeling right now, but this is one hell of a coincidence if he isn't." Luke looked at Lacey. "By the way, I hate coincidences." Luke lowered his voice, "Unfortunately we have absolutely no evidence against him. The girls, Miss Abigail, and Miss Frankie all claim he's harmless, so I can't even call him a person of interest, much less a suspect. Right now, he's just a name on a list of folks I need to talk to. All we can do is ask him some questions, but I doubt he'll confess to anything—if he is guilty of anything. He may not have anything to do with Jasmine's death or Megan's injury. We need more evidence." Luke looked over at Lacey again and continued, "I just have this nagging feeling that something is very wrong here, and Stanley Robbins is smack-dab in the middle of it."

"So, what are you going to do when we confront Mr. Robbins?"

Luke returned his gaze to the road. Lacey wasn't a police officer and couldn't be placed in potentially dangerous situations. His thoughts were interrupted by beeps from his cell phone. Luke slowed down a little and flipped it open.

"Detective Brasch. What can I do for you?"

"Doctor Williams here, Detective. Good news. Your mystery gal has come out of whatever coma she was in. She's getting stronger now that she's awake and eating. She says her name is Megan Fisher, but won't say anything else. Just thought you'd like to know."

Additional confirmation of Megan's identity. Luke's annoyance subsided. "Did you get the court order for the sexual assault exam?"

"Yes, I did. Thanks. I conducted it a few hours before she woke up and faxed the report to your office. Didn't you get it?"

"I've been out all day. Can you give me the highlights, Doctor?"

"Sure, glad to. Inconclusive, I'm afraid. Some evidence of bruising, but not definitive for sexual assault. No semen or sperm. He could have used a condom, or just not ejaculated if there was penetration. Or, she wasn't sexually assaulted at all. As I said, inconclusive."

"Thanks, Doctor. Is she strong enough to talk to me?"

"I think so, but she really isn't very talkative."

Glancing over at Lacey again and smiling, "That's okay. I know someone who can get her to open up. Thanks again, Doctor."

◻ ◻ ◻

The house located at the address Miss Frankie gave for Stanley Robbins was in a nice neighborhood in Seminole, a municipality about ten miles northwest of downtown St. Petersburg. Luke told Lacey to stay in the car while he approached the door alone. Pleasant chimes announced him when the button was pressed. After a few moments a woman's voice spoke through the closed door, "Yes, who is it?"

"My name is Detective Lucas Brasch with the St. Petersburg police department. May I come in to speak with you, please?"

"Can I see some identification first?" The door opened as far as the chain would allow.

Luke angled his badge and ID so the woman could see them through the slim crack. "Thank you." Then she closed the door enough to remove the chain and ushered Luke inside. Lacey watched all of this from inside the locked SUV. She could see the lady was in her mid thirties wearing a pink bathrobe. She had ash brown hair pulled back in a ponytail.

"Thank you for seeing me, Ms… "

"Sorry, I'm Mrs. Nancy Kemp." Luke wrote her name in his notepad as she led him into a small den and they both sat down.

"Do you live here, Mrs. Kemp?"

"Yes, my husband and I bought this place about two years ago."

"What's your husband's name, ma'am?"

"Trevor. Trevor Kemp. May I ask why you're questioning me? What's all this about?"

"I'm just following up on some leads in a routine investigation. Do you know a man named Stanley Robbins?"

Hesitation as she looked at Luke. Nancy couldn't figure out why this detective was asking about a person she never heard of. She eyed him skeptically, "No. I don't recognize that name."

Luke kept scribbling in his pad. "Do you and your husband live here alone?" Luke was fishing for a houseguest hoping it was Stanley Robbins.

"Yes. It's just the two of us. We don't have children."

"How long have you been married, Mrs. Kemp?"

"We married in February of last year." Each new answer was more difficult to illicit than the last. Nancy's mood was becoming hostile and defiant.

"Detective, I really don't see why you're asking me all these questions. I don't know who you're asking me about, and my personal life shouldn't be questioned as part of any routine investigation."

Luke ignored her objections. "Just a few more questions, Mrs. Kemp. Do you know the previous owners of this property?"

A short hesitation, then, "My husband and I never met them. We saw the house with our real estate agent and our lawyer handled the closing." She was eyeing Luke with even greater skepticism now.

"Do you know the previous owner's name, ma'am?"

"Sorry, I don't remember, but I'm sure there are records."

"Yes, there are. Thank you for your time, Mrs. Kemp." Luke rose and extended his hand, "Please take my card, and if you think of anything else, kindly give me a call."

Nancy took the card, looked at it, shook hands, and led Luke to the door. "I really am sorry I couldn't help you, but I don't know anything relevant to your investigation."

"Thank you again, Mrs. Kemp." Nancy slammed the door behind him.

Luke called the station and ordered a property search to see who owned the house before the Kemps.

"Seems like a dead end with Stanley's address. I'll see what the property records turn up, but I'm not holding my breath. Looks like good old Stanley just picked an address to give to Miss Frankie. So, now we have to find him some other way." Luke called the station again and ordered a Be-on-the-Lookout, a BOLO, for Stanley using the description Miss Frankie provided and the information about his Honda she'd given him. He'd get a copy of Stanley's driver's license and car registration when he returned to the station later that day. With that done, Luke's thoughts returned to questioning Megan now that she was awake.

"We're going to interview Megan at the hospital," said Luke nonchalantly to Lacey. "Can you talk to her?"

"Sure, I can try. Maybe she knows things about Stanley that Miss Frankie doesn't."

"Miss Frankie knows a lot," countered Luke.

"Yes she does, but girls talk to other girls about some things they won't talk about to a mom or mother figure."

"Don't girls tell mom everything?"

"For normal girls, **almost** everything. Abused girls aren't normal. These girls are getting hurt, sometimes with the knowledge and consent of mom. Many abused women don't want to upset or lose their man, so they look the other way sometimes when daughter is concerned. Daughter quickly learns mom can't be trusted. No trust, no confiding."

"Soooo, how do we get through to Megan?" Luke drew out his question.

"We have to gain her trust. Show her that we won't hurt her; that we're not a threat to her physically or emotionally." Lacey was calm and collected.

"I'll bet you're going to tell me that gaining her trust will take time."

"You catch on fast, Doctor Detective." Lacey chuckled at her own clever use of titles.

"Cute. So, do you even want me in the room when you try to gain her trust?"

"Of course. She needs to trust you too, and understand that this is serious business."

"Fine, I'll try to follow your lead."

"Luke, I know you. You can pretend to be a tough cop, but deep down you're really sensitive and a genuinely nice person. Just be yourself when you do your job. You can show compassion. Kids are very perceptive, especially ones that live by their own wits. I suspect Megan can spot a phony a mile away."

"Then why didn't she spot Stanley?"

"Good question. Maybe Megan doesn't think he's a threat, and maybe that's a clue. We really don't know if he's involved with any of this, do we?"

"You're right. You're right. But, I have my suspicions. Interviewing Stanley Robbins is near the top of my list, but that can only happen after we find him. By the way, let's try to get a better description of Stanley from Megan. Driver's License photos don't do anyone justice."

"Certainly, I'll try. What's next on your agenda? I can tag along if you think I can help. I'll just reschedule a few more appointments." Lacey was almost pleading.

Luke had his opening, "No thanks, Lacey. Not today. When we're done at the hospital, I'll drop you back at the station. I've got some paperwork I need to finish up, so I'll hunt down Robbins for a friendly chat tomorrow if the BOLO doesn't produce him sooner. Let's just head for the hospital now. When we're done there you can keep your appointments. Your clients are also important."

They arrived at the hospital ten minutes later. Luke glided smoothly into a parking space, turned off the engine, and trudged around to help Lacey out.

◻ ◻ ◻

Megan was propped up in the bed watching TV. Her long straight mousey blond hair was combed neatly. Her hospital gown was haphazardly draped, exposing a thin white thigh. Megan turned to survey the two strangers as they cautiously entered the room. No one was in the second bed.

"Megan, my name is Lacey Hirsch. This is Detective Lucas Brasch from the St. Petersburg Police department. We'd like to talk to you about what happened over the weekend."

Click—the TV went silent and Megan just stared. Luke spoke, "We're here to help you. We won't harm you in any way, and you're not in any trouble. Will you talk to us?" Shoulder shrug from Megan.

Lacey moved closer to Megan and gently pulled the gown over the exposed thigh.

A shy, "Thanks," as Megan absently smoothed the gown even further.

Lacey pressed on in spite of Megan's uneasiness. "How are you feeling, Megan?"

"Okay, I guess." No eye contact by Megan.

"Are they taking good care of you here? Do you want anything? Books? Music?" Lacey was trying hard to gain Megan's trust.

"I'm okay."

"Do you know why you're here in the hospital?"

"I know where I am, but I don't remember how I got here. I know I have some cuts, and I was asleep for a long time." Megan touched her injured thigh as she spoke, and looked directly at Lacey for the first time.

"Do you remember anything? What was the last thing you do remember?"

"I don't want to get anyone in trouble."

"Don't worry about that. Miss Frankie is just very worried about you. She's not in trouble either and would welcome you back."

"No, not Miss Frankie. She's cool." Megan looked away.

"Then who, Megan? Who don't you want to get in trouble?"

"I just wanted to go for a ride."

"Did you? Did someone take you for a ride?"

Slow head nod.

"Who took you for a ride, Megan?" Lacey asked softly but sternly.

Megan looked away and whispered, "Mr. Stanley."

Lacey backed away when Luke stepped in front of her. "Megan, what can you tell me about Mr. Stanley? Was he always nice to you?"

No answer.

"Megan, we can't help you if you won't talk to us."

Violent head shake then a stare at the far wall.

Lacey stepped forward again. "Megan, look at me," as she gently pulled Megan's face around. Megan didn't resist. She just stared directly at Lacey, and then her eyes darted to Luke. Lacey quickly assessed the problem. "What if Detective Brasch stepped out and just you and I talk for a while? Girl talk. Would that be okay?"

Luke understood immediately. "I'll get us some sodas. Any preference, Megan?"

Very softly, "Diet Coke, please."

"You got it. I'll be back in five or ten minutes. Water for you, Lacey?"

Lacey replied in the affirmative.

Luke nodded at Lacey indicating he approved of her approach and headed for the hallway.

About eight minutes later, Luke returned with three plastic bottles, stopped just outside the doorway, and craned his neck to listen. He could make out Lacey's calm voice. Megan's whispering was dotted with gasps and sobs. He couldn't really understand what either was saying, so he decided to let Lacey continue on her own for the time being. Strolling to the lounge about 50 feet away, he opened his soda and took a long swallow.

The TV in the visitor lounge was tuned to Bay News 9, the Tampa Bay 24 hour news, weather, and sports channel exclusive to Bright House cable customers. The anchorman was introducing a Breaking News story. The bright flashing lights on the TV screen caught Luke's eye. A female reporter was on scene at the Pinellas County side of the Gandy Bridge that connects St. Petersburg to Tampa. The Gandy Bridge is about four miles to the south of the Howard Frankland Bridge. Traffic was a mess as it merged into just a single eastbound lane. Police and emergency vehicle lights flashed haphazardly behind her. Westbound gawkers slowed to a crawl looking for anything gruesome. Yellow police tape flapped in the wind.

He chose a chair near an end table but where he could see the TV. The bottles were set down on the table as Luke settled into his chair. No one else was in the room. The sound was low, but Luke could make out most of what the reporter was saying as she described how the body of a young, unidentified girl was found behind some bushes an hour or so ago. The St. Petersburg police weren't commenting, but the Parks Department worker who found the body said the girl was naked and that he saw blood. It appeared she'd been there overnight.

Luke instantly realized that this tragedy occurred just a few days after Megan was assaulted and Jasmine was killed. Brain synapses flashed into overdrive as he thought about the similarities in two, maybe all three cases. First Jasmine, then Megan, and now this unidentified girl had something in common besides their age—all three were found near the end of a long bridge. Coincidence? Luke returned his concentration back to the TV, but nothing else was reported during the ten minute cycle between the *Weather on the Nines* reports. He'd have to check it out himself later.

Luke grabbed the three bottles and headed back to Megan and Lacey. He knocked gently while opening the door. "How're you two girlfriends doing?" Big smile while holding up the drinks.

Both Lacey and Megan turned to face Luke. Lacey smiled back and mouthed, "Okay," as a signal that the situation was improving. Megan said nothing and remained expressionless.

Luke approached and handed the diet coke to Megan. A soft, "Thanks," preceded Megan sheepishly reaching out to take the bottle. "You're very welcome, Megan."

Luke handed the bottled water to Lacey and said, "We need to talk as soon as you're done here." Another head nod as she turned back to Megan.

Lacey addressed Megan, "Is it okay if I leave with Detective Brasch?"

Megan looked down at her lap and whispered, "Yes, if you have to. Thanks for talking to me."

"Can Detective Brasch and I come back to talk to you some more tomorrow?"

A little louder, "I'd like that."

"Good. Now I need a hug. How about it?" Lacey spread her arms wide while smiling broadly and leaning towards Megan.

With a hint of a smile Megan hugged Lacey in a long, tight embrace.

Back on the road Lacey recapped what she learned from Megan, including a general description of Stanley that was similar to the one Miss Frankie gave them. Lacey explained that the kids didn't think Miss Frankie knew that Stanley occasionally snuck the girls out for a drive and a bite to eat. It was always one girl at a time to avoid suspicion. Megan had been out with Stanley before this last time, and he hadn't acted inappropriately on those two previous excursions. After about an hour or so Stanley always returned the girls to the shelter. Megan confided that some older girls who were out with Stanley more often than Megan hinted at being touched inappropriately. One girl said Stanley asked her to undress and she did just to be nice to him. The girl said Stanley touched her all over, and asked her to touch him inside his pants, but she claimed there was no intercourse. Maybe there was and the girl was afraid to admit it even to the other girls. Lacey concluded with, "Who knows."

All of this seemed to startle Luke and he struggled to regain his composure, "So what do you think? Stanley's a pedophile who gets his kicks playing around with teenage girls?" Luke's initial suspicions about Stanley was proving to be right.

"Probably, but there's more."

Luke shook his head in disbelief, "It just gets better and better all the time. Keep going. You're doing fine." Luke gripped the steering wheel tighter as he strained to listen closely.

"Okay, here goes. Stanley snuck Megan out Saturday evening and took her to the McDonalds about two miles from the shelter. After burgers and fries Stanley drove to the Skyway and parked on the fishing pier. Another man Megan had never seen before was waiting there in a dark colored SUV. All three sat around drinking and just talking. Beer for the guys, just water for Megan. Megan doesn't remember much after that. The only thing she vaguely remembers is banging on a car window before collapsing and blacking out again. The next thing she clearly remembers is waking up in the hospital."

Luke offered, "There's no mention of checking Megan for drugs in her system, so we can't be sure if, or why she blacked out." Luke was getting annoyed again, and Lacey was about to make it even worse.

"Date rape drugs and most other street drugs that cause blackouts don't remain in the system very long. That's why it's so hard to prosecute such cases when the girl waits a day or so before coming forward."

Luke banged his palm on the steering wheel and just shook his head. "Oh, shit. Now we've got two of them, at least according to Megan. It's a good start but we still need at least some corroborating evidence. Megan is a scared little girl who was in a coma for several days. Any district attorney will want more than just her account of what happened and who did, or didn't do anything to her. Plus, she doesn't remember anything bad happening to her."

Luke calmed down a little after a few deep breaths and changed subjects. He replayed the news about the murdered teenage girl just found near the Gandy Bridge, and reminded Lacey about Jasmine, the dead teen from Tampa. Lacey was now visibly shaken, but Luke needed her opinion. "I think these three cases might be connected somehow. There's something about the bridges that keeps gnawing at me. Something we haven't discovered yet. What do you think?"

Lacey was settling down now, but had nothing to offer. "I don't know. You're the detective. What's your gut feel?"

"I really prefer to follow the evidence when we have any, not my gut."

"Does your gut tell you where to look for evidence?"

"Sometimes, but I never thought about it that way." Thoughtful hesitation. "Yeah, I guess it does."

"If there's a connection, has your gut told you anything about *how* the girls got to the bridges?"

"Of course. The cars. I do intend to look into Stanley's car and the SUV Megan told you about." Luke felt compelled to justify his plans.

"You're welcome," said Lacey to the unspoken, "Thank You," with satisfaction.

□ □ □

Less than a mile from the Station Luke's phone beeped again. Detective Ronny Sinclair was reporting in. "Detective Brasch. Hi. How's it going on your end? I'll share with you if you share with me." Chipper wasn't the mood Luke was in, and Luke was getting annoyed at Detective Sinclair's seeming lack of seriousness. "Hi, Detective. What do you have for me?"

"Made a trip over to Avalon. Man, that road construction by the airport is a bitch. Anyway, I found out who rented your abandoned SUV. Some dude from North Carolina. Seven day rental, but must have been abandoned on day six since the guy hadn't reported the damn thing stolen before it was found. No forensics. Avalon was glad to get it back so they just cleaned it as they always do and put it back in service. They hit up the Visa for the abandonment expenses, but the card was already maxed out. I'm faxing the report to your office."

"Thanks. Here's what I've got for you." Luke proceeded to summarize what he and Lacey found out about Jasmine Griswold, and finished up just as they were parking in the police department lot. Luke decided he should tolerate Sinclair; the guy did come through. They both hung up with an exchange of pleasantries.

Luke pondered the new information: an SUV on one end of a long Tampa Bay Bridge where a naked dead teenage girl was found at the other end. Too much similarity to be just a coincidence. He ran that by Lacey, and she agreed he should pursue the leads wherever they went, even to the surrounding counties.

Luke needed to talk to his lieutenant.

Luke walked Lacey to her Jaguar and gave her a tentative peck on the cheek. "You were a big help today, Lacey. I really appreciate what you've done."

"Just doing my job, Partner," as Lacey playfully punched Luke's arm.

Luke pretended to grimace in pain and rub his arm, smiled, and held the door open for Lacey. She got in and Luke watched her drive away before he headed for the police station entrance.

◻ ◻ ◻

Luke briefed Lieutenant Nick Thompson and answered a few simple questions before the conversation turned to Lacey. "So, Luke, has Dr. Hirsch helped you out?"

"Yes, she has. Lacey…uh…Dr. Hirsch has a way with teenage girls." Luke was leery of where Nick might be going with this.

"Good. Keep bringing her around. Maybe she can help out on some of the other cases."

"Sure, Loo. I'll do that."

"So, where are you headed with all this?'

Luke was relieved to return to his cases, "Nothing solid yet. Still interviewing the players and trying to collect evidence. Hillsborough County may be involved."

Loo made a face and puckered his lips, "Okay. Keep me posted."

"Yes, sir. I will."

Luke walked out of Nick's office in no better position than when he walked in. He needed to talk to some of the other detectives and do some research before going any further with cases he wasn't assigned to investigate.

But first, he needed to get to his Advanced Criminology Class at St. Petersburg College. Luckily, he'd planned ahead and had his books and notes with him.

CHAPTER EIGHT

Wednesday, First Week in October
Police Station
St. Petersburg, FL
10:49 a.m.

What Luke had learned after an extensive computer search only complicated the situation. Stanley Robbins had no criminal history, he held a valid Florida drivers license with no Wants or Warrants out against him, and no recent traffic violations. Luke reconfirmed that Stanley owned a properly registered six-year old white Honda. There were no pending court cases with Stanley Robbins as a plaintiff or defendant. There was no real estate in his name anywhere in the Tampa Bay area or surrounding counties. A credit check revealed that Stanley had a reasonable credit rating, no bankruptcies, a modest debt on a Visa card, and no mention of employment other than *self employed*. The listed address on his driver's license was the same as Miss Frankie gave—the Kemp home. Nothing to corroborate what Megan told him, so Luke couldn't move Stanley to the top of the suspect list yet. But in reality, Stanley Robbins was still the only suspect, and Luke wanted to find and talk to him more than ever. There was still no confirmation of, or information about the mystery man Megan told them about, so Luke couldn't spend much time on him. In reality, Luke couldn't figure out how to even begin looking into this new mystery man.

Talking to other detectives was no more fruitful. None of the other detectives were working cases involving stolen or abandoned vehicles, or murdered teenage girls except the one from yesterday near the Gandy Bridge. Luke got no more information other than what the news reported. Luke knew he had to wait until the murdered girl could be identified, or new information developed before he could change focus.

He should schedule an interview with the teens who found Megan. At the same time, Luke was starting to question his own suspicions. Maybe there *isn't* a connection, and Stanley Robbins *is* just a coincidence. Maybe Megan is wrong, or confused, and there isn't a second guy. None of the other girls at the shelter mentioned a second guy. Luke decided to withhold judgment for a few more days. Maybe some new evidence would turn up.

A phone call to Randy Swanson's home was answered by his mother, who usually works from home. Mrs. Swanson was cordial and informed Luke that Randy would be home by 3:30. Luke was welcome to stop by then. Mrs. Swanson also offered to contact Randi Kingston and have her come home with Randy. "Thank you, Mrs. Swanson. I appreciate your help. I'll see you around 3:30."

Nothing on Stanley's BOLO. Luke checked again to see if there was anything new on the Gandy murder victim. There wasn't, so Luke picked up his sport coat and headed out to lunch at the St. Petersburg Pier. Luke often went to this iconic landmark to relax in its easygoing pace. He could be surrounded by tourists, yet be alone. He could gaze out on the scenic Tampa Bay, watch expensive yachts come and go, and marvel at smaller motorboats and sailboats of every size and color as they glided around in no particular direction. He could just think. Sometimes he would take out his fishing gear and try his luck. If Luke ever caught anything he would immediately release it back into the blue waters of Tampa Bay. Luke rarely spoke to the other fishermen, and never to the tourists that sometimes mobbed the shops and restaurants. He usually just preferred to be alone with his thoughts.

Today, Luke just wandered around. He watched excited tourists climb aboard a tourist charter boat that advertised, "See the Dolphins up close". Next, he sauntered over to where the recreated pirate ship, the Bounty, was docked. Luke's thoughts drifted to the Gasparilla festivities, the event named after the famous early 1800's pirate, Jose Gaspar. Area officials made a really big deal about the February and

March activities. Fun and games for all. There were re-enacted pirate invasions using this very ship, a fake kidnapping of the Tampa mayor to steal the key to the city, pirate themed parades where thousands of colorful beaded necklaces were thrown by the handful to cheering children and adults by pirates and dignitaries walking the parade route and riding on imaginative floats. There were costume balls, and much more.

Luke smiled at himself as he realized how pirate themes were a favorite throughout the Tampa Bay area. The most prominent being the Tampa Bay Buccaneers professional football team. The Bucs even have a pirate ship built into their stadium, and proudly fire fake cannons when the Bucs score. Why not? That makes good sense. Tampa Bay *was* a pirates' haven in the old swashbuckling days a mere few hundred years ago.

Back to the present. Sitting alone at a window table facing Tampa Bay, Luke ordered one of his favorite meals. Gazing out the expansive third floor window, Luke reviewed what was still to be done: interview the remaining girls at the shelter, interview the teens who found Megan, talk to Megan again, confirm or debunk the existence of a second guy, and do something more to find Stanley. None of which he wanted to tackle by himself. Luke took a sip of his iced tea, whipped out his cell phone, and punched in Lacey's number, "Lacey, hi, it's me, Luke."

A little surprised. "Hi, Luke. Nice to hear from you. What's up?"

Luke explained his interview plan, and asked if she had the time to go with him. "I'm due in court at 1:00, but should be done by 2:00, or so. Judge Corey is a stickler for being on time. I also have some reports to write, but they can wait until this evening. Where should I meet you?"

Luke was thankful Lacey had cut back on her professional workload a year or so ago and was willing to go with him. The most convenient place was St. Petersburg Regional Hospital. They could talk to Megan again, head off to talk to the teens, and then hit the shelter. Stanley Robbins would have to wait until Luke gathered more evidence—or suspicions—against him. Besides, you can't talk to someone you can't get your hands on. The BOLO still hadn't turned up anything yet. Luke's lunch arrived with flair, so he bid farewell to Lacey and dug in with gusto.

◻ ◻ ◻

Lacey was waiting in the lobby of the hospital as Luke walked in. Today, she was a vision in black. Black pant suit, black top, black sandals, black jewelry. Only a hint of white in her earrings, a lapel pin, small purse, and shiny bright white teeth. What a smile.

Luke returned the smile and they momentarily embraced. The ride up the elevator and down the hallway was peppered with idle chit chat. The door to Megan's room was open and they walked in. Still no roommate. Megan was staring at the TV and didn't notice them until she heard her name called. Big smile when she recognized Lacey. "Hi, Megan. How are you feeling today?"

Most of the girls at the shelter had the odd habit of calling everyone by a title and their first name, except for Miss Frankie, which was a twist on her last name that sounded like a first name. "Oh, much better, Doctor Lacey." Perky and poised. A good sign. Lacey had already checked and found out that Megan would be released around 4:00 p.m. The only issue was to whom she would be released. Social Services hadn't found a foster home yet. Megan still refused to divulge where her family lived.

"I hear you're about to be released. Do you want to go back to Miss Frankie?"

The smile disappeared, "Will Stanley be there?"

Luke answered, "No, Megan. Stanley won't be allowed to go to the shelter ever again."

Thoughtful pondering. "Well, okay. I like Miss Frankie, and the others there are nice to me, too."

Lacey responded to Megan, "Good. We'll check on the arrangements after we leave here."

"Dr. Lacey, will you come by to see me?"

"Certainly, Megan. I'll stop by as often as I can. I promise." Lacey held up her hand in a swearing motion. Megan smiled again.

"Megan, Detective Luke has a few more questions. I'd appreciate it if you answer them. Will you?"

Sheepish shrug. "I'll try."

Luke moved closer and smiled, "Megan, Dr. Lacey told me about the night at the Skyway. You know she told me those things so I can help you, don't you?"

Looking down at her hands folded in her lap, "I understand."

"Good girl. Do you remember anything about the man Stanley and you met at the Skyway?"

"He was just some skinny guy. I'd never seen him before."

"Was he tall? Short? White? Black? Did you hear a name? Anything you can remember."

Megan rested her chin on a small palm and then looked up, "He was an old white guy."

Lacey asked, "Is he older than Detective Luke?"

"It was kind of dark, but yeah, old like Detective Luke, much skinnier, and almost as tall." Lacey looked away as both she and Luke chuckled into their hands. Thirty-something is old to a young teenager.

Returning to Megan, Luke repeated, "Did you hear a name?"

More pondering by Megan as Luke and Lacey waited. Finally, "Mike. Mitch, maybe, but I don't remember." Another shrug.

"Okay. Would you recognize the man if you saw him again?"

"Yeah, I think so." Head bob for emphasis.

"Do you think you could describe the man well enough so an artist can draw a picture of him?"

A slower head bob. "I might be."

"Will you at least try? It's okay if it doesn't work out."

A long look at Lacey, then back to Luke. Lacey's nods reassured Megan. "Okay. I'll try."

"That's good, Megan. We'll work out the details and get back with you soon."

Luke was leaning back towds believing Megan, and wished he had a photo to show her, but the reality was that Luke had no idea who this second guy could be. He thought about showing Megan photos of known pedophiles in the Tampa Bay area, but decided against that. There were too many of them and the photos might unreasonably influence or confuse her. He had no choice but to wait for the composite by the police sketch artist.

❑ ❑ ❑

Randy Swanson and Randi Kingston both looked younger than they actually were. Both were well dressed and nice looking. They were good, wholesome teens and could be poster kids for what's right with American youth. The teens sat together on a red flower-patterned sofa. Randy was calm and collected and almost slouched. Randi was stiff and obviously uncomfortable. Randy's mom had laid out homemade cookies and offered a variety of canned sodas. Glasses and ice were nearby. Mrs. Swanson perched on a nearby chair in peach colored slacks and a white top with flowers of the same peach color. Luke and Lacey were seated on the only remaining chairs in the neat room.

Lacey started with small talk to put everyone at ease. She talked about the schools in the area, the declining local home prices that were common knowledge everywhere, the October weather, and such. Luke surveyed the nicely furnished room and noticed the display on a card table in the corner. Then he saw a red ribbon. "Is that your science project, Randy?"

"Yes, it is, sir." Randy and Luke got up and went over for a closer inspection.

"Second Place. Impressive. What's it about?"

Randy stood a little taller. "Well, sir, I've been interested in big things all my life, so I tried to compare small things everyone recognizes with something bigger. On a project like this I couldn't deal with *really big things* like huge stars and galaxies, so I concentrated on more familiar items."

Randy explained to Luke how even very thin things, like a dollar bill, can become taller than the Washington Monument when millions of them are stacked on top of each other. Randy continued enthusiastically and showed Luke how objects that weigh very little, a dime for instance, can weigh more than an elephant when millions are piled together. Randy moved on to the very small size of atoms and the staggering number of atoms and molecules in a single drop of water.

These were the most impressive examples, and Luke's head was spinning with memories of his science and chemistry classes and the complicated formulas and relationships he'd learned about. He needed to refocus. "These are impressive comparisons. Sounds like a first place prize to me. What did the first place winner do?"

"First place went to a gal that designed and built a fuel cell that ran on trash. But that's cool. I won $500. I'm proud of second place."

"As you should be," exclaimed Luke. He looked at the ladies before he clapped his hands together and walked back to the group. With the pleasantries over, Luke started the official questioning. "Okay. Let's get down to why we're here."

Luke leaned forward and began in measured tones speaking directly to the teens, "Both of you know that you are not in trouble with the police. We just need to ask you some questions about what you saw or heard last Saturday night. Okay?"

Both Randy and Randi nodded and said in unison, "Yes, we know."

"Good. Start from the beginning on last Saturday evening, and be as specific as possible."

The teens generally took turns describing what they did, saw, and heard that night, smartly leaving out what Randy's hand was doing under Randi's shirt. Luke interrupted only a few times to flush out more details. Part way through Randi said, "I sure hope that poor young girl is okay." Lacey assured everyone that she was, but gave no other information. Randi thanked her and returned to other aspects of that evening.

The teens insisted they neither saw nor heard anyone at the Sunshine Skyway Pier other than the young girl, at least not until the officers and paramedics arrived. The only new piece of information was the dark SUV the kids saw leaving as they were arriving. Could this SUV be somehow linked to Megan's SUV? Luke drew a big "?" next to his notes as a reminder to check it out.

"Can I see your car, Randy? I'd like the forensics team to check out the red stain you two told me about."

Randy looked around puzzled. "Uh...I ran the car through the car wash this morning when I filled up."

"Were the technicians here already?"

"No, sir. But it's been four days, and I like to keep the car clean. I just figured the police weren't interested."

"Didn't the officers at the scene ask you not to disturb the evidence?"

"Uh...Nooo. They didn't say anything about that." Randy's eyes darted around for help that never came.

Luke looked up at the ceiling then back at Randy, "That's okay. Don't worry about it." More scribbling in his notepad as Luke worked to control his anger at what appeared to be sloppy police work.

After Luke finished up his questioning, Lacey and Luke were ready to leave. Luke thanked the teens and Mrs. Swanson for their cooperation and hospitality. "If you think of anything else, please give me a call," as he handed each a business card. Luke and Lacey shook hands with the trio and headed out.

The mood in Luke's car was sour. Lacey thought the investigation was going along just fine. She didn't realize that it was spinning out of control. Luke just drove stone-faced and silent.

Miss Frankie was as cordial as the last time, but she was careful not to bring up the subject of Stanley Robbins. The interview with the remaining young girls elicited no new information. No mention of sneaky escapes with Stanley. No mention of any improper or sexual activity either. No mention of a second mystery guy. In fact, when pressed, each girl emphatically denied having anything to do with Stanley other than casual conversation at the shelter. To them, Stanley was just a sad little man who fixed things around the shelter. Luke wasn't sure if he should believe them or not. Lacey had no immediate impression either.

Luke was now worried that anything Megan said would be contradicted by these girls. Either these girls were not being completely truthful or Megan was mistaken. Someone may be lying. Luke was leaning towards believing Megan, but three high school girls against one young teenager aren't good odds.

The ride back to the station was even more tense. Lacey offered, "For what it's worth, I think the girls are holding something back."

"So do I, but I don't know what I can do about it. Extreme interrogation techniques aren't allowed against teenage girls anymore. I can't just make them tell the truth if they're determined to lie."

Lacey ignored Luke's sarcasm. "I think the girls are afraid to talk in front of Miss Frankie. They don't want to get kicked out by admitting to breaking the house rules. Some of the girls told Miss Frankie about the little forays with Stanley, but the other girls don't know that. Most think that Miss Frankie doesn't know anything about their escapes, and are afraid to speak up and tell the truth."

"Makes sense. So how do we get them to open up?"

"Easy. I talk to them at school, away from the shelter and Miss Frankie."

They were stopped at a traffic light, so Luke leaned over and kissed Lacey on the cheek as she stared straight ahead pretending not to notice, except for the broad grin on her face.

"How about tomorrow afternoon, Partner?" Lacey just kept grinning and continued looking straight ahead.

Chapter Nine

Thursday, First Week in October
Police Station
St. Petersburg, FL
9:14 a.m.

Luke finished his paperwork and started a new computer search, this time expanded to include all surrounding counties during the past five years. The five year period was a total guess, but it was a reasonable selection. Not too far back, but back far enough. He was looking for fairly recent unsolved murders or suspicious deaths of teenage girls. It took a few minutes for the computer memory banks to find the records, so Luke just rocked slowly and sipped coffee while he waited. Then the screen spit out a list of cases. There were seven new ones, and including Jasmine and the unidentified teen found on the Gandy Bridge, who was now dubbed Jeanie Doe, made nine unsolved teenage girl deaths in the past five years. Megan wouldn't show up when the criteria was a death, but she certainly couldn't be discounted just because she didn't die. Not yet anyway.

Luke mentally summarized his findings. There were eight unidentified teenage girls murdered in the Tampa Bay area over the past five years. There was one identified girl murdered, Jasmine, and one girl, Megan, injured during the past week or so. That made ten total unsolved cases. Not the kind of minimal field work Luke was limited to by his doctors. Luke decided to ignore the doctor's advice; he felt fine and needed to do this.

Luke read each computerized summary with intense interest, and a touch of surprise. Five of these seven girls were found at one end or the other of a Tampa Bay Bridge. Counting Megan, Jasmine, and Jeanie Doe from Tuesday there were eight such girls.

What other secrets were the long Tampa Bay bridges hiding? Luke's head started spinning just thinking about the number of girls and the similarities of each case; a long Tampa Bay bridge was now an added factor in each. Luke took a deep breath and pressed on. One of the non-bridge girls was found in an alley near the downtown St. Pete area, and the other was near the Tampa Bay Port, also in Hillsborough County. Neither was at the end of a long bridge, but both were less than two or three miles from one. Only Megan and Jasmine had been identified, so there was no way to determine where the others came from. Runaways, kidnappings, locals, or what? Luke continued raising his own questions out loud. More importantly, "Is this a pattern, and why hadn't anyone noticed the similarities before? Additionally, is there any connection with Stanley Robbins and a second guy?"

Each case was printed out in its entirety and re-read again. A black and white picture of the victim accompanied each file. Luke couldn't help but stare at each. What a damn shame. So many young lives snuffed out almost before they began. By 11:30 a.m., Luke was still trying to find connections between Megan, Jasmine, Jeanie Doe, and these seven new cases but couldn't spot much. The girls were all teens, but ranged in age from about 12 to 17. Three were black, two Hispanic, one Asian, and four white. No indications if any others were living at a shelter. None of their bodies were claimed by their families, possibly because they were unidentified and their respective families couldn't be notified. On the flip side, the families either did not know or care what happened, so no inquiries were made by the families. Maybe the families didn't even know to look in the Tampa Bay area. It seemed unlikely that all these families didn't care about a missing child? Luke put that unanswered question on the back burner.

Luke's desk phone rang. "Detective Luke Brasch. How can I help you?"

He was greeted by cheery voice on the other end, "How formal, Detective Brasch."

Luke relaxed back in his chair, "Hi, Lacey. Force of habit. I should've checked the Caller ID before I picked up. Sorry."

"Don't be silly. I'm just playing around with you."

"Lacey, please forgive me, but I'm just not in a playful mood right now."

Lacey asked a few questions but got even fewer answers. "We're in this together. I'll stop by the station and take you to lunch before I go to the high school to talk to the girls."

Luke really wanted to see Lacey again and run a few thoughts by her. Lacey's insights from a psychological standpoint were proving to be helpful. "That would be great, but chicks don't take me to lunch. I take them. Is that clear, ma'am?"

Lacey laughed out loud. "We'll see. I'll be there by 12:30. Be ready, sir."

◻ ◻ ◻

Lacey was ten minutes early. Luke was still looking over the printouts and making notes as she strolled to his desk. No surprise. Lacey was as elegant and glamorous as ever dressed in black, white, and grey.

"Give me a second to clear up this mess." The mess was a few neatly arranged computer printouts, grim looking head-shots of dead girls, handwritten notes on a pad of paper, and a noticeably thicker official file folder. Lacey waited while Luke put everything away and slipped on his sport coat. "And where am I taking you for lunch today, ma'am?"

◻ ◻ ◻

Lacey directed Luke to an Italian restaurant Luke would normally avoid because he thought it was too fancy and upscale for his taste. During Lacey's intermittent directions to turn left here or turn right there, Luke relayed what his computer search revealed. Lacey listened until Luke asked, "Well, what do you think? How does your psychological voodoo link all this? Should I even try to connect them?"

Lacey glared at Luke. "It's not voodoo, Luke, just insight and experience."

"Come on, Lacey. You know what I mean. No offense."

"None taken, thank you."

"So, what do you think?" Luke repeated.

Lacey had a simple answer. "Did you find out anything about the vehicles?"

"There you go again. Typical shrink-speak. Answer one question with another." Deep sigh. Lacey waited in silence as she stared directly into his eyes.

Luke finally blinked. "No. Not yet. I've been concentrating on the ten girls."

"All of those girls had to get to wherever they were dumped somehow, didn't they?"

"Sure. It's unlikely they drove themselves to their own deaths. But there's nothing to connect the three vehicles we know about with any of the murders. Even the SUV the kids saw may not mean anything, and we don't have any leads pointing us towards any particular vehicle. Nothing but a vague description of a dark SUV. Don't know what make or model. No license plate info. Not even a partial. Zippo. Nothing."

"Don't be sarcastic. I'm just trying to help you."

Luke sighed. "Sorry, I know you are. I'm just frustrated. I agree the vehicles may have some relevance. I just don't know if they do." A pause as Lacey remained quiet. "I don't even have any leads that might show relevance."

"You've already started, haven't you? You've got the abandoned SUV from Tampa, the SUV the teens saw before Megan was found, and the vehicle Megan described, plus Stanley Robbins' car. Want to hear my idea?" Lacey cocked her head and batted her eyelashes.

"Do I have to answer that?"

"Of course not. Did you try to correlate other abandoned or stolen vehicles with the dates of the murders?"

Luke was silent for several moments as he mulled over Lacey's suggestion. Finally, "That's a compelling angle, Lacey. Thanks."

"You're welcome."

"Remind me to kiss you when we get to the restaurant."

Giggle. "I will if I have to, but I suspect you won't need to be reminded." Lacey was right. He didn't.

Luke had to admit to himself that he was concentrating on the girls while almost ignoring the vehicles. He should pursue both angles at the same time. That's why partners are so important; a second opinion is invaluable in complicated police work.

Luke and Lacey kicked around a few other ideas, and the few pieces of information they had trying to get a better handle on these cases. Luke reminded Lacey that the only kids that had information about the Megan and Jasmine cases were all teens with serious incentives to shade the truth, or outright lie. Especially the girls at the shelter. Lacey agreed and assured him she would press the shelter girls for more answers when she saw them later that afternoon.

Then Luke repeated his prior thought. "I wonder how many of the girls in the new cases were living in shelters when they were killed? There's one or more in each county. Right?"

Lacey set down her fork and smiled at Luke. "Why, detective, I think you're on to something," as she reached over and squeezed his hand. Luke returned the gesture and held on longer.

"Checking out that theory will take some doing. How do we even find them? Most of the shelters aren't listed in the Yellow Pages."

Lacey thought for a few moments. "Maybe my connections with the courts might pry some addresses loose."

"You really think so?"

Lacey answered matter-of-factly, "Of course. The courts trust me. I'm no threat to the girls, and I know how to keep secrets. I'll let you know when I get them." Lacey picked up her fork and took another bite.

Luke just looked down, shook his head, and grinned before returning to his own lunch.

On the ride back to the police station, Luke again went over what he wanted Lacey to find out when she talked to the three shelter girls. Then he added, "I'll make a set of pictures of the eight unidentified murdered girls. See if the shelter girls recognize any of them. If they do, get whatever information you can."

"Will do, but keep in mind these girls would only know the ones that were in Miss Frankie's shelter. Even then, these girls may not have been in the shelter at the same time."

"That's right. So when can we hit the surrounding shelters?"

Lacey gave him a funny look. "Okay, I get it. I'll start this afternoon with one of the judges I know personally. Hopefully I'll have the addresses for you tomorrow."

"Now you're talking."

Lacey had called the principal at the High School earlier in the day and explained what she wanted to do. Dr. Tanya Birch was in her mid 50's and had been the principal there for four years. She alone knew that the three girls were actually living in the shelter. The teachers were not told, and the girls were warned to keep the secret with a threat of being kicked out of the shelter if they betrayed the secret.

The three girls were notified during their respective last period class to report to the principal's office after class. No reason was given or needed. The three girls trickled in one-by-one and were ushered into Dr. Birch's office. Lacey was waiting for them with Dr. Birch. The girls remembered meeting Lacey at the shelter and noticeably turned stiff and cool.

When all three teens were assembled and settled into chairs arranged in a circle in the center of the room, Dr. Birch thanked them for coming and re-introduced Lacey as a friend who needed their help. Lacey had toned down her appearance so she wouldn't present such a stark contrast to Dr. Birch, but more importantly with the girls. The girls were reluctant to be completely open and honest the last time they met and Lacey was determined to avoid the same outcome this time.

Lacey started with questions about their classes and the school experience in general. The girls seemed eager to discuss their feelings about school. Next, Lacey asked about the shelter, Miss Frankie, and finally Stanley Robbins. The hesitancy was back, so Lacey reminded the girls that one of their friends was hurt and another dead. The three girls looked at each other, shuffled their feet, slumped guiltily in their seats, but remained silent. Lacey tried another approach. "Stanley Robbins is not coming back to the shelter, not to do odd jobs, or to sneak any of you out for, shall we say *field trips*." No change in the girl's expressions. "You won't ever see him again. I also know that none of you will be punished in any way for anything you've done in the past." Lacey looked directly at each girl as she spoke. "More importantly, you will not be punished for anything you tell me now. I promise." Lacey covered her heart and raised her left hand as a show of honesty.

The three girls looked at each other again. The flood gates were opened and the girls poured out information for almost an hour. They told Lacey and Dr. Birch about the tricks used to sneak out when Stanley took them for rides and fast food. Eventually the girls revealed the touching and groping. All three had given him oral sex and two had agreed to go even farther. Only on one occasion could Stanley actually perform. No other men were mentioned. Lacey thought that was odd since Megan said that Stanley took her to meet another man. When asked by Dr. Birch why they allowed Stanley to treat them that way, they just shrugged, "No big deal." Their Moms were doing the same things, and more, with their boyfriends, so why not. At least Stanley was nice to them. All their mothers' boyfriends were awful and disgusting, and more often than not, the boyfriends beat up the moms and the kids. These three girls all ran away to escape the beatings. Stanley never hurt them, so trading sexual favors was just the price the girls were willing to pay for a ride, fresh air, and a burger.

This was not what either Dr. Birch or Lacey expected to hear.

Next Lacey produced the photos Luke gave her. Each girl looked closely at the first two and handed them back. No recognition. All three girls were visibly shaken when Lacey handed them the third photo. The dead teen was easily identified by name. Photo number five elicited the same shaken response and another name. Photo number six was recognized only by the oldest shelter girl from almost two years ago when she was there for the first time. When pressed by Lacey the girls said they thought the dead girls just ran away from the shelter. They didn't suspect any of the girls had been hurt or killed. "Girls just leave all the time. Nothing to get excited about when they do."

None of the girls knew if Stanley took any of the dead girls out for a ride, so Lacey couldn't figure out what any of this meant. She had no choice but to just report what she learned to Luke and let him sort it all out.

Lacey's notes concluded: "These girls have so little self-worth that they think the only way they can ever get anything is to give up their own bodies for the momentary pleasure of some man who was nice to them. Tragic, but not unheard of."

Chapter Ten

Thursday, First Week in October
Luke's Condo
St. Petersburg, FL
10:22 p.m.

Luke had just returned home from his Thursday class when his cell phone jingled. A quick peek at the caller ID informed him it was Lacey. Luke plopped down in his favorite chair as he flipped open the phone. Lacey's familiar cheerful voice greeted him, "Hi, Luke. How was class?"

"Hi, Lacey. Same old, same old. I'm beginning to think that I hate school."

"I liked school and vaguely remember my classes, so I sympathize with you." Lacey paused and giggled before adding, "But that was soooo long ago." Lacey enjoyed the good-natured jibes and was sure Luke did too.

Luke just sighed so Lacey continued, "I knew you were in class most of the evening, so I didn't call to report in until I thought you would be home."

"I appreciate your sensitivity to my schedule. Really, I do."

"I know you do, Luke." Lacey was all happy and bubbly. "So how was class?" she repeated in a soft sweet voice.

Luke laughed and momentarily forgot about why she probably called in the first place. They chatted leisurely and actually made a real date for the upcoming weekend; dinner and a movie on Saturday night.

After about fifteen minutes Lacey sensed that Luke was more relaxed. "So, want to hear about what the girls and I talked about?"

Luke sat more upright. "Yes, but can the details wait until tomorrow? How about just the highlights now?"

Lacey hit all the major points, some of which were a surprise to Luke. He had his suspicions, but here was some actual confirmation. He finally commented, "Trading sex for something in return. Lots of folks do that every day. Usually some pimp is at the tip of that iceberg." Stanley Robbins' status as a prime suspect just got stronger. Luke continued, "Unfortunately, just fooling around with teenage girls isn't evidence of murder. Any ideas about how to tie Stanley to the murders, or corroborate Megan's injury story?"

Somewhat dejected, "No, not really."

"Now, don't knock yourself down, kiddo. You did good. Be proud. Chin up. Shoulders back. Chest out, and all that rubbish."

Lacey smirked. "My chest is out, or hadn't you noticed?"

Luke had noticed. He'd admired, and had been impressed with Lacey's female attributes since the 10th grade when he first noticed how well she filled out her sweaters. Back then, Luke and Lacey were only casual acquaintances. It took a year for Luke to get up the courage to ask out one of the most popular girls in their Jewish youth group. Since then Lacey had matured into full curvaceous womanhood. Now he was really torn between treating her as a trusted colleague or a girlfriend. He couldn't see how she could be both. "Lacey, we need to focus on this case first. Our personal relationship will sort itself out."

Silence from Lacey. She knew that relationships don't just **sort themselves out**. Those in the relationship have to work hard to just maintain, much less grow their relationship.

"Lacey, don't get me wrong. Doing my job is very important to me. Someone has to catch these murdering bastards, and that someone is me."

"But, what about us?"

"What about us? We like being together. We're getting to know each other again, aren't we? Hell, I got you this consulting job so I could spend more time with you. Doesn't that count?" Luke's voice was louder and he spoke more rapidly.

Lacey backed off. "Look. I'm sure you're tired. So am I. I didn't mean to push you into anything. And by the way, I think what you did about my consulting with you was sweet. That does mean a lot to me."

"I did it because I do want to see more of you. Your resume and skills were just an excuse."

A few moments of silence. "I've got the addresses you asked for."

Luke took a deep breath. "Let's not discuss details like this over the phone."

"Of course not. What was I thinking?"

"No problem. How's your schedule for tomorrow?'

"I've got a session with two brothers at 11:00 a.m., but they've cancelled before. Should I drop by the station around nine?"

"No. I'm busy then. I've got other plans."

Startled. "Oh. I'm sorry. I didn't know that."

"Something very important with a special lady."

Lacey's blood went cold, and she waited in silence.

Luke chuckled, "I'm meeting you for breakfast tomorrow morning."

What a relief. Luke played silly games too. She should have known he was kidding her. Lacey smiled at the phone. "You are?"

"Yes, I am, if you'd be kind enough to join me."

"I'd like that." Lacey was impressed with Luke's approach.

They decided on a place and time, and that Luke would also pay for breakfast. Lacey fantasized about what it would be like to wake up next to Luke and have breakfast with him. But, such dreams would have to wait. They had murders to solve.

<u>Friday, First Week in October</u>
<u>A Local Restaurant</u>
<u>St. Petersburg, FL</u>
<u>7:26 a.m.</u>

Lacey was clad in a less dramatic outfit this morning. A fairly conservative dark grey pantsuit with a black top sporting a gold sunburst pattern. Minimal jewelry. No scarf. She was beginning to realize that her glamorous clothes weren't necessary for police consulting work. Luke complimented her anyway as if nothing changed, and Lacey thanked him with a kiss on the cheek. After five days of seeing each other every day, Luke and Lacey had yet to kiss each other on the lips.

The restaurant was conveniently located, reasonably priced, and served good food. Unfortunately sometimes the service was slow, but Luke frequented the place regularly anyway. Others had the same breakfast idea, so Luke and Lacey waited about fifteen minutes to be seated. Neither wanted anything fancy for breakfast. They both wanted coffee and orange juice. Lacey ordered a few pancakes and Luke ordered the featured breakfast.

As they chatted, Lacey was reluctant to flirt, but relented when Luke covered her hand with his as they joked around. Police work and shop talk was off limits until they were finished eating. Both enjoyed the leisurely breakfast and their time together.

At about 8:30 Luke paid the bill and left a generous tip, as he always did. The weather was cool with a light breeze, so they sat in Luke's SUV with the windows down. Luke took out his pad and pen to take notes as Lacey rummaged through her purse to retrieve the neatly printed report she'd prepared last night. When both were settled in and ready Lacey began reading out loud from her report. That way she wouldn't forget anything or mix up any of the facts. The details for the secret shelters in the surrounding counties were on a separate piece of paper. Very professional.

Luke took few notes because the report was so thorough. He decided to just include it in the file. He interrupted her occasionally only to find out his question was answered later in the report. She thought of almost everything and covered several angles. Lacey showed Luke the two photos the girls said they knew from the Pinellas County shelter. She had carefully made notations on the back of each, including a name in capital letters. A third photo had a note indicating that only one of the girls knew the victim from two years ago. None of the shelter girls recognized the four dead girls in the other photos.

Lacey really did a good job and Luke commented on her proficiency and professionalism. "Thank you. I'm here to serve and please, boss." Both grinned as Luke squeezed her hand.

Neither was sure about the rest of the day or if Lacey would need her own car, so Luke asked Lacey to follow him back to the police station to do some more computer searches along the lines Lacey suggested and Luke expanded upon. They would try to correlate abandoned and stolen cars with the murder dates, and would proceed further if promising information turned up.

◻ ◻ ◻

Lacey's appointment had cancelled, so she was free until the afternoon. By 11:15 a.m., Luke and Lacey were combing through over one thousand stolen and abandoned vehicle reports in the Tampa Bay area during the last five years. Most were closed because the vehicle was found and returned to the rightful owner. Apprehending the thief was not a priority, so little, or no forensics was collected. Seventy-three were reported as joy-rides involving rambunctious teens. Twenty-nine were thefts by family members; mostly teenage kids where the car was returned, but only after a police report had been filed. Thirteen involved a rental car company vehicle. Of course, there was no way of telling how many thefts went unreported. Luke knew there were too many reports to track down individually.

Luke pondered his dilemma, then decided to sort by dates of interest, carefully eliminating any car theft or abandoned vehicle that was more than two days before or after a murder. The list dwindled to a mere 87 reports. Much more manageable. Next Luke eliminated any car not found within two miles of a bridge. Down to 28. Lacey was getting excited. Luke knew that this was only the first step. They still had to connect the vehicles with the murders. No easy task with the meager evidence they had.

A good time to break for lunch. Lacey insisted that she at least be allowed to pay her own way. Luke reluctantly relented when Lacey made a pouty face and stamped her foot. It was an act, but one that was witnessed by two other detectives who looked away and snickered when Luke stared them down.

As they were walking out, Luke realized something else; he could try to correlate these 28 vehicles with the other side of the bridge from where a body was found. He knew the bridges connected different counties, and each county had different law enforcement agencies. If the police departments of the three counties investigated what each thought was a separate homicide or vehicle crime in their county, a dead body wouldn't be associated with a vehicle in another county.

Light bulbs went off in Luke's head. What a great theory: ***a murder in one county and a stolen or rental vehicle dumped in another***. But, didn't Luke just learn that all the law enforcement agencies in the Tampa Bay area were working to modernize their computer systems to be able to share information like this more easily? Luke made a note to check out how the computer upgrades were coming along.

If his theory was right nine murders, one injured girl, and ten vehicles—20 possible cases—could be reduced to 10, maybe even fewer. Possibly only one killer, or one group of killers, and car thieves.

Maybe now we might start learning the secrets of the bridges. Luke and Lacey were out in the parking lot before Luke snapped back to the present time. "Lacey, would you mind putting off lunch? I've got some more research to do—right now."

Lacey stopped and looked at him quizzically, then told a little white lie. "No. It doesn't matter to me one way or the other. Do you want me to help you, or should I just go by myself?" There was no anger or annoyance in her voice.

"I don't want you to waste your time. I don't know how long this might take, or even if it will lead to anything useful. You probably have more important things to do."

"My work isn't any more important than yours, but I'll just leave you to your research anyway. I've got three sessions at my office later today and I need to prepare for them."

"Sorry. I'll make this up to you somehow, and I'll call you this evening."

"I'll be waiting, Luke. Don't give it another thought. Good luck with your research."

Lacey moved closer to give him a peck on the cheek, but his cell phone beeps stopped her.

Luke snatched his phone out, glanced at the Caller ID, and made a face. "Hi, Mom. What's up?"

"Lucas, don't be so grumpy. Did I catch you at a bad time?"

"No, Mom. I've got a few minutes." Luke made another face to Lacey, who just shrugged.

"Can you get here by six tonight for Sabbath Dinner?"

"I'll try. No guarantee."

"Don't be late, Lucas," mom said sternly.

"I'll do the best I can."

"Are you bringing that nice Lacey Hirsch?"

"I haven't asked her yet."

"Why not? What are you waiting for?"

"I've been busy, Mom."

"Too busy to have a life? Call her right now, and I'll see you both at six. Bye, Lucas." The phone went silent. Luke looked at the phone before closing it. Lacey heard the entire conversation, turned to look directly at Luke, and cooed in a sing-song tone, "Anything you want to ask me, Lucas?" They both laughed so hard they bent over holding their sides.

When they calmed down, Lacey giggled, "Pick me up at 5:30." Then they broke out in laughter again.

Chapter Eleven

Five years earlier
An Apartment
Clearwater, FL
7:12 p.m.

The male voice was calm but stern, "Stanley, it's been over five weeks since you brought me a girl."

"I just can't keep sneaking girls out. Miss Frankie will find out."

"No, she won't. Not if you're careful."

"I don't like doing this."

"I don't give a shit about what you like or don't like. Just remember your poor mother and the jail cell she'd be sitting in."

Stanley's mom had several run-ins with the law a few years back. Drugs, prostitution, and petty theft, but no lengthy jail time. Stanley was scared and nearly hysterical each time his mom got arrested. The man was an old boyfriend of Stanley Robbins' mother, Martha Robbins, and used Stanley's fears to his advantage. The guy was about fifteen years older than Stanley. He punched her around when he felt like it, got her hooked on a variety of illegal drugs, and pimped her out whenever he was low on cash. They were occasionally seeing each other when Martha finally sought help at Miss Frankie's shelter. The guy had moved out of town to avoid getting arrested, but he was able to track her down the few times she tried to get away from him before. He did so again after she left the shelter. Now Stanley was older and could be manipulated with threats against Martha. Stanley loved his mother and would do anything to protect her. Cynics would call him a mama's boy. Stanley's weak mental abilities also worked against him.

The man was even getting Stanley hooked on the young girls. Touching at first and then whatever Stanley could get the girl to do. Mostly the girls were eager to cooperate, especially when they were rewarded.

Stanley finally relented. "Okay. I'll meet you at the west end of the Courtney Campbell Causeway Saturday night around 9:00. The eastbound side."

"See how easy that was. Good boy, and say *hi* to your mom for me." A sickening grin crossed his face.

◻ ◻ ◻

On Saturday Stanley met Serena Ramirez right after dinner a block away from the shelter. Serena was antsy and didn't eat much at the group dinner, but no one really noticed. They had made the clandestine plan when Stanley was re-painting an upstairs bedroom the day before. Miss Frankie was downstairs in the kitchen fixing lunch with two other girls and didn't see or hear anything going on upstairs.

Serena was dressed casually in cut-off jean shorts, a tee shirt, and rubber flip-flops on her feet. No purse or ID. Three metal hoop bracelets adorned her right wrist and silver-dollar sized metal hoops hung from her earlobes. Stanley greeted her warmly. "Hey, Serena. How about Burger King?"

"I like Burger King. Thanks." Serena buckled her seat belt and settled in for the ride. They made childish small talk; the kind that teeny-bopper girls love.

Fifteen minutes later Stanley guided the Honda into the drive-thru lane. He didn't want to risk anyone seeing him with Serena any more than necessary. He ordered two cheeseburgers, two orders of fries, and two cokes. They waited behind the lone car in front of them until the lady drove away.

Serena started eating as soon as Stanley was out on the street. He was headed for the Courtney Campbell Causeway, but Serena didn't know that, and didn't care.

This was only the second time Stanley had taken Serena for a ride and a burger. He was smart enough to know that the first time with any girl was always to gain the girl's trust. A ride, burgers, and fries were the only order of business on the ***first date***. Stanley made no overtures or advances, sometimes not even on the second, depending on how the girl reacted. Suggestive clothing worn by the girl usually moved things along more quickly.

Serena, now 15 years old, was dressed provocatively and showing a lot of bronze skin. Her clothes also showed off her young maturing body. Her hair was pulled back in a tight ponytail. Stanley, being socially and sexually immature, was sure she was ready for, and wanted more.

Stanley parked in the lot on the eastbound side of the Courtney Campbell Causeway near the Pinellas County end, with a view south towards the expansive Tampa Bay. Moonlight peeked through passing clouds. Stanley struggled to contain his urges while they sat and just talked for about a half hour. Serena seemed to be enjoying the outing with Stanley and didn't notice the dark SUV parking two spaces to their right because she was looking at Stanley seated to her left. Then she heard the tapping on the passenger side window. She turned and could only see the outline of a person bending to look inside. Stanley reached across Serena's startled body and opened the door from the inside. "What are you doing?" screamed Serena.

"Don't get excited, Serena. He's a friend who wants to get to know you better."

Serena whipped her head back and forth between Stanley and this stranger. She was scared and tried to jump out of the car. The stranger grabbed her arm and jerked her over to the SUV. Serena screamed again, "Help me. Someone help me, please."

No one was in earshot, except Stanley and the stranger. Neither man tried to silence her. They were over a hundred feet from the roadway, so any passing motorist couldn't hear anything over the din of the cars whizzing by at near highway speeds. The stranger wrapped an arm around Serena's waist and hoisted her into the open side door. Serena screamed louder. Still no one else was close enough to hear. If anyone looked in their direction the poorly lit parking lot wouldn't reveal anything.

Stanley scrambled inside the SUV and tried to restrain her flailing arms and legs. He wasn't a big man, but he was bigger and stronger than Serena. The stranger climbed behind the wheel, started the engine, and headed out of the lot. Serena's screams persisted until Stanley slapped her hard across her face. Stanley was not a violent man, but Serena's screaming unnerved him. The screams stopped immediately. Serena stared motionless and wide-eyed at Stanley who was acting like someone she never met.

And then it began. Slowly at first; crude touching and clumsy kissing. Every time Serena protested Stanley smacked her again in the face. By the time he was fiddling with the hooks on her bra Serena was completely passive and she let him do anything he wanted. She just stared out the side windows at the unfamiliar dimly lit storefronts and occasional passing car. Her eyes were glazed over while she waited for this nightmare to be over.

Soon Serena was completely naked. Her shorts, top, and underwear were on the floor in the back seat. Stanley didn't stop at just touching and kissing and Serena had learned not to resist.

Finally, the stranger turned around. Serena hadn't noticed the SUV had stopped in what looked like a very large deserted parking lot. She had no idea where they were. "You done yet?" the stranger snarled.

Stanley wasn't done, but he was so afraid of him he relented. "Sure. She's all yours. Let's switch places."

The stranger got out and came around. He reached across Stanley to hold Serena inside the car while Stanley stumbled out rubbing his throbbing crotch. Once behind the wheel Stanley started the engine and headed out of the lot. The stranger now took his turn with Serena and he didn't stop until exploding inside of her with a shuddering spasm. As he rolled off her, Serena pitched forward and projectile vomited all over herself, the stranger, and the back seat.

"You goddamn f--king bitch." Serena didn't see or feel his palm slam upward into her face breaking her nose and shoving bone fragments and cartilage up into her brain. Death was instantaneous. So was the flow of bright red blood.

Stanley stomped on the brakes and jerked around at the stranger's outburst accompanied by the sounds of cracking bones. "What the hell did you do?"

"The bitch had it coming. She was trouble from the start." The stranger looked at his clothes, now drenched in vomit and blood, and cursed even more.

Stanley could only stare at her naked body, also covered in blood and vomit. "Is she dead?"

"Who gives a shit? Just go back to the causeway and dump her like the garbage she is."

"What about this SUV? The cops will find us."

"No they won't. We'll leave it on the other side of the causeway. The idiot cops in Tampa don't talk to the stupid cops in St. Pete."

"What about fingerprints? They'll track us down just like they do on those cop shows on TV." Stanley was panicking.

"Get it together, Stanley. No one will find us."

"Yes, they will. The cops always do."

"How? Neither of us have our fingerprints on file, and the SUV is stolen. Nothing but dead ends. To those fools we're invisible." He laughed out loud, confident that he could evade being identified.

Stanley couldn't see the disgusting smirk that stretched across the stranger's face as Stanley said. "Man, I'm not so sure about all of this."

They soon reached the parking lot on the causeway where the distressing episode started. "Come on, Stanley. Suck it up. Nothing's gonna happen to us. Just toss the girl over there, drive your car to the other end of the causeway, and pick me up after I dump the SUV." The stranger pointed to a stand of palm trees, snatched her clothes from the car floor, and flung them in the opposite direction as far as he could.

Stanley was nearly hysterical gripping Serena's limp body under her shoulders, but he couldn't look at her as he half-dragged and half-carried her behind the palm trees as ordered. He laid her face down.

He was too scared to check for a pulse or any signs of breathing. The stranger drove away slowly towards the Tampa side of the causeway and Stanley followed in his Honda shaking like a leaf.

Stanley's only fear was getting caught. This evening clearly didn't go as well as Stanley had expected.

❏ ❏ ❏

Serena's beaten and bloodied body was found the next morning by a middle aged couple out for a stroll in the sea air. They called 911. EMS arrived within a few minutes and quickly determined the girl was dead. A single police officer arrived seconds later with lights flashing and siren wailing. A criminal investigation started immediately but just as quickly ground to a halt. There were no witnesses, no useable clues, no fingerprint or DNA matches to anyone in their database, no identification of who the dead girl was, no one reported a missing girl with her description, and no idea where she came from. The St. Petersburg police had nothing to go on.

After three months of spinning their wheels and getting nowhere, Serena's murder became a Cold Case. There would be no more investigation unless new evidence or leads turned up.

The reality of setting realistic priorities set in. There were more immediate problems for the police; three gang members killed during gang warfare, five innocent victims caught in the crossfire with two of them killed, increased prostitution and drug activity, and a rogue police officer caught in an alley with a hooker—with his and her pants down. The public and the media were hounding the mayor and the chief of police to stop this wave of violence and clean up the St. Pete police department. Apparently, one unidentified, murdered Spanish teenage girl, where there weren't any clues and that wasn't claimed by her family, wasn't a high enough priority.

❏ ❏ ❏

The Tampa Police investigated the stolen vehicle dumped on the Hillsboro County side of the Courtney Campbell Causeway. They identified and contacted the owner who thought his oldest son, a delinquent with a history of taking the car on joy rides, had done it again. Dad suspected a drunken party in the vehicle. No one believed the teenage son when he vigorously denied taking the car. The vomit all over the back seat mixed with and concealed the blood so the police didn't suspect anything sinister. They turned the car over to the rightful owner, the dad, who promptly had the mess professionally cleaned up. The strong chemicals and steam cleaning destroyed any hope of finding usable fingerprints or DNA. The Tampa police closed their stolen vehicle case.

Chapter Twelve

About four and one half years earlier
An Apartment
Clearwater, FL
6:18 p.m.

The stranger called Stanley for the first time in about six months. "Stanley, it's time to bring me another girl."

No exchange of pleasantries. "You gonna kill this one, too?"

"That Spanish kid was trash. She deserved what I gave her. Bring me someone who enjoys partying this time."

"I can't. I don't want to be involved."

"You getting any, Stanley? I know what you're doing to those girls. The stranger didn't know anything about what Stanley was or wasn't doing with the girls; just a wild guess that was right on the money. Stanley didn't answer.

"Stanley, your mom says hello. Want me to tell her what you're doing with those young girls the next time I'm fuckin' her?" A gasp from Stanley.

"I guess I'll just have to haul her fat ass down to the police station and turn your mom into the Drug Bust Unit. She'll look nice in an orange jumpsuit with a number on the back, don't you think?"

"Okay. Okay. I'll bring you a girl. Where should we meet?"

The stranger gave Stanley instructions, and then added, "There won't be any trouble this time if the girl knows what we want from her up front. Just do it, Stanley."

Miss Frankie never called Stanley; she didn't even have his phone number, only an address. Stanley called Miss Frankie when he wanted to come around and help out. That arrangement worked fine for Miss Frankie since Stanley called every two or three months, sometimes more often.

The next day Stanley was at the shelter working on a window that wouldn't open when Lilly James strolled in. Up until that time he didn't have any opportunities to talk to, or select a girl. Stanley remembered that Lilly turned 17 years old a few months ago. She'd been at the shelter for over five months, and most importantly had been out with Stanley twice already. The last time he asked her to stick her hand in his unzipped pants, which she did without hesitation. She let him kiss her, rub her chest, and slip his hand between her legs, but only after he'd bought her a burger and fries, and promised to take her out again.

Lilly approached Stanley with a grin and a flirtatious hip wiggle. "Hi, Stanley. How you doing?"

"She'd do fine," Stanley thought to himself. He stopped working on the window and set down the screwdriver. "Hey, Lilly."

Cutesy head cock to the side. "So when are you taking me out again?"

"She is the right one," he repeated to himself. To Lilly, "How about this evening?"

"You can buy me a new pair of jeans?" No negotiation. Lilly set the price. If Stanley was to get what he wanted he'd have to pay for it.

"Sure. We can do that. I'll pick you up at the same place at 8:30."

"I'll be there. Buy me a hamburger, too?" The price went up.

"We can try. See you then, Lilly." Stanley went back to his screwdriver and window as Lilly bounced out of the room humming softly and looking forward to the outing. She didn't care if he tried to fool around. Actually, it was kind of fun messing around with an older guy who could buy her stuff. Lilly knew the power of her sexuality and how to wield it.

Stanley followed Lilly to the check-out line near the front of the store as the monotone voice came over the loudspeaker. "We will be closing in ten minutes. Please take your purchases to a check-out counter. Thank you for shopping with us."

.The cashier scanned the tag on the jeans when it was their turn. Stanley forked over two $20 bills and the harried cashier counted out the indicated change. The jeans were bagged and handed to Lilly. Stanley took the receipt. Cash only was his motto with the girls. Stanley understood that credit cards leave trails. So do paper receipts. As they headed for Stanley's Honda he wadded up the receipt and tossed it in a nearby trashcan.

"How about Wendy's? I love their hamburgers, don't you?" Lilly was cheerful, obviously in a good mood. The new jeans in the bag underneath her feet helped.

"Yeah, sure. We've got time. There's one on the way to the Skyway."

"I love the Skyway. What a view. Especially from the tippy-top." Lilly was referring to the 200 foot high main-span. You can see over 16 miles in all directions.

After a quick trip through the drive thru at Wendy's Stanley headed south on the long bridge towards Manatee County. Approaching the gentle slope to the top, the high-rise condos on Tierra Verde could be seen on her right. Lilly swiveled her head around as she looked back towards St. Pete. Then she looked to her left trying to make out landmarks at MacDill Air Force Base and Tampa in the distance. Turning forward to gaze at the Manatee County lights, "What a view," she repeated, eyes wide with excitement as she absorbed the spectacle of night-time lights.

Stanley pulled off at the service road that led to the fishing pier on the south end of the Sunshine Skyway Bridge, the end closest to Manatee County. It was deserted except for two other cars. One pulled out a few minutes later. Stanley parked as far away from those cars as possible, shut off the lights and engine, and turned toward Lilly. She spoke first. "Thanks again for the jeans. I'll wear them the next time we go out."

"That'd be great. I'm sure they'll look nice on you."

Lilly ran her hands up and down her hips. "Yes, I'm sure they will. How can I repay you?"

Stanley reached over and caressed her arm. "You can repay me the same way you did last time." He continued rubbing her arm with one hand and unzipped his pants with the other. Lilly looked down at his crotch, leaned over, freed him, and went to work. When Stanley's hand moved to her breast, Lilly stopped only long enough to help him unhook her bra before returning to the task in his lap.

After ten minutes Stanley hadn't climaxed and Lilly was getting frustrated and bored. "Enough already," she thought to herself. Her firm breasts were sore from what Stanley was doing to them, and her hand was tired from working on him. Lilly let go and sat up. "Let's go back. I've had enough," as she re-fastened her bra and pulled her shirt down.

Stanley was caught by surprise. "You're not done. We're not going back yet."

"Why not? I'm not getting you off, so why stay here? We'll try again another time." Lilly just sighed, "See, it's no use," as she looked at his crotch and pointed.

"We can't go because we're waiting for someone."

"Waiting for someone? Who?" Lilly stiffened and stared at Stanley.

"He's a friend who wants to meet you."

"A friend, huh. Is he a friend like you? Does he want what you want? Huh, Stanley?" Lilly was angry about being pimped out. Fooling around with Stanley while getting something in return was one thing, but with some other guy she never met before was another matter entirely.

"Just be nice to him, please. For me, Lilly. Please." Stanley was zipping up his pants as he pleaded with her.

"Why should I?"

Stanley wanted to say, "To save your life." Instead he said, "I'll buy you whatever you want, Lilly."

Lilly thought about that for a moment. "I need an entire outfit, including new shoes. At least two pairs."

"That'll have to wait a few days. I can take you out again on Thursday evening."

"Deal." Lilly stuck out her hand and waited for Stanley to shake in agreement. With the bargain struck the cheerfulness returned.

"Okay. Where's this guy? And, I promise I'll be nice to him."

"He'll be along soon. He knows we were coming here." Stanley was relieved. Hopefully, there wouldn't be a killing tonight.

Lilly cocked her head and thought to herself, "Was all this planned? What an idiot I am. Well, at least I'll get more nice clothes and shoes."

◻ ◻ ◻

Stanley and Lilly watched the moonlight flickering on the waves in relative silence. The car radio was tuned to a station that featured a syndicated evening show playing requests as the hostess chatted with listeners about their lives and loves. After about 15 minutes the sound of an approaching vehicle attracted their attention and both looked to their left. A dark SUV pulled into the space next to the Honda and a man got out. He was barely visible in the almost nonexistent lighting.

Stanley opened his door and motioned for Lilly to get out. Reluctantly she did. "This is Lilly. Lilly, my friend," as he pointed at each. Lilly nodded tentatively. The stranger looked her up and down and smiled. He liked what he saw. Dark brunette hair hanging below her shoulders, slim body, long legs, skintight low rider jeans showing an inch or so of flesh at her waist, and nice boobs. "Let's get in the back seat and get acquainted," he said opening the back door for Lilly. To Stanley, "You drive."

As they did six months earlier Stanley headed for some deserted unlit parking lot a few miles away. The stranger started groping Lilly immediately. His hands were all over her body. Within minutes one hand was under her shirt. A few seconds later Lilly's jeans were unzipped and around her thighs exposing light green bikini panties. Lilly wanted to open the door and jump out but resisted the urge. He wasn't gentle or romantic in any way, and there was nothing pleasant about what the stranger was doing to her. Total animal instincts with no emotions. In fact, he reminded her of the last boyfriend her mom had. That guy was a low-life pig who cared only about himself, and thought he could do whatever he wanted to her mother and her. That's why she ran away from home. Now another disgusting asshole was pawing her.

But something told Lilly to just chill out. Maybe she sensed how dangerous this stranger could be if he didn't get what he wanted. Mom's boyfriend scared Lilly. This guy terrified her. Lilly relaxed somewhat and let him do his thing. Next, the jeans were down to her ankles and off of one leg. Her panties were yanked down so hard they tore. Lilly stiffened and alternated between closing her eyes and looking at the ceiling of the SUV, desperately trying to ignore what was being done to her. But, to no avail.

She didn't see him unzip his pants, but she heard it, and braced for what she knew was coming. He jerked her legs further apart and climbed between them. Within seconds he was slamming his hips into hers. Up to that moment Lilly had considered herself to be a virgin. Now she no long was. She squeezed her eyes shut even harder as her rigid body withstood the terrifying onslaught. She forced herself to think about something else; anything but what she was enduring. Lilly whispered softly to herself, "Stanley is gonna pay for this. That piece of shit is gonna buy me an entire goddamn store, or I'll get his smarmy ass in so much trouble with the cops he'll wish he didn't have a dick."

Then Lilly smiled at the grotesque image she conjured up in her mind's eye about this thin guy on top of her, "I'll just think of this jerk as a **Prick on a Stick**. Yeah, a **Prick on a Stick**. That's all he is." That helped, but she still hated what was happening to her.

After what seemed like an eternity, but was actually less than two minutes, Lilly heard her tormentor moan, then felt him convulse and shutter before he collapsed on top of her. Lilly gently pushed him off, pulled on her torn panties, slipped back into her bra, tugged up her jeans, and pulled down her shirt. She was too disgusted to even look at the guy, so she stared out the side window. Within a few minutes she could tell the SUV was back on the road headed towards where they started 20 minutes ago. Stanley parked next to his Honda, got out, and opened the door for Lilly. The stranger got out on the other side and went around to the driver's door. He got in, started the engine, and backed away. No goodbyes, no thank you for a good f—k, no acknowledgement that Lilly even existed. Nothing. "What a goddamn friggin' asshole. Just a **Prick on a Stick**," she thought again trying to calm her anger at being used in such a despicable way.

Lilly knew that she alone now held Stanley's fate in her hands—and the other jerk's. She could put them both behind bars with a single phone call, but decided to play Stanley for the foolish idiot and dumb sucker he was. That decision was a mistake; she didn't think about or consider the well-being and personal safety of the many other girls that might follow her into Stanley's and his friend's clutches.

From that moment on Lilly knew she was in charge of what Stanley would, and wouldn't, do around the shelter and for her, and she never let Stanley touch her again. Not only did she threaten to cut off his favorite appendage, she kept reminding him that she knew the phone number of the St. Petersburg Police Station, and that she was a minor. Guys convicted of Statutory Rape don't fare very well in prison. Every time she ran into him Lilly made Stanley buy her something new; clothes, shoes, CD's, and whatever else she wanted. When Lilly finally turned 18 she gathered her loot, walked out of the shelter, and left Stanley and St. Pete in her wake. At least she was alive, but no matter how disgusting the experience was to her, she never realized that her decision to cooperate on that lonely night actually saved her life.

From that night on, the stranger and Stanley had the trick figured out. Stanley got whatever he wanted whenever he found a willing girl for little more than a ride and a burger. Occasionally, the stranger got a girl provided by Stanley. If the girl cooperated, no additional physical harm would be done to her—other than the sexual assault. Protests were met with swift lethal actions. The stranger started carrying a large hunting knife that he didn't mind using to silence those that didn't cooperate willingly. If a failed attempt resulted in a killing,

Stanley would find another girl within a few days for the stranger. Occasionally they would resort to date rape drugs to improve the likelihood of cooperation.

Stanley found willing girls every two to three months. About half of them were from the shelter, with the rest being girls Stanley found on the streets in Hillsborough County, Pinellas County, and Manatee County, always being careful to never repeat the same county twice in a row.

Over the years that followed, two girls from the St. Pete shelter refused to cooperate. Both had their throats slit. Five girls picked up on the streets met the same fate. None of the seven girls were dumped in the same place. Two in Hillsborough County, four in Pinellas, and one in Manatee over a five year period. The mostly stolen, or the few rented vehicles used when they committed a murder were dumped in an adjacent county at the other end of a long, connecting bridge. There was no obvious pattern to the cases the individual county police departments investigated. It looked like seven separate, but random unrelated murders, and another seven random and unrelated vehicle cases to the police in three separate counties. The three most recent cases made it look like 20 separate crimes.

CHAPTER THIRTEEN

Three years ago
An Apartment
Clearwater, FL
4:49 p.m.

The stranger called Stanley for his now bi-monthly sex fix; he wanted another teenage girl. They made plans for the next evening. Stanley would troll the streets of Tampa this time, but he was becoming increasingly concerned that they would be identified and arrested by the police. How long did he really think this scheme would hold out? Stanley wasn't very smart, but he knew enough to not push his luck too far.

Plus, he had seen a woman he wanted to get friendly with, but had not yet actually met face-to-face. He didn't know her name and was pretty sure she didn't know who he was. He saw her at the bank almost every time he went on Saturday morning. They smiled at each other and nodded *Hello* but nothing more. He wanted that to change.

Playing around with young girls just wasn't doing much for him anymore. He spent the next two hours trying to figure out how he could keep finding girls for the stranger while having what he considered a normal life with an adult woman. Then it came to him; all he had to do was change his identity just like in the old movie he'd watched the other evening. He recreated the dramatic scene by snatching the phone book he kept in a drawer and opened it without looking. He placed the open telephone book on his desk, held his hand over his head while pointing downward, closed his eyes again, and stabbed at the book. With his finger resting near the middle of the left page he opened his eyes and looked at his new name. Trevor Kemp.

Now he only needed fake ID's and he was in business. Stanley knew he wasn't smart enough to steal the real Trevor Kemp's identity and personal information but that didn't matter. He only wanted to *use* the name. Fortunately for Stanley he had heard of a guy who knew a guy who could produce a fake driver's license and Social Security card. That was all he needed to get a bank account and maybe some loans for his small business. Stanley, now Trevor, was all set for a mere $650. He could start a new life as Trevor Kemp while remaining Stanley Robbins to find girls for the stranger so he could keep his mom out of jail.

▫ ▫ ▫

Nancy showed up at the bank on the second Saturday after Stanley started looking out for her armed with his new identification.

Stanley, now Trevor, approached the lady with a thin smile and an outstretched hand. "Hi, my name is Trevor Kemp. I've seen you here a few times and was hoping you'd let me buy you a cup of coffee."

The lady took his hand tentatively and looked him up and down. He seemed to be on the up-and-up and she remembered seeing him here before. It had been almost a year since she broke up with her last serious boyfriend and hadn't done much dating since. "Nice to meet you, Mr. Kemp."

"How about that coffee, Miss…?"

"I'm Nancy. Maybe, when I get done here. Thanks." Nancy let go of Trevor's hand and went over to the chairs where patrons waited to see bank officials and customer service representatives. Trevor called out to her back, "I'm not busy. I'll wait." Nancy smiled to herself but didn't turn around as she walked away.

Trevor retreated to the other side of the bank pretending to fill out deposit slips as he sneaked peeks in the direction of the chairs. After about ten minutes a CSR called out a name as he read it from the sign-in sheet. Nancy rose, extended her hand, and followed the man to his cubicle. Trevor craned his neck to watch. After another ten minutes Trevor sauntered over to an empty chair and took a seat. He could see Nancy's back as she talked to the agent about her banking situation. Nothing serious, just straightening out some bumbled phone information. A bank statement was showing the last four digits of her home phone number as 7592, which were the last four digits of her cell phone number. The last four digits of her cell phone number were listed as her home phone.

The CSR efficiently made the corrections. Finally, Nancy stood up and shook hands with the CSR. Exiting his cubicle she immediately saw Trevor sitting in a nearby chair and stopped short. Trevor saw Nancy and pushed himself out of the chair. Nancy stood still as Trevor approached, staring at him as if she couldn't believe her eyes. Her mind flip-flopped back and forth between being flattered that a nice looking man was showing interest in her and fearing that she was being stalked. Her mind settled on flattered as he approached, "Hi, again Nancy. The offer to buy you a coffee is still open. You can pick the place."

◻ ◻ ◻

The first shared coffee led to a second and then a third. Holding hands and a quick peck on the cheek was as far as Trevor went. That surprised even him. On the fourth date Trevor attempted a kiss on the lips. Nancy did nothing to prevent it. Over the next several months, Trevor and Nancy saw each other almost weekly; dinners at various restaurants, movies at neighborhood theaters, walks on the beaches, and drives around the scenic portions of Pinellas County. The dates became more serious as each grew more comfortable with the other. But, no sex. Both seemed to accept, and even enjoy, that unspoken arrangement. Stanley didn't think about the teenage girls and what he used to do with them. He, as Trevor, just wanted to spend time with Nancy.

The Stanley alter-ego was grateful the stranger hadn't called for another girl, nor had Stanley felt the urge to take out one of the girls at the shelter for some food and…whatever. He concentrated on Nancy. Maybe she could become more than just a new friend.

❑ ❑ ❑

Stanley had completely converted his life and business over to Trevor Kemp, except for when he worked at the shelter or had to service the stranger with girls. During this time Trevor's handyman and subcontracting business was experiencing the same downturn as the general economy. Trevor openly confessed his financial situation to Nancy, who was quite sympathetic. She was living in a small one bedroom apartment and had been thinking about moving into something larger for several months. Her lease was up in two months so she proposed a solution to both of their problems; she and Trevor could buy a house together. Trevor hesitated at first but soon relented. They started looking at homes for sale and settled on a small 3-bedroom, 2-bath house within a week. Trevor had a small savings account and contributed $7,500 for the initial deposit. Nancy had over $50,000 in stocks and savings mostly from an inheritance. At closing she put up over $20,000 to cover the remaining down payment and closing costs.

Trevor and Nancy took two days after the closing to move all of his and her belongings into their new digs. They finally made love the first night both slept together in the same bed in their home. Trevor proposed marriage the next weekend and they were married two months later. Trevor's mom was unexpectedly admitted to the hospital with an emergency appendectomy. Nancy had no living relatives she was close to, so no relatives on either side attended. Neither had any close friends; the marriage ceremony took place in Las Vegas with only strangers present. Neither cared. Trevor had not told his mom about his new identity and dreaded doing so if she showed up for the wedding. He couldn't think of any lie he could tell his mom about why he changed his name.

Within months both Nancy and Trevor settled into a routine many married couples try to avoid—scheduled familiar sex. For Trevor and Nancy sex was relegated to once, occasionally twice on the weekend, and maybe Wednesday night. Neither expected spontaneity or sexual acts that some might consider *different*. Trevor always initiated the sexual activity and both were fine with that since Stanley/Trevor was still experiencing occasional bouts with erectile dysfunction. Nancy was on the pill so condoms or other preparations weren't needed. Foreplay was almost a joke. Neither was upset with this dull predictability.

After a year of married life they were fully entrenched in the rut of mediocrity. There was no excitement and everything that happened in their lives was expected or planned. No spontaneity, no surprises, basically boring. Trevor still loved Nancy and would never consider hurting her. To compensate, and without thinking about it, Trevor gradually reverted to old habits. The stranger was now calling about every two months, and Trevor, pretending to be Stanley, filled the stranger's needs as he had for the past several years. Without noticing it, Stanley started taking out some of the girls again. Messing around with teenage girls was pleasurable and exciting again. Perhaps what some experts say is true: *Once a pedophile, always a pedophile. They can't be cured, so they must be stopped*.

Trevor's handyman and subcontracting business was picking up so he had money to spend on the girls. Trevor took great pains to keep his secrets from Nancy. Their mediocre and mundane lifestyle suited Nancy. She hated controversy and avoided anything that even smelled of a crisis. If she suspected that her husband was involved with teenage girls she never let on, and she had no desire to snoop around to try and uncover another truth. Nancy was happy with her life as the dutiful housewife living a quiet and uncomplicated existence with a man she loved and thought she knew.

Chapter Fourteen

Friday, First Week in October
Near Lacey's Condo
Treasure Island, FL
5:21 p.m.

The drive west across St. Pete on Central Avenue was quick and easy. Luke made a stop to buy a present, and then drove across the inter-coastal waterway to Treasure Island. He encountered moderate traffic but it didn't slow him down. He had never been inside of Lacey's condo, but had frequently driven by imagining the luxury **those folks** lived in. Until recently he didn't even know Lacey lived there. Her particular high rise building was one of three and closest to the shore line of the Gulf of Mexico. The grounds were immaculate, lush, and gorgeous. Stately palm trees swayed in the coastal breeze, some of the pink azaleas were still in bloom, and the greenery was stunning. The complex looked more like an upscale resort than a condo complex. Luke hated the garish buildings and businesses built on the west side of the coastal islands. They hid the beauty of the gulf waters from view, and prevented normal folks from enjoying the beaches, except in specific designated places.

Lacey's condo complex was different. In addition to its modern design and open areas, there was a pathway that snaked its way onto the white sands open to anyone willing and able to walk a few hundred yards on a concrete walkway. The entire scene was soothing, pleasant, and inviting.

Lacey gave Luke specific directions so he could easily find her building and the visitor parking area. Luke found an open space and eased in. He got out, slipped on his sport coat, picked up his package, locked his car, and headed towards the entrance.

Lacey's unit was on the twelfth floor of the sixteen story building. The lobby was spacious, decorated in muted earth-tones, and was surprisingly as inviting as the grounds. A few splashes of colorful art, pottery, and flowers added a brightening touch. The interior decorators certainly earned their fee on this project. Luke spotted the double elevators and strolled over. He stepped in as the shiny bronze-colored doors silently slid open.

After a smooth ride up, the elevator doors opened into a spacious hall area. There were eight units on every floor, each with their own double door entrance. All units were on the west side with their backs towards the Gulf. Lacey's was the southern end unit. Luke walked the 40 paces and stopped in front of the doors marked 1208. He softly pressed the doorbell button and heard a delightful chime announce his arrival.

Almost immediately Lacey opened the door with a warm smile, "Welcome. I see you found the place okay," as she ushered him inside with a grand sweep of her arm.

Lacey was dressed in black slacks and a white bulky sweater, not too big to hide her figure, and not too tight to be considered trampy or provocative.

Luke stepped in with a smile of his own. He bent to give Lacey a peck on the cheek, but Lacey quickly turned her head and kissed him on the lips. They looked deep into each other's eyes and embraced again with a longer kiss and a tight hug. After a few moments Luke pulled away and held out the box of candy for Lacey. "Sweets for the sweet". Corny, but sincere.

"Thank you, Luke, but you didn't have to buy me anything."

"I know. I just wanted to. And you're very welcome."

"Well, fine—this time. Should I take it with us to your mom's?"

"Good idea."

"I'd show you around now, but we don't want to keep your mom waiting, do we?" Lacey wagged a finger at Luke as she spoke.

Luke looked at his watch. "You're right. We should get moving."

"I'll just grab my purse," as she turned to retrieve it from a nearby chair.

Lacey locked the door and turned to Luke, "I'll show you around when you bring me back. The grand tour." Luke smiled down at her.

Luke's mom, Arlene Brasch, was a widow living alone in the modest home she'd shared with her late husband until he passed away six years ago. The drive from Treasure Island took less than 20 minutes so Luke and Lacey arrived a few minutes before 6:00 p.m.

Luke pulled into the driveway, got out, and went around to open the door for Lacey. Lacey slipped her arm under his as they walked up the short walkway. Luke patted her hand and kept walking. Arlene was waiting for them with the front door open. When Luke and Lacey were still three paces away, Arlene threw her arms wide and rushed out to greet them as if they were long lost relatives she hadn't seen in 40 years.

Big hugs all around. "Come in children. Come in," as Arlene ushered them inside.

"Hi, Mom," said Luke as he gave her another hug and kiss on the cheek. Arlene almost ignored him as she focused on Lacey. "What a beautiful woman you turned out to be. Any man who lets you get away is a fool." Her smile at Lacey turned into a scowl when she glared at Luke.

"Thank you, Mrs. Brasch. I appreciate the compliment," said Lacey as sincerely as possible.

Luke broke in, "Mom, Lacey has some chocolate candy for you."

Arlene looked at the package Lacey was holding, reached out, and took it with a broad grin. "Thank you, Lacey, dear. Everyone calls me Arlene. Will you help me finish setting the table?"

Before Lacey could answer, Luke piped up, "I'll do it, Mom."

"Lucas, go rest in the den. Lacey can help me," making a shooing motion in the opposite direction.

"I'd be happy to help you, Arlene," as Lacey winked at Luke and headed off toward the dining room with Arlene.

Luke busied himself in the den watching the local news on the TV. He tried unsuccessfully to ignore the chatter, punctuated with laughter, coming from the adjoining rooms.

About a half hour later both Arlene and Lacey came back into the den still chatting. Arlene was wearing a yellow apron and Lacey had on a frilly white one. Neither apron had even a single spot or stain. Arlene was drying her hands on a dish towel. Lacey spoke first, "Luke, we're ready to light the Sabbath candles. Come join us." Lacey held out a brightly colored kippah, a Jewish head covering. Arlene returned to the dining room as she bobby-pinned a lace doily on her head.

Lacey almost hung on Luke's arm as they joined Arlene. It was obvious Lacey was ecstatic to be included in this ancient Jewish tradition with Luke and Arlene. The dining room table was set with Sabbath china and polished silver tableware at all three places. Glass goblets were filled with water and wine. A beautiful tablecloth sprawled along the entire length of the table that could easily accommodate ten diners. Two identical gleaming silver candle holders held two Sabbath candles. Extra wine was in a glass decanter and a decorative cloth bread cover almost completely hid the Sabbath challah bread.

Luke surveyed the room with a sense of nostalgia. "Mom, it's been too long since I've been here for Shabbat."

"Yes it has, Lucas. Maybe Lacey can bring you around more often."

"Mom, don't start."

Lacey raised her hand to her mouth to stifle a grin and a chuckle. Arlene motioned for Lacey to come over to the where the candles were arranged. "Say the blessings with me, dear." Lacey let go of Luke and went over, clearly delighted to stand at Arlene's side at this solemn moment. The two women of different generations stood together to recite a prayer that was thousands of years old. Arlene lit both candles and began rolling her hands in front of her face indicating that she was bringing the light of the Sabbath candles into her body. Lacey did the same three times in unison before closing her eyes and holding both hands over her face. Lacey started singing the candle blessing and Arlene joined in. Luke marveled at the sight as he traveled back to almost forgotten memories of his childhood and the hundreds of Sabbath dinners he shared with his parents.

Luke snapped back to the present as the ladies finished the blessing. Arlene lowered her hands and turned to Lacey, embraced, and kissed her on the cheek "Good Shabbas, my children." She then went over to Luke and kissed him on both cheeks. Luke returned the kisses. Lacey followed Arlene over to Luke, "Good Shabbas, Luke," as she reached up to pull his face down to her level where she could kiss him on the lips.

All three knew that the Kiddish, the prayer over the wine, was next. Luke picked up his wine goblet and held it high. Arlene and Lacey picked up their wine goblets and turned to face Luke. When Luke finished the prayer they all said, "Amen" in unison and took a sip of wine from their goblet.

Finally, Luke uncovered the challah bread and broke off a large hunk. Ripping off a small piece for himself, he handed the larger piece to Lacey who tore it in half. Lacey kept one half and handed the other to Arlene. All three were smiling broadly as they started chanting the Hamotsi, the prayer over the bread. All three sang the prayer, again said, "Amen," and took a bite from the piece of the bread each was holding.

Arlene dashed around the table and almost pushed Lacey down into her chair. "You children sit. I'll bring in the dinner," as she hustled off to the kitchen.

Lacey peeled off her apron as Luke took his seat at the head of the table, the traditional place for the man of the house. No one considered such respectful traditions to be sexist or derogatory to women.

Arlene brought in two bowls of chicken soup with carrots, celery, and small thin noodles. She placed one in front of Lacey, then the other on Luke's plate. "Eat while it's still hot. I'll be right back," she said as she scurried back into the kitchen for her own bowl.

The Sabbath meal was slow and delicious. The conversation was friendly and touched on many subjects. Mostly, Arlene told stories about Luke's early years in school and Hebrew classes. Luke pretended not to be interested and attacked his meal instead. Lacey explained her work with children caught in the middle of their parents' breakups, emphasizing how rewarding the successes were to her. When Luke could get a word in he talked about his fishing and free time. No one spoke of Luke's police work or of the frustrations surrounding the current cases. Arlene knew better and Lacey just wanted a quiet evening with people she cared about.

Around 7:45, and during a momentary lull in the conversation, Lacey rose and picked up her plate, "I'll clear the dishes, Arlene. You've done enough tonight."

"Don't be silly," as Arlene stood, picked up her plate, and reached for Luke's before Lacey did. "You're welcome to help me with coffee and dessert, dear."

Luke watched in amazement. His mom was treating Lacey like a daughter-in-law, not just a guest. "Can I help?" Luke asked to their backs. He got no response so he got up, gathered a few dishes, and headed for the kitchen. Lacey met him at the doorway, "I'll take those, thanks," as she blew him a kiss.

With that, Luke returned to his seat and just watched as the women made a few more trips back and forth until the table was cleared. In Arlene's house, as in thousands of other homes, the women are proud to take care of the men who take care of them. Shared love, mutual trust, and respect for each other are the powerful glue that holds a family together.

Out came the coffee cakes, brownies, and coffee with a clean set of china and silverware. All three sat down again, took something from each platter, and started eating again. Lacey poured the coffee while Arlene labored to pass around the sugar and creamer. Luke could tell that his mother was running out of steam. Making and serving this elaborate dinner was hard on her. Even though Arlene was only in her early sixties she was not used to all this activity.

By 8:30, Luke was stuffed and ready to head off. "This was great, Mom. I'm glad we came."

Lacey chimed in, "Dinner was delicious. I'll have you both over to my place for Sabbath dinner soon."

"That would be lovely, dear." Arlene matched Lacey's sincerity.

Luke and Lacey headed for the door and Arlene followed. "Good night, Lucas," as she kissed him on the cheek. "Thanks, Mom. I'll call tomorrow to see how you're doing."

"Oh, pooh. I'm fine, but you call anyway, Lucas," scoffed Arlene. Luke smiled and laughed.

Lacey stepped forward and hugged Arlene. "Thanks again for having us. I really enjoyed being here."

"It was nothing. I like having you young people over. It keeps me young. You're welcome any time, my dear."

With the farewells over, Luke and Lacey strolled hand-in-hand to his car.

❐ ❐ ❐

On the ride back to Lacey's condo, she couldn't stop talking about the good time she had sharing a Sabbath dinner with Luke and Arlene. "I really like your mom, Luke."

Lacey reminisced about their time in the Jewish youth group and how happy she was with all her friends back then. Luke commented about how involved the different parents were. Without active parents there wouldn't be a youth group. Lacey sat back and faced forward in deep concentration. Luke drove about five minutes in silence before Lacey spoke again. "I envied you and several other kids, you know."

"You did? Why? Your dad is one of the most prominent lawyers in the city. You had everything. In fact, some of us envied what *you* had."

"Luke, I had material things. My parents loved me and gave me whatever I wanted if it could be bought and paid for. Don't misunderstand me. I really liked having all those things: the clothes, a new car when I turned sweet sixteen, Caribbean cruises, the trips to exotic places, a good college, and grad school."

"Exactly. That's what some of us envied. Our parents were comfortable, but not rich. We didn't summer in Europe. We worked our asses off to buy the clunkers we drove—at least those of us who could scrounge up a few hundred bucks for a piece of junk with an engine."

"Money isn't everything, Luke."

"Really! How would you know? You've never been poor."

"No, I haven't been poor financially. But having money in the bank isn't the same as being **rich**."

"And what do you base that philosophical gem on? If you have money, you're rich. Seems simple enough to me."

Exasperated, Lacey pressed on, "What I envied was the total involvement of other parents in their children's lives. My parents loved me, but were usually too busy with one benefit or another to support me in-the-flesh. They were very generous with their checkbook, but pretty skimpy with their time."

"I remember your mom and dad showing up at lots of events."

"Yes, they showed up—whenever a donation or financial support was involved."

Luke looked over at Lacey to see her quickly wipe a tear from her left eye.

Luke continued undeterred, "Your parents bought an entire table at our senior play. They donated substantially to our youth group." Luke persisted by reminding Lacey how most parents of their friends back then helped out in whatever way they could. "Your mom and dad were, and still are, good people."

Lacey countered by telling Luke she just wanted her parents to spend time with her and support her activities. The tears were flowing freely now as Lacey buried her face in her hands. Lacey's unexpected outburst momentarily startled Luke, so he turned off into an almost deserted strip shopping center parking lot. Luke hadn't known Lacey felt that way. He unbuckled his seatbelt, turned to Lacey, and pulled her hands away from her face. Luke smiled at her as Lacey stared back through watery eyes. Slowly Luke pulled her close and wrapped his arms around her slender body. After a few moments Luke gently pushed Lacey away and held her shoulders at arm's length. "I'm very proud of your parents, and I know you are too."

Lacey looked around as if trying to find the words. "I am proud of them. I don't know what came over me. Sorry."

"There's nothing to be sorry about."

Luke looked at Lacey caringly. "You okay?"

Lacey pulled a tissue from her purse, dabbed at her eyes, and tried to laugh, "I probably look terrible."

Luke took her chin in his hand, turned her head back and forth, and up and down, "You look fine to me." Her eyes stayed trained on his.

"No, I don't." They both laughed again as Lacey hugged him tight. "Okay. Enough of this commiserating. I owe you a tour of my home." The crying fit was over.

Luke sat up, re-fastened his seatbelt, and restarted the engine. Lacey dabbed at her eyes again.

Chapter Fifteen

Friday, First Week in October
Lacey's Condo
Treasure Island, FL
9:48 p.m.

Lacey's condo was more spacious than Luke expected, and the view of the Gulf of Mexico from this height was spectacular, even in half moon light. Luke was surprised by all the color; flowers, and greenery everywhere. He couldn't imagine one person taking care of so much. The flowers had to be fakes. But, if they weren't real they were expert imitations and absolutely gorgeous. Every wall, drapery, and piece of furniture screamed of color. Various shades of pastels, yellows, greens, and blues were all tastefully blended together and color coordinated to make a cheery and homey mosaic. No black, gray, and white combinations anywhere to be seen except on Lacey herself.

Lacey led him through the entire condo pointing out this knickknack and that piece of artwork, proudly explaining where specific pieces came from or some other detail. They leisurely walked hand-in-hand from the living room to the dining room, through the den, the hall bathroom, the kitchen, the study she used as an office, and both spare bed rooms.

Back into the living room, Lacey stopped in front of a free-standing chrome and glass cabinet and flipped a switch on the back. About two dozen stunning objects sparkled and shined in the glow of the overhead light. Lacey pointed to several items and proudly proclaimed that she purchased them in Israel a few years ago. Then she lovingly picked up a pair of elaborately carved silver candlestick holders and showed them to Luke, "These were my grandmother's, one of the few treasures she was able to smuggle out of Europe in the mid 1930's."

Lacey put the candlestick holders back with a sigh and flipped off the light. "I feel comforted and I get a strong sense of my Jewish identity just looking at these beautiful things."

Luke was impressed. His collection of Jewish art and cherished items was limited to the decorative wine cup he received at his Bar Mitzvah from the Sisterhood, two colorful Chanukah manorahs, a Tallis and matching kippah he bought while on leave in Germany about six years ago, and a few Jewish pictures hanging in his living room.

Lacey moved away from the cabinet, and had purposely saved her bedroom for last. Luke wasn't sending any sexual signals, so she didn't expect anything intimate to happen, but was sure she wouldn't put up a fuss if it did. Lacey led Luke by the hand to her master bedroom, then into her bathroom.

Luke marveled at the size of her master bathroom and the huge sunken Jacuzzi tub situated under a large picture window. No curtain or frosted glass was needed for privacy because there was no chance anyone would be peeking into a twelfth floor bathroom window that overlooked the Gulf of Mexico. Lacey loved to relax in the Jacuzzi and watch the sunset.

Lacey's private phone rang, startling both of them. Lacey could tell what line it was from the type of ring evoked by the incoming call. She only gave that number to other professionals and some very select clients. "Who'd be calling me at this time of night?" They looked at each other, and then Lacey marched over to the nightstand where two phones stood. She snatched up the one that was flashing a red light and making noise, visibly annoyed by the intrusion.

"Hello, this is Dr. Hirsch. How can I help you?" Lacey tried to be pleasant, but couldn't quite pull it off.

After a few moments of stunned silence the female voice on the other end introduced herself as a doctor at Children's Hospital. She apologized and said she was sorry for the lateness of the call. She explained that her patient had pleaded with her to call Lacey, so she did. The girl provided the phone number scribbled on a piece of wrinkled and folded paper. Her patient was a teenage girl whose parents were going through a nasty divorce and things were getting violent at her house. The girl had gotten into the middle of a fight between her parents and was banged up with a few cuts and some bruises. The doctor identified the girl by name and Lacey immediately recognized the family and the girl. Lacey had four, maybe five, weekly sessions with the girl about five or six months earlier; she wasn't sure of those minor details. She did recall that the sessions stopped when the parents claimed they wanted to stay together and were trying to get the marriage back on track. Lacey wasn't so sure that the parents could make the marriage work, but that wasn't her job; the girl's wellbeing was her only concern. If both of the parents could stop physically and mentally abusing each other the best place for the girl was with her parents in their home.

Now it seems the father had reverted to his old destructive and abusive behaviors and was smacking the women around again.

Lacey proclaimed flatly, "Doctor, I can stop by the hospital tomorrow morning. I'll look up my notes from before so I'll have a better idea of what I'm dealing with."

"Dr. Hirsch," the doctor stated emphatically, "The girl is an emotional wreck right now. If I can't get her calmed down I'll be forced to just medicate her. I'm sure this isn't an ideal time for you, but if there is any way you can come here now, maybe we can avoid the addictive meds."

Lacey hesitated and didn't answer immediately. Instead, she lowered the phone and shook her head while looking at the carpet. She then looked at Luke and shrugged while returning the phone to her ear. "I can be there within an hour, Doctor. Where can I find you?"

Lacey and the doctor exchanged rapid details about when and where they should rendezvous before Lacey hung up. Lacey turned to Luke with sad eyes, "I haven't had a nighttime call in over three months. It's just our luck I get one right now."

Luke took her in his arms, "In our jobs it's always business before pleasure. In fact, it's more likely that I would have gotten a call when I didn't want one."

"I am sorry but I do have to go—like immediately." The look in Lacey's eyes screamed the longing she felt.

"I can go with you if you want. Maybe I can be of some help to you?"

"You'd just be wasting your time standing around. I have to see her in private. I am sorry," Lacey repeated looking up at him.

Luke pushed her away gently. "Go find your notes. I'll show myself out."

"Thanks for being so understanding."

"Don't mention it. We're still on for tomorrow night, right?"

"Yes, we are. I'll see you around 6:00." Lacey's mood was somewhat brightened by the thought of starting again tomorrow where they left off tonight.

"Wild horses won't keep me away." A quick embrace and kiss then Luke was out of the bedroom.

◻ ◻ ◻

Luke was in no hurry to get home, so he just drove aimlessly along the familiar streets while heading in the general direction of his condo in Largo. Thoughts of Lacey in his arms were dashed when he spotted a group of five teenage girls milling around the parking lot of a convenience store along a commercial part of Madeira Beach. They were obviously joking around with each other, laughing, and just having a grand old time as teenage girls everywhere should be doing.

"Damn it! It's just not right," Luke muttered to himself. "My girls shouldn't have been brutally murdered. They deserved a full life just like these girls are experiencing."

This case was becoming very personal to Luke. Luke was now focusing even more on the dead teens. It was his current mission in life. Luke clenched his jaw, squeezed the steering wheel tighter, and was more determined than ever to get to the bottom of these murders—whatever it took.

Chapter Sixteen

Saturday, First Week in October
Police Station
St. Petersburg, FL
5:18 p.m.

Luke had already spent a few hours at the police station going through the case file trying to find something he might have missed earlier. No success. He finally gave up around 5:30 and headed over to Lacey's condo for their date. Luke forced himself to focus on Lacey and not his murdered girls, but it was hard to do. He also decided he would not put himself into the uncomfortable position where they might get intimate, at least not until they stopped working together. He needed Lacey for her insights and opinions about teenage girls, and refused to allow his feelings and desires for her complicate or interfere with the job he had to do.

Lacey had no such misgivings. She saw no reason why she and Luke couldn't be romantically involved and work together at the same time. So Lacey was surprised when she greeted Luke at the door and he declined her offer to just sit around her condo and relax together before going out to dinner. He also had only kissed her on the cheek, further raising her concern about the status of their relationship.

The mood in Luke's SUV was tense. Lacey couldn't read Luke's thoughts, and he flatly refused to discuss what was bothering him. She knew how wrapped up he was in solving the murders, but that hadn't changed since last evening. Or, had it? Gradually, she started fearing that she had said or done something to turn him off, but what?

Lacey couldn't think of anything, so she just sat in the chilly silence wondering what relationship catastrophe might strike next.

Dinner at a steak place was no better. Conversation was almost nonexistent, and neither seemed to look directly at the other. There also was no flirting or touching. Both just focused on the meal. After an excruciating disastrous hour of what was supposed to be a pleasant time together Lacey couldn't take it anymore. "Luke, why don't we call it an evening? I think I should just go home."

"Whatever you want." No reluctance or emotion in his voice.

Luke paid the bill and Lacey marched three steps ahead of him to the parking lot. When Luke pressed the remote to unlock the car, Lacey jerked the passenger door open and climbed in before Luke even arrived on her side of the SUV.

Luke was aware of the chill between them, but didn't know what to do about it. His head just wasn't in their relationship, and he was now unsure about how Lacey felt, or what was upsetting her. It was a classic lack of communication tugging at the shreds of their relationship, tearing it apart.

They rode in silence about half way to Lacey's condo before Luke finally spoke. "I spent about three hours at the station just before I picked you up." His tone was somber, but Lacey detected the intensity in his voice.

"At least he's paying attention to something," Lacey thought to herself. Some otherwise good psychologists sometimes have trouble dealing with their own complicated personal situations. Lacey was experiencing that paradox now. She turned to Luke and said, "I thought this was your day off?"

"It usually is, but I don't punch a clock—especially now." Luke swiveled his head to glare at Lacey before returning his gaze to the road.

Lacey froze momentarily, "Especially now? What do you mean by that?"

Luke turned to look at her again and almost sneered, "**Now** is the middle of nine unsolved murders, Lacey. **Now** is the dead girls. **Now** is the case we're working on. Remember?"

Then Lacey got it; Luke was totally focused on the case. She finally realized that there wouldn't be any time in his life for her until he did solve the murders. Lacey didn't like it, but she reluctantly accepted this new reality. She resolved then and there that they would continue to work together to solve the murders, and then maybe…

After a long sigh, Lacey replied, "What can I do to help you, Luke?"

Luke looked down momentarily as he shook his head dejectedly, "I really don't know. I can't figure out how to connect the cases. I just have a gut feeling that they are all linked somehow, but I can't find anything to substantiate my theory beyond the obvious fact that all the dead girls are teens, and probably homeless or living in a shelter. That's all I have."

Lacey was looking intently at Luke as he stared at the road ahead of them. He looked more tired than when he was recovering from the gunshot wounds. Lacey's professional psychologist mode never really shut off. "You look beat. Have you been getting enough sleep, Luke?"

"I guess. About five or six hours a night lately."

Most people over-estimate how much sleep they actually get. Lacey knew Luke needed more, even if he did get as much sleep as he thought. "Luke, you're pretty wiped out. When you drop me off come up and I'll give you a few of the strong over-the-counter sleeping pills I give some of my patients. I keep a supply on hand for emergencies."

"I'll sleep when this damn case is over."

Lacey was an expert, with extensive experience in childhood sleep deprivation. She knew the adverse effects it had on a child's ability to function normally. She also knew that sleep deprived adults suffered just in similar ways. "No, Luke. You'll work much better after a good night's sleep. Take the pills home and promise me that you'll take one tonight before you go to bed." Lacey had reached over and was gently holding his bicep.

Luke glanced at Lacey, but didn't say anything for the rest of the ride to her condo. On the elevator up to her floor Lacey clutched his hand and leaned in close. "Luke, you're my friend. I care about you, and I understand how important this case is to you. It's important to me, too."

"I'm not being much of a friend right now, am I? I want us to be more than just good friends, Lacey, but I just can't be when I'm in this… mood." Luke threw his hands in the air in disgust. "And you're right about this case."

"I'm also right about getting enough sleep. Take the pill tonight when you get home, please."

Luke actually smiled for the first time this evening. "And if I don't?" He was trying to improve his mood by playing their little game again.

Lacey kissed him on the cheek as the elevator doors opened. "Then I'll just make you take one right now, and simply wait until you pass out before I start ravaging your body."

"A hard choice. Okay. I give up. I'll take the pill when I get home."

Lacey didn't expect a different answer, so she smiled as she unlocked the door. Luke waited in the living room for Lacey to return with a small plastic bag. A white label was stuck to it. Inside were three oval shaped pink pills. Lacey handed Luke the plastic bag, "Sure you don't want to take one right now?"

"I really am sorry but I should go home." It was obvious that Luke was torn by the choices.

"I'm sorry, too. Call me when you take the pill tonight and again when you wake up tomorrow so I can check how much sleep you actually got." Lacey was still the professional.

"Yes, ma'am." Luke made a half-hearted salute before he bent to kiss Lacey on the lips. Luke had every intention of doing as Lacey ordered.

Both knew that a sleeping pill for Luke at his own home was the best thing right now for the case and their budding relationship.

Even as a professional psychologist, Lacey should have, but didn't notice the depth and frequency of both Luke's and her own mood swings. Therefore, she didn't realize that such instability in her own life could be destructive to the very relationship she was trying to protect. The stress both were under was making matters worse.

Luke took one of the pills at 11:50 that night and immediately called Lacey staying on the phone for only two minutes before he laid his head on the pillow. The much needed deep sleep overcame him almost immediately. It was 9:53 the next morning before he called to check in with Lacey. After the pleasantries, Lacey inquired, "How'd you sleep, Luke?"

"Like a baby. I haven't slept more than seven hours at a time in over six months except when I had bullet holes in my body and I was drugged."

"You were drugged again last night, Luke," Lacey asserted nonchalantly.

"Well, yeah. I guess I was." His laugh was short but real.

"How do you feel? Do you feel rested?"

"Yes, I feel great. Those pills are like magic."

"Yep, they are. Good, now you can get your head cleared so you can function effectively."

"Thank you, Doctor. I appreciate all you're doing to help me."

"You're very welcome, Detective." Lacey returned the playful jibe before returning to serious business. "Now I've got to run out on you. I need to see that girl from Friday night, then I've got hours of paperwork waiting for me."

"Not to worry, Lacey. Take care of whatever you need to. I'll call you this evening if I need your help on Monday."

"Sounds like a plan. Just remember to take those pills only when you really need one, and don't expect to do anything but sleep soundly for eight to ten hours afterwards."

"Got it. Thanks again. Bye, Lacey."

"Remember to call me if you need me. Bye, Luke." Both hung up.

Luke showered and shaved before deciding what to do on this pleasant Sunday morning. He batted around the idea of going to the police station for more research or just hanging out at the St. Petersburg Pier. After vacillating for a few minutes he opted for the pier to just fish and think. His fishing rod, reel, and tackle box were already in the SUV, and he could buy bait when he got there. With that decision made, he rummaged through his closet and dresser for clothes he could get wet and stinky in. He put on his fishing duds, snatched his floppy hat hanging on a hook in the closet, then headed out with a clear head and a spring in his step.

Luke found a spot on the northeast corner of the St. Petersburg Pier and started preparing for a few hours of fishing, and to be alone with his thoughts. A man with a young boy, maybe 7 or 8 years old and probably his son, was already fishing about 25 feet to his right. A shirtless man and a woman in short shorts, a skimpy loose fitting top, and colorful platform shoes were fishing with four poles about 40 feet to his left. Tourists strolled by or just milled around taking in the view. Everyone minded their own business and no one paid any attention to anyone else. Luke ignored them all once his detective instincts assured him everything around him was fine.

Luke selected the fish hook he felt was best and attached it to his line. A small weight was hung about 18 inches higher up the line. Next he plucked out a live shrimp from the dozen or so he bought from the pier bait shop and weaved the hook through its hapless body. When he was satisfied that the shrimp was secured he looked behind him to make sure no one was in his way. He flipped the pole over his right shoulder and flung it overhand as hard as he could. The line spun out a hundred feet into Tampa Bay, and Luke watched as the line settled into the water. About three minutes later he started slowly reeling in the line as he jerked the pole up and down or side to side trying to simulate the swimming motion of the shrimp. It took about ten minutes to get the line wound in enough for Luke to check on his shrimp. It was still there. Luke reeled it in completely and repeated the entire process several more times before he allowed himself to think about the case.

By noon, Luke had reviewed everything about the case in his head, and was convinced he needed additional help in tracking down leads in Pinellas and the two surrounding counties. Actually, he had only suspicions and hunches, and he knew he had no investigative authority in Hillsborough or Manatee Counties to confirm or refute anything. His authority didn't extend beyond right there in Pinellas County. In Luke's mind these cases were now just too big for Luke to handle entirely by himself. He had no choice but to bring all this to Lieutenant Thompson and ask for help. If he didn't get help, he feared he wouldn't solve the cases. But, were these murder cases Luke should even be involved in? They weren't assigned to him. He was assigned only to the Megan Fisher case and a stolen SUV. He needed help and some kind of expanded authority to pursue all of them.

Satisfied with his decision on how to proceed, Luke glanced over at the man and his son. The man was trying to console the boy about something. Luke watched as the man pointed to their bait bucket and started collecting their fishing gear. The boy was now crying, "But Daddy, why can't you buy more shrimp? I want to keep fishing with you."

The man knelt in front of his son while holding the boy gently by the shoulders. Luke couldn't hear what the man said, but the boy just looked sadly at the sidewalk. Then Luke realized what the problem was; the man couldn't, or wouldn't, spend more money on bait.

Luke glanced at the seven shrimp in his own bait bucket then back to the man and boy. Luke took a few steps closer. "Excuse me, sir, but I have to get going and find myself with some extra shrimp. Could you and your son use them? I'd hate to just throw them over the side."

The man looked at his son then back at Luke. "Thanks mister, we just ran out." The boy smiled from ear to ear as he looked up at his dad then back at Luke.

Luke strolled over with the bait bucket and handed it to the boy. As he tousled the kid's wind-blown mop of hair, "Catch a big one for me."

Luke shook hands with the father and returned to collect his fishing gear. The scantily clad woman jiggled over to him holding her bait bucket. "That was a very nice thing to do." Her southern drawl was delightful. The lady bent over and handed her bait bucket to the boy. The boy held up the second bait bucket for his father to inspect after a brief exchange with the pretty lady. The lady kissed the boy on the forehead and stood up to go back to her fishing spot. Father and son waved at the lady as she looked back over her shoulder. The lady winked at Luke as she returned to her fishing buddy and their poles. Doing good deeds and being kind to others can be contagious.

◻ ◻ ◻

Luke got home by 12:45, stripped off his fishing duds, and was in the shower by 1:00. Lunch in front of the TV was a thrown together sandwich and a few sides. A cold drink rested on the TV tray. The Tampa Bay Bucs were playing the Dolphins in Miami. By the 3rd quarter the lead had changed hands four times and was now tied at 23. Then play was stopped to attend to an injured Dolphins' linebacker who had a leg bent in an unnatural angle when he tackled a Bucs' receiver at the ten yard line. At least he prevented a touchdown. The lull in the action gave Luke enough time to trudge into the kitchen with his empty plate and glass. When Luke returned to his chair a modified golf cart was parked next to the medical team attending to the injured player. Several large guys lifted and strapped the injured player onto the cart, and then the golf cart headed for the locker rooms. About half of the medical team jogged beside the cart while the others headed for the Dolphins' bench. The action ratcheted up as players from both teams hustled back onto the field, re-fastened their helmets, and started huddling in preparation for the next play.

Luke watched the game, immersed in the back and forth action as each team fought for yardage and points. The Bucs finally scored and were now in the lead by a single point. The stadium was in a frenzy anticipating the kick-off.

Then Luke's cell phone rang. It was laying on the coffee table a few steps away. Luke kept jerking his head from the TV to the jingling phone refusing to get out of his chair. The Dolphins kick-off return specialist caught the ball at the 8-yard line and raced over to the sideline where he fell in behind seven huge Dolphin players that had formed a v-shaped wedge.

By midfield the scoreboard clock showed 00:00. No time left, but the play would be allowed to finish. The wedge eventually disintegrated completely and the ball-carrier was streaking alone down the right sideline towards the end zone. The Bucs fastest player was speeding from the other side of the field heading towards the 5 or 10 yard line where he hoped to intercept the runner and keep the Dolphins from scoring. When Luke saw the two men tumble out of bounds at the 4-yard line he jumped up with a loud, "Yes", threw both arms in the air, and rushed over to grab the phone on the fifth ring.

"Hello."

"Is this Detective Brasch?"

"Yes, I'm Detective Brasch. To whom am I speaking?"

The caller identified himself as a St. Petersburg police officer. Luke didn't recognize the name.

"Good afternoon, Officer. What can I do for you?"

"I was on a call to chew out a teenage kid who took his parents' car for a joy ride without permission. The parents freaked out when they discovered the car missing and called us."

"And, what does that have to do with me?"

"I'm getting to that, sir."

"Okay, go on, Officer."

"As I was rolling up to the kid's house I spotted your BOLO Honda parked on the street a few houses away. At least I think it was your BOLO."

"Did you check it out?"

"No, sir. By the time I finished brow-beating the kid the Honda was gone."

"Where was this, Officer?"

The officer relayed the address and Luke scribbled it down.

"Thank you, Officer. This could be very helpful."

"You're welcome. Glad I could help. If I spot the Honda again I'll try to detain the driver and call you immediately."

"I hope you get the chance. Thanks again." Both hung up, and Luke went back to his TV for another football game, satisfied with two successes—well, almost two. In less than three minutes the Bucs won a squeaker and Stanley's Honda might still be in the northeast St. Petersburg area where he had hoped to find it.

There wasn't anything else he could do until the Honda was spotted again. Running out there right now just to look around for a Honda that might not even be Stanley's, and had disappeared again, would be a futile exercise. Luke had no stomach for chasing smoke.

Chapter Seventeen

Monday, Second Week in October
Police Station
St. Petersburg, FL
8:22 a.m.

The detective room was buzzing with activity. Luke was the last detective to check in this morning. The others were already hard at work making phone calls, clacking away on their computer keyboards, rummaging through file folders, or talking with each other. A few looked up and waved or nodded, but no one rushed over to greet him as Luke headed for his own desk on the other side of the large room.

Luke had been working on Megan's case for a week now with little real progress. This was not a simple case or the easy solve he first expected. He wrapped his sport coat around the back of his chair and got settled in behind his desk. He knew exactly what he had to do and set about preparing for the task ahead. Luke's plan was finalized last evening after he finished watching a second football game, had eaten dinner, and settled in for the rest of the night. Luke took out his case file and reviewed its contents for the umpteenth time, and set about carefully assembling the documents and photographs he thought would be the most useful. Satisfied, he called his lieutenant's extension.

When Nick Thompson picked up, Luke started in a friendly manner, "Luke, here. Good morning, Loo. Have a good weekend?"

"Oh, good morning, Luke. Yes, I did. Spent some quality time with the wife and kids. Don't get to do that enough lately. How was yours?"

"Very productive, sir. I'd like to brief you if you have the time."

"Sure, I need an update anyway. How about 9:30?" Luke turned his wrist over to check the time.

"Good for me, Loo. 9:30 it is." Loo hung up first with no goodbye. Luke looked at the receiver with a scowl before replacing it. Another confirming quick check of his watch told him he had about 20 minutes before the meeting. Luke immediately began arranging his papers and photos as he mentally prepared for his pitch.

At exactly 9:30 Luke rapped on Loo's open door. The Lieutenant was on the phone and motioned for Luke to come in and take a seat. Lieutenant Thompson spent almost half of his time on the phone coordinating his detectives and kissing up to various politicos and local officials to keep, or stem the decline of, his dwindling budget. These perpetual phone interruptions were a nuisance, but nothing new to Luke, so he just waited until Nick was done.

Three minutes later Nick Thompson replaced the receiver shaking his head. "The assistant to the Mayor is on my ass again grousing about how many detectives we have, but how few cases we actually solve. Where the hell does he get his numbers from? Our solve rate is the second highest in the entire state."

Luke had heard this all before. "We do our best, Loo."

"I know you all do. I'll just have to re-educate the Mayor—again." Loo slumped back into his chair. Today Loo was dressed as always. This time with a light purple sport coat, dark purple shirt, purple and white tie, and black slacks. Actually, this was one of his more coordinated outfits.

Loo finally leaned forward and placed his hands palms down on his desk. After a quick glance at his momentarily silent phone, "Okay, Luke. Let's have it."

Luke went through everything he had: the nine photos of mostly unidentified dead teenage girls, Stanley Robbins probable involvement but still in the wind, the dark SUVs, the mysterious second guy, what Megan and the other girls said, what Randy and Randi said, the computer searches he had done, and his own theories and suspicions. Loo listened intently, looked at the photos, the computer printouts, and the several reports and summaries as Luke handed each to him.

The entire presentation took over 30 minutes. Loo had not spoken except to urge Luke to keep going and explain some of the details. Only two short phone calls interrupted Luke's rhythm, which he regained almost immediately after Loo abruptly hung up on each caller after a brief exchange.

When Luke was finished, Loo made his first serious comment, "Very interesting and good police work, Luke. So what's your next move?"

"Well, sir. I still have to find Robbins and the guy with him. The police sketch artist isn't done yet, so I'm waiting on that. I'll follow up on the location of the BOLO this afternoon. The Honda hasn't been spotted again since yesterday afternoon. Maybe the Honda will be back. Who knows? I could use some help with the rest of it."

Loo flopped back into his chair as he looked directly at Luke contemplating what to say. Finally, "Do you have anything else?"

"No, sir. The sketch artist is still working with Megan. They've had two sessions already so I might get something from him soon. There are no easy leads with the nine murdered teenage girls. That's where I need some help. Otherwise, this is all of it right now." Luke swept his arm over the materials on the desk.

Loo was silent for a long moment. Luke could see Loo's chest puff in and out as both men waited for the other to speak. Loo broke the uncomfortable silence. Gesturing with a sweep of his arm across all the papers and photos, mimicking Luke's motion less than two minutes ago, "This just isn't enough, Luke, and you know it isn't."

Luke sat silently as he gripped the arms of his chair and his blood began to boil. Loo continued with more sensitivity, "Luke, I know how you feel about all this. Off the record, I probably would feel exactly as you do. But, we both know there just isn't enough evidence to justify my putting more detectives on this, or asking other counties to get involved."

Luke focused his hot stare at Loo but said nothing. Loo continued, "Let's review this from the prospective of the prosecutor, okay?"

Tersely, Luke snapped at his superior, "Sure, let's do that."

Loo hesitated a few seconds, and then started with Luke's assumption that all the cases are connected. "First, there is no evidence linking the ten murder, or attempted murder, cases and the ten or more stolen or abandoned SUVs that have possibly coincidental dump dates. True, all the victims are teenage girls, but it ends there. We know that some, but not all, of the girls came from a shelter, so we can't use that to connect all the cases." Loo was holding the photos in his hands, looking sadly at each once again as he spoke. It was obvious that Nick was taking this case as hard as Luke, but he had to be more objective.

Next, Loo picked up the computer printout listing the time of each murder. "The murders occurred over a five year period. That's two a year on average across three counties. We get dozens of murders, or suspected murders, right here in Pinellas each year. It's just as likely these girls are only a part of the larger statistic and not a pattern by themselves." He put the computer printout down, but picked it up again almost immediately.

Pointing at the printout, Loo stressed, "All ten girls were found in a different location in the three surrounding counties. No pattern here either."

Loo put down the printout and picked up Luke's summaries. "Then there are the SUVs. They can mean anything—or nothing. There are only three that are close to being suspicious, and the rented one you can identify produced no evidence at all. There is no evidence of SUVs, vans, or any other kind of vehicles in the other murders. Plus, you can't show that the SUVs you identified have any connection with any of the murders."

Smacking the summary with the back of his hand, Loo continued, "Then there's Stanley Robbins and the phantom guy with him. Robbins has a driver's license, but the address is bogus. You don't have a valid home or work address for him. Other than the lady in the shelter, no one has seen or heard from him in a few weeks. The BOLO hasn't turned up anything solid yet. Plus, we don't have an ID on the other guy, if there is another guy. On top of all that, there's no DNA from Megan's sexual assault exam, and no identifiable fingerprints from the one SUV you have the most information about, which as I recall you can't link to any murder. Then, add the fact that there are nine separate murder cases, none of which were connected to each other when they were first investigated, nor were any solved. So, to sum all this up as a defense lawyer will, you ain't got shit." Loo glared back at Luke daring him to challenge his conclusion.

Luke said dejectedly, "I know, but…"

Loo cut him off by slapping his desk with his right hand. Some of the loose papers fluttered about. "But nothing, Luke. We've got to sell this to a district attorney eventually. They expect solid evidence, not just coincidences, supposition, and conjecture. Gut feels, regardless of how real they seem to be, don't hold any weight either. Besides, we're investigating one of those murders, Jeanie Doe, as an unrelated case because there's nothing to make us think it's anything more."

Luke was really fuming now. "Loo, I just need help getting the evidence. I am well aware that I don't have enough for the DA yet."

"There's no one to help you, Luke. All the other detectives are smothered with their own cases."

"I can't just ignore all of this." Luke pushed papers and photos around on Loo's desk. Standing straight up, "So what do you want me to do?"

"Unofficially, I want you to keep digging until you positively connect these cases and catch those bastards. Officially, there isn't enough evidence for me to elevate Megan's case and an unrelated dumped rented SUV, the ones you are assigned to investigate, high enough to put a team of detectives on it. This may still turn out to be nine other unconnected murders and a bunch of unrelated stolen cars regardless of how many guys investigate them."

"It is getting harder now that there are so many murders and stolen cars for me to investigate across three counties without help."

"I know, Luke. You and I unofficially are the only ones who think there *might be* a connection. Based on what you have so far, no one else will agree with us." Loo paused for effect before continuing, "And, you're on restricted duty, remember?"

Both men just looked at each other, and then Luke offered, "How about this? I keep working the two cases without help from any of the other St. Pete Detectives, and you keep my limited duty order to yourself?"

Nick Thompson didn't hesitate as he pointed to the scattered array of papers and photos covering the top of his desk, "It's quite possible that I misplaced the doctor's note—for a week or so."

"No kidding? Then I'll just keep working on Megan's case and the rented SUV from the Tampa rental company dumped in Pinellas County. If something else turns up, I'll let you know."

Loo showed a thin smile. "So, why are you just standing around jabbering with me?" Both men started collecting the papers and photos as Luke shoved them into his file folder.

Luke knew what he had to do now, and where the boundaries of his investigation were set. He needed more evidence before he could *officially* pursue the other cases.

It was after 2:00 p.m. when Luke finished his quick lunch at a family owned sandwich shop. He punched in the location on his GPS where the officer spotted a white Honda he thought might be the one from Luke's BOLO. As he got closer, Luke realized he was in the same neighborhood where Stanley's driver's license said Stanley lived. Could this be a coincidence? Luke didn't believe in coincidences when it came to police work. He smacked the steering wheel with his hand and looked up and down the block. As Luke drove around the four-block area looking for the Honda he was certain this was where Stanley was supposed to be living, but he consulted his notes anyway. The Honda was spotted on a street one block south from Robbins' bogus home address. The actual house was the fifth one from the corner on the south side of the street, the one now owned by Trevor and Nancy Kemp. Luke circled the four blocks slowly three more times, but didn't see the Honda anywhere.

Luke parked about a half block further south from where the Honda was spotted on Sunday, and decided to wait no more than an hour to see if it turned up again. There were several reasons for this minimal stake-out decision: it was the middle of the afternoon and most folks drove their cars to work making it unlikely the Honda would be here now, the Honda seen by the officer may not have been Stanley's, and the Honda may have been there only once and might never return again. He didn't want to waste too much of his valuable time on what might turn out to be a great big wild goose chase.

Luke kept switching his gaze between the rear view mirror, looking out the windshield, and reading his notes. He maintained this routine for 45 minutes or so, and then he spotted something suspicious and sat up straighter to get a better look. Coming at him was a white car that could be a Honda. Luke waited to see if the car was in fact a Honda, and where it was headed. When the white car turned right in the direction of the Kemp home, he could make out very clearly that it was a Honda. Luke started the engine and inched towards the corner where he turned west in pursuit but there was no Honda in sight. Luke immediately stopped his SUV and looked around in all directions. "Where the hell could it have gone?" Luke hissed to himself as he scanned each open and closed garage door for any signs of recent movement. Nothing.

Luke knew that he had no probable cause to just start knocking on doors asking to look into closed garages, much less get a warrant to do so. For all he knew the driver of the Honda had spotted him and just high-tailed it out of there as soon as the houses blocked Luke's view. Or, maybe it wasn't Stanley's Honda. Luke smacked the steering wheel again, and slumped back into his seat. So close, but just another setback. Why couldn't he catch a break?

Luke drove back towards the police station muttering obscenities under his breath. His cell phone ring snapped him out of his funk.

"Hello. Detective Brasch."

"Hi, Detective. This is Mike Hardy, the police sketch artist."

"Hi, Mile. How's the work with Megan coming?"

"Done. It was a good idea to go slow with Megan. She dropped by with a lady she said was her mom's friend, made one minor adjustment, and reconfirmed that the computer drawing was the guy she remembered."

"Good work. Will you print out a few dozen copies for me?"

"Sure, they'll be waiting for you in ten, maybe fifteen minutes."

"Thanks, Mike. I appreciate that."

"Glad to help, Luke. See you soon."

Finally some good news. Luke's mood improved. He decided to share what might be a possible break in the case with Lacey. Luke had her cell and home phone numbers in speed dial, but he got her voice mail on both. He left basically the same message twice. "Hi, Lacey. It's Luke. I'm picking up the artist's rendering of the guy Megan saw with Stanley. Stop by the station before 6:00 or so this evening and I'll give you a peek." After a long hesitation "…or just call me and we can figure out when and how you can see them. Talk to you soon. Bye." Luke flipped the phone closed and kept driving south towards the police station.

CHAPTER EIGHTEEN

Monday, Second Week in October
Police Station
St. Petersburg, FL
5:48 p.m.

Most of the detectives were either out in the field or had left for the day. All seven of the detectives rotated the graveyard duty, and this was Lakesha Johnson's month to work the late shift. Lakesha was the only other person still working in the office. She was the lone female and one of the two black detectives in the department. She was a seventeen-year veteran of the St. Petersburg police department and was almost legendary. Lakesha was credited with taking down several well known dangerous criminals with good detective work. Rarely did any of Lakesha's cases land in the cold-case files, and her conviction rate was often the highest year after year. She'd been seriously injured twice; a gunshot wound in the left thigh and a stab wound in her right bicep. Both injuries occurred long before Luke joined the force. Lakesha was 42 years old and married for over 20 years with two teenage boys. Her record as a police officer was impressive: six citations for meritorious service, and no black marks against her. She was a good cop. Some called her a cop's cop. All the other detectives sought out her advice and wanted to be her partner whenever possible. Lakesha's only fault, if it is a fault, is that she had the annoying habit of calling her colleagues by their last name.

As Luke marched to his desk, Lakesha looked up, "Hey, Brasch. How's your case going? I heard you ID'd the girl." Somehow she always knew what the other detectives were up to.

Lakesha was the only person Luke addressed by their last name, "Hey yourself, Johnson. Yes, I did. I also found out where she lives. Hope to get it wrapped up soon."

"If you know who she is and where she lives, what's left to do?"

Luke was ordered to keep the other detectives away from his case, so he was cautious about how much to tell Lakesha. Finally, "I don't want to bother you with my problems."

"Not a problem, Brasch. We're all in this together. You help me when I need it, and I help you."

Luke really didn't want to disobey Loo's order. "It's getting late and it's a thick file. Maybe I can go over the particulars with you tomorrow."

"Any time. Look me up when you're ready."

"Will do, Johnson. Thanks."

Lakesha nodded and went back to her own work.

After settling in and checking his messages—none that required immediate attention—Luke went off to find Mike Hardy and collect his sketches. By 6:15 Luke was back sitting at his desk intently studying the sketch. No recognition of the face staring back at him. The guy looked very average, nothing like a stereotypical sinister pedophile or sadistic killer. Luke wondered if Megan described the guy well enough for this sketch to be accurate. He put the picture down on top of the pile, let out a huge sigh, and made a note to check with Megan about the sketch tomorrow.

Luke rubbed his temples and hoped he wasn't getting a headache from all the stress. He felt tired and worn out. Time to go home.

Luke's Condo
7:49 p.m.

The dirty dishes were in the dishwasher and Luke attacked the few pots and containers in the sink. Finished with that task, Luke went into his living room and flipped on the TV with the remote as he plopped into his chair. He surfed through the channels searching for anything interesting, but not requiring much concentration or thinking on his part. He finally landed on a Discovery Channel show about dinosaurs being the ancestors of birds. Why not? He'd heard stranger theories.

Luke's home phone rang fifteen minutes into the show. Lacey was calling. Luke muted the TV and grabbed the phone, "Hi, Lacey. Thanks for calling back."

"Hi, Luke. Partners check in with each other, don't they? Sorry I couldn't call sooner. Another emergency run to see a patient." Lacey was obviously in a cheerful mood.

"Yes, they do, partner. And, I know you have your practice and other responsibilities." Luke tried to match her mood.

"So you've got a sketch of the guy with Stanley?"

"Yeah, but no ID, and nothing about where or how to find him. Plus, I'm not sure if Megan described him accurately."

"I am curious. I'd like to take a look the next time I see you." Lacey paused then added, "So, what else have you been doing?" Lacey was quick to move on since this sketch wasn't much of a lead, at least not yet.

"I had an interesting development this afternoon." Luke went on to explain about the white Honda, and where it was spotted twice; once by a St. Petersburg police officer over the weekend, and then again by Luke himself a few hours ago. He mentioned the coincidence of it being very close to the address listed on Stanley's driver's license. Then Luke reminded Lacey of his encounter with Nancy Kemp, and how she'd never heard of Stanley Robbins. Luke also told her he wanted to check back with Megan to be sure the sketch was accurate.

Lacey asked one simple question, "Did you talk to Trevor Kemp?"

"No. He wasn't at home," Luke said slowly as his mind shifted into a higher gear. Lacey continued her thought.

"Maybe Trevor knows Stanley but his wife doesn't."

Lacey's idea hit Luke like a freight train. "That's an interesting possibility, Lacey." Luke continued excitedly, "I hadn't thought of that. It's possible Stanley is a relative, or just a friend using the Kemp address for some reason, and Nancy Kemp honestly doesn't know about it."

"Those are strong possibilities. So, what's your plan?"

"Well, I'll see Megan about the sketch in the morning. I don't think she's started back to school yet. I can't give the sketch to our media department until I'm sure about it. I have to call the police departments in Tampa and Bradenton about unsolved cases they might have. Then I need to go back and have another chat with Nancy Kemp, and maybe Trevor Kemp, if he's home. What're you up to?"

"I've got two late morning sessions with kids and three early afternoon ones, but the last one might cancel. Want some company?"

"Probably not with Megan, but the Kemps are another matter."

"I'm sure I'll be free after 4:00, more likely 3:00. I should know for sure by noon if my last appointment will show."

"All right. Call me as soon as you know your schedule. We'll meet somewhere and go over to the Kemp's together."

Lacey was relieved that Luke wasn't annoyed with, or avoiding her.

With their police business settled, Luke and Lacey talked about other things. Both carefully avoided their relationship issues, and no dates were arranged for the upcoming weekend. Ten minutes later they said their goodbyes and retreated into their own separate worlds.

<u>Tuesday, Second Week in October</u>
<u>Police Department</u>
<u>St. Petersburg, FL</u>
<u>7:43 a.m.</u>

Luke made a point of arriving early. He had a lot to do, but he needed coffee before he got started. As Luke filled his mug, Detective Rocky Kowalski popped his head into the small break room. "Morning, Luke. How's your case going?"

"Good morning, Rocky," Luke twisted around to address his colleague, but didn't answer the question.

Rocky persisted, "Need any help?" It seemed like everyone wanted to help out, but Luke had his orders.

"Nope. Everything's under control. Thanks anyway."

"Let me know if I can help."

"Will do, thanks."

Back at his desk, Luke arranged the photos and papers while deciding who to contact first. Hillsboro County, and Tampa in particular, had more unsolved teen girl murders than Manatee County, so the odds favored starting there. A call to Ronny Sinclair found him out for the week on vacation. Luke left a message and then consulted his police directory for another Tampa police department phone number. A few seconds later a pleasant female voice greeted him. Luke introduced himself and explained in generalities what he was trying to find out. Within minutes Luke was connected to Hector Jimenez, another Tampa detective.

Both detectives tried to talk about their own open cases, but quickly concluded that the conversation would be much more productive face-to-face. Detective Jimenez suggested they meet at Westshore Plaza, just off of I-275 about a mile from the east end of the Howard Frankland Bridge. They agreed on a specific time and place in the huge shopping, entertainment, and restaurant complex. Luke had 45 minutes to get there. More than enough time.

Westshore Plaza
Tampa, FL
10:35 a.m.

Luke arrived about ten minutes early, and Detective Jimenez showed up a few minutes later. They exchanged greetings and looked around for a quiet, secluded place to talk. The mall wasn't crowded yet, so they settled on a cute café that had outdoor tables where they could spread out their papers and files. Each ordered a coffee and sweet roll.

Luke started first since he had requested the meeting. He explained about Megan and how he got involved. Luke told Hector about the shelter, but not its location, and his interviews with the girls, Stanley Robbins probable involvement, and the several SUVs. Then Luke pulled out the pictures to discuss the nine murders.

Hector Jimenez took the pile tentatively and looked at each one for a long time before turning it over to check the name printed neatly on the back, if there was one. Luke watched Hector intently without saying anything.

On the eighth photo Hector slumped back in his seat and stared at the picture much longer than the others. He didn't turn it over to check for a name. Luke finally asked, "Are you okay, Detective?"

"I'm just a little surprised. I know this girl," as he showed the gruesome photo of a dead Hispanic girl to Luke. No name on the back.

Hector continued sadly, "Her name is Rosa Marie Alvarez. I went to her house about a year and a half ago on a domestic violence call. Her mother's boyfriend had beaten her up pretty badly. Mom was knocked unconscious and somehow Rosa called 911. I had to physically restrain the guy after he threatened to kill Rosa for calling the cops."

"What happened to Rosa?" Luke was printing her name on the back of her photo and started taking notes.

"She ran out of the house crying. I found her again a few hours later wandering around the streets not far from here actually," Hector pointed in a southern direction. "She said a girlfriend would take her in and swore she would never return home; not to her mom's boyfriend, not to her mom either."

"Did you keep up with Rosa?"

"I tried for a few months, but she just eventually disappeared. Do you have a file on her?"

Luke shuffled through the papers, pulled out the police report, and summarized the contents. "Her naked body was found in north Manatee County. South end of the Skyway. No clues. Whatever DNA there was didn't produce anything useful. No fingerprint matches either."

"Can I see the file?"

"Of course," as Luke handed it over. Hector read every word carefully and then looked up at Luke.

"Did you notice this?" Hector pointed to a line on a computer printout.

Luke took the file back and reread the item Hector identified. He didn't see anything unusual. "What's your point, Detective?"

"The fingerprint file checked only for ID matches. When none came up there was no check for other cases in Manatee County, Hillsborough, Pinellas, or anywhere else for the same fingerprints."

Luke looked back at the file, "Are you sure? Why not?"

"Yes, I'm sure. And I think I know why not. That's part of the upgrade we're undertaking. The new software will clearly ask the user if they want such a check, rather than assume you know to ask for one."

Luke was shaking his head, "I never paid any attention. I click on the ICON and let the computer do its thing."

"Most people do exactly that. Are you aware of the team making these upgrades and trying to get all our computer systems to talk to each other better than they already do?"

"I've heard it was happening, but haven't paid much attention."

"Well," said Hector sitting up straighter, "I'm part of the team."

Surprised. "You are?"

"Yes. My role is not to deal with the computer codes or any of that. I don't know Jack about that mumbo jumbo stuff. I do, however, know that a particular item in your database is the same as in ours even if they have different names in their respective programs. Database incompatibility has been a big problem in law enforcement for years. I also am helping to identify what information might be missing in your database that we have in ours, and visa versa." Hector tended to talk with his hands, gesturing and pointing—very distracting. Luke tried to ignore the excessive motion and concentrated on the words coming from the over-animated body.

"I'm no computer expert. I just point and click and hope for the best."

"You and 99% of everyone else. That's why it's taking so long. We're working very hard on making the final version what the Geeks call **User Friendly.** You know, being more intuitive, anticipate what we all need, and stuff like that."

"So when will the upgrades be ready?"

"They tell me the roll-out date is by the end of November. I think they're on track to meet it."

"What can we do in the meantime?"

"It would be a pain in the butt to re-run all those fingerprints and DNA yourself. I know the guys who are setting up databases to do some testing of the final program. Maybe they can take data from you and use it for their tests. You know, kill two birds with one stone."

"That would be helpful. How do I get in touch with them?"

"I'll dig their contact info out and send it over to you this afternoon."
"Great. Thanks, Hector."
"Maybe this is the help you need to nudge your case forward."
"I sure hope so. Thanks again."

Luke and Hector quickly went over Hector's obviously unrelated cases, gathered their papers and files, and shook hands before heading in opposite directions.

Luke's cell phone jingled three blocks from the station. Lacey was checking in. "Hi, Lacey. What's up?"

"Good morning, Luke. My 3:00 appointment just cancelled, but I'm stuck in the office until 3:00."

"Do you want to go with me to the Kemp's place?"

"Yes, I do. Can I meet you some place?"

"Great. Do you know the big home improvement store on Park Street just west of 34th? That's a convenient place. I'm headed to the station now, then lunch on my way to see Megan."

"Okay. I know where the store is."

"Fine. I'll meet you at the northwest corner of the parking lot. We can leave your car there."

"I can get there by 3:30 at the latest."

"Thanks, Lacey. See you soon."

"Looking forward to it." Lacey was getting bubbly.

"I gotta go, Lacey. Bye." Luke flipped his phone closed before Lacey could object. He just couldn't allow their personal relationship to cloud his judgment or derail his concentration. He did allow himself a long sigh—he felt bad about hurting her feelings.

<u>Secret Girl's Shelter</u>
<u>Pinellas County</u>
<u>1:21 p.m.</u>

Miss Frankie was waiting for Luke as he knocked on the door. She knew he was coming. Megan looked like the little girl that she was. Her hair was in a long French braid. Her tasteful knee-length shorts and loose fitting shirt suited a young lady. Her smile was somewhat forced when Luke told her Lacey couldn't visit this afternoon; he had come by himself. Miss Frankie hovered around Megan but didn't interfere with Luke. After a few minutes of the idle chit-chat, the kind Luke watched Lacey use when talking to the girls, Megan seemed to be a little more comfortable. Luke was a careful observer and a fast learner.

"I want to thank you for helping the police artist draw a picture of the man you said was with Stanley Robbins. You thought his name was Mike or Mitch, right?"

Seated primly, she responded softly with hands folded in her lap "Yes."

Luke opened a folder and handed the sketch to Megan. "Is this what the man looked like?"

Again, "Yes," handing it back immediately as if the picture was toxic.

"Can you think of anything you might want to change about how the man looked?"

"No."

Luke was getting frustrated with the lack of elaboration. "You understand that when I put this picture in the newspapers and on TV someone will recognize this person. You don't want the wrong person recognized, do you?"

Megan faced Luke, but her eyes sought out Miss Frankie, then back at Luke, "No."

"Okay, Megan. If you're sure this is a good picture of the man you saw with Stanley, I'll send it out to the newspapers and TV." Luke was giving Megan one last chance to change her mind.

Megan looked at Miss Frankie, then back at Luke again. Finally she pointed to the picture, "That's him."

Luke glanced at Miss Frankie who was nodding her head up and down in approval. She believed Megan and was encouraging Luke to do the same. Luke reached out and patted Megan on the shoulder, "Good girl. Thank you, Megan. You've been very helpful."

Luke stood and thanked Miss Frankie. Turning to Megan, Luke said as cheerfully as he could, "Dr. Lacey asked me to tell you that she'll try to stop by in a day or two."

Megan perked up, "I'd like that. Thank you for telling me."

As Luke walked to his SUV he marveled once again at how well Lacey connected with young girls.

Chapter Nineteen

Tuesday, Second Week in October
A home improvement store parking lot
Pinellas Park, FL
3:23 p.m.

Luke turned into the vast parking lot and headed toward the black Jaguar parked as far from the main building as possible. Lacey was watching from behind designer sunglasses and waved when she spotted Luke's SUV, as if Luke couldn't find her unless she signaled to him. There wasn't another car within 200 feet. Lacey pressed the button to put the top up and stepped out as Luke approached.

Luke pulled up and reached across the inside of his SUV to open the passenger door. Lacey didn't complain about this type of gentlemanly courtesy. At least he did open the door for her. Lacey slid in and leaned over to give Luke a quick peck on the cheek. She was relieved when he leaned sideways to accommodate her and reciprocate with his own kiss. A good sign.

"Hi, Luke. Thanks for picking me up."

"My pleasure, Lacey. Ready to meet the Kemps?"

"Sure. Let's do it." Lacey was getting excited about working so closely with Luke again. She hadn't seen him since Saturday.

They drove off following the voice commands of Luke's GPS, even though he had a good idea of where he was going. On the fifteen minute ride, Luke told Lacey about his meeting in Tampa and that he had identified another girl. Then he moved on to Megan. He commented on how she looked like a typical 13-year old young lady, she seemed to be doing well with Miss Frankie, she genuinely felt the picture was accurate, and that she looked forward to seeing Lacey again in a few days.

"I'm glad Megan's doing so well. I will go see her soon."

"She's looking forward to that," Luke repeated.

They rode in silence for a few more minutes. Then Luke got back to Trevor and Nancy Kemp. "Trevor wasn't at home when I went to their house last week looking for Stanley. Nancy Kemp said she never heard of Stanley Robbins and was annoyed that I thought he lived there."

"Yes, I remember you telling me all of that. So what do you plan to do differently this time?"

"Well, we can't assume Trevor will be at home this time either—or Nancy for that matter. If he isn't, we'll concentrate on Nancy if she's there. I'll ask her a few questions again; show her a picture of Stanley Robbins, and the sketch Megan said was his accomplice. Maybe she'll recognize one or both. If Trevor is also there we'll talk to both of them."

"Okay, what do you want me to do?"

"I don't want them to know you're a professional psychologist unless we have to. Just flash your ID and hope they won't ask for a closer examination. Once we start the questioning watch their reactions. Can you get a sense of what they might be feeling? Are they telling the truth? Are they holding anything back? Stuff like that. We can discuss your impressions after we leave."

"Yes, I do that with my patients every day. Body language is an important element of communication. How quickly a person responds. How they use and hold their hands. Facial expressions. Even how little or how much they sweat tells me something about the individual. Sometimes body language tells me more than what a person actually says."

"Good. I thought you were an expert at this." Luke thought for a few seconds and then continued, "I'll concentrate on the questioning and you pay attention to their reactions."

"What if I think of a question you haven't asked yet?" Lacey was getting into the investigation mode.

"I hope you do. Just ask it. It won't hurt my feelings. We're partners, aren't we?"

Lacey leaned over and jabbed Luke in his bicep as she smiled and giggled, "Yes, we are." Lacey was having the time of her life.

Luke looked over at her momentarily and returned her smile with one of his own. They rode in silence except for the voice from the GPS until it finally informed them, "You have arrived." Luke pulled into the driveway and killed the engine. Both got out and walked up to the modest well-kept house.

Nancy Kemp opened the door a few seconds after Luke pressed the buzzer. She was wearing a light blue sweat suit with an orange stripe running down each leg and sleeve. The University of Florida Gator seemed to growl at them from the emblem over her left breast.

Nancy Kemp instantly recognized Luke through the crack in the door, and her expression changed from one of surprise to annoyance as she glared at him. She opened the door just to give him a piece of her mind. Luke greeted her with a smile and an outstretched hand, "Good afternoon, Mrs. Kemp."

No pleasantry from Nancy Kemp as she ignored his hand with a downward glance that screamed her disapproval at another intrusion, "Why are you back here? I told you that I couldn't help you."

Luke dropped his hand. The gesture at civility was slipping away, but Luke wasn't giving up that easily. "I know that, ma'am. But we have a few more questions you might be able to help us with." Luke pointed between himself and Lacey as he spoke, "May we come in, please?"

Nancy continued to glare at Luke and Lacey before she flattened her back against the open door. Luke followed Lacey into the small living room. Nancy closed the door behind them and scurried inside herself. She didn't offer them a seat or any refreshments, nor did she ask for identifications. Instead, she said with a terse, "Let's get this over with."

Luke pressed on by introducing Lacey to Mrs. Kemp, then he turned to face Nancy, "Is your husband home, Mrs. Kemp?"

With arms folded tightly across her chest, "No, he's at work. Why are you asking about Trevor?"

Luke answered as calmly as he could, "We have reason to believe that your husband may know Stanley Robbins, the man I asked about last week."

Nancy was still tense, "Trevor never mentioned that name to me."

"Could Mr. Robbins be a relative or old friend that your husband didn't talk about?"

"I doubt that. We have no secrets from one another."

Luke glanced over at Lacey whose head shook back and forth almost imperceptibly. Lacey detected a chink in Nancy's armor. Luke turned back to Nancy, "We'd like to ask him ourselves just to clear our records. When will Mr. Kemp be home?"

Nancy looked to her right where a modern stylish clock hung on a wall surrounded by an array of photographs in mismatched frames. Luke and Lacey followed her gaze to the far wall. Turning back to Luke she said, "Probably not for about two hours or so."

Luke continued, "May we show you an artist's rendering and ask if you recognize the man in the sketch?"

"Well, I guess so."

Luke opened the folder and took out the sketch Megan helped to create and handed it to Nancy, "Do you know this man, Mrs. Kemp?"

Nancy took the sketch in both hands and studied it intently. She hoped that she was convincing the detectives that she was cooperating, and maybe then they'll leave her alone. After staring at the sketch for ten seconds Nancy handed it back, "Sorry. I've never seen this man before."

Lacey turned to Luke and held out her hand, "May I have the file, please?"

Luke handed it over with a quizzical look. Luke and Nancy watched as Lacey leafed through the file until she found what she was searching for and pulled it out. Lacey carefully showed a small one-inch photocopy of Stanley Robbins' driver's license photo to Luke while concealing it from Nancy. Luke nodded his approval for Lacey to continue. He knew she wanted to show it to Nancy, but wasn't sure of her motive since Nancy had already said she didn't know Stanley Robbins.

Lacey turned to Nancy as she handed her the tiny picture, "This is a driver's license photo of Stanley Robbins. Do you recognize this man?" Lacey's voice was soft and motherly.

Nancy's hands started trembling and her eyes bulged as she stared at the small photo in the center of a regular size piece of paper, "No. No, I don't recognize the person in this picture either." Nancy quickly handed the paper back to Lacey, but couldn't look her in the eye. Both Luke and Lacey knew Nancy wasn't being entirely truthful; she was lying to them and they didn't know why. Luke alone knew they couldn't do anything about it at the moment. If he pressed her further she would just become defiant. He needed to find a different way to get the truth out of Mrs. Kemp.

In a noticeably shaky voice, Nancy said, "It's getting late. Please leave now. I've answered your questions and I have nothing more to tell you."

Luke stood his ground and persisted, "Just one more thing, Mrs. Kemp." Nancy glared at Luke and just stood there like a pillar of stone. "Where does your husband work, ma'am?"

After a long sigh, "Trevor runs his own contracting business and goes from one job to another. I don't know where he is or where the jobs are."

"How do you contact Mr. Kemp when he's working?" Luke was fishing for a cell phone number.

"He calls me once or twice a day. I never call him. He doesn't want to be interrupted while he's working." Shut down again. Luke's frustration level ratcheted up another notch.

"What's the name of his business?"

"He operates under his own name. He uses our third bedroom as his office." No offer to show it to them. Luke didn't press the issue. There was no reason to suspect anything sinister yet. There's no law against protecting your husband or using a bedroom as an office. He'd just have to wait some more to talk to Trevor Kemp.

Luke sensed he wouldn't get anything more from Nancy Kemp, "Thank you for your time, Mrs. Kemp." Nancy kept her hands tightly at her sides so Luke didn't try for a handshake. Instead, Luke grabbed Lacey's upper arm and ushered her towards the door. Nancy rushed past them to open the door. She couldn't get rid of them fast enough.

❏ ❏ ❏

Luke and Lacey discussed the implications of their encounter with Nancy Kemp on the ride back. They both thought that Nancy had recognized the photo of Stanley Robbins but Nancy lied about it. Neither thought Nancy recognized the second man. Luke tossed out some possibilities relating to Stanley Robbins, "It's possible that Stanley is what we thought—a relative or friend. But if he is, why would Nancy try to hide that?"

Lacey responded with what her training taught her, "People tend to avoid things that embarrass them, or to hide something they don't want others to know. Often it involves illegal activity, or some real or perceived immorality."

"That makes sense. The black-sheep brother, or the cousin stepping out on his wife." Luke was pondering what to do about his dilemma.

"That's right. So, why can't you push Mrs. Kemp harder and make her tell you the truth?"

"We only **suspect** she's lying. We don't have any proof she actually lied. We have no evidence of any criminal activity involving the Kemps, so we're stuck with believing her. We would have to find some compelling contradictory evidence before we can confront her, which of course we don't have. Maybe we'll find some, maybe not. Until then, I repeat, we have no choice but to officially believe her. And I should remind you that a jury would do exactly that—believe her."

"Sooooo?" Lacey drew out the word not following Luke's thought.

"So, I can't harass people without probable cause. If Nancy Kemp says she doesn't know the guys in the photos, I can't just keep asking her questions about them without a good reason to do so. I don't have a good reason, Lacey."

Lacey was perturbed about all this, "Isn't lying a good reason?"

"Sure it is. This is a great big Catch 22. I just have to prove she's lying first. Surprise, surprise. We're back where we started. Only now we have more suspicions we can run down." Luke glanced at Lacey then back to the road ahead, "Before you jump all over me, gut feel and women's intuition, even based on skillfully observing body language, does not count as proof of anything."

Lacey snickered and smacked her knee with a hand, "Damn. I thought we had her."

Luke laughed, "Sorry, Lacey. I wish it was that easy."

"So, what can we do?"

"Well, our options are limited, but we're not totally dead in the water."

Lacey was getting it now, "We need to find and talk to both Trevor Kemp *and* Stanley Robbins."

"Right you are. Plus, I've got to get with the computer guys about checking to see if all these cases are connected through whatever forensics we do have."

"Okay. We know where Trevor lives so how do we find Stanley?"

"It might be hard without help from the department. A little luck is always a good thing. I still need a lot more evidence before Lieutenant Thompson can assign anyone else to help us. Maybe the BOLO will produce him. Maybe not since it hasn't so far. For now, it's just you and me, babe."

That was fine with Lacey. She was enjoying her time with Luke. "Is there anything I can do in the meantime?"

"I can't think of anything. I need to get back to the station and call the computer guys, send them the files, and wait for results. Since we have no clue where Stanley might be, a stakeout is a waste of time. Besides, we don't know where or what to stakeout. Same for Trevor. We could sit outside his house and wait for him to come home. But, Nancy may have tipped him off and he won't show." Luke momentarily let go of the steering wheel, threw his hands in the air, and shrugged. Luke knew better than to let go of the steering wheel, but what the hell. They were only traveling at 30 miles an hour on lightly used neighborhood streets. "Besides, I've got class tonight. If the chance of doing anything productive were higher than next to nothing I'd skip the lecture." Luke was gripping the steering wheel again before Lacey could protest about his driving skills—or lack of them.

Lacey put Luke's driving out of her head. "And, I thought I had problems dealing with mixed up teens taking sides with one parent against the other, and hiding their feelings about the mess their parents made of their lives."

"Different circumstances, same outcome. Frustration at not making much headway, and annoyance at not being able to do much else."

"So true, Luke. So true." Lacey's mood was turning sour to match Luke's.

Eight minutes later, Luke was guiding his SUV towards Lacey's Jaguar parked all alone on the vast parking lot. More parking places were filled with cars, vans, and pick-up trucks, but Lacey's Jag was still the only vehicle in her little corner of the lot.

Lacey gave Luke a big hug and a quick kiss on the lips before sliding into the driver's seat of her car. With only a few wispy clouds over head, she lowered the top, perched her sunglasses on her nose, and headed off with a wave. Raven hair billowed around Lacey's elegant face.

Luke grabbed a sandwich on the way to class.

CHAPTER TWENTY

Wednesday, Second Week in October
Police Station
St. Petersburg, FL
8:36 a.m.

Luke had called the computer guy at the phone number provided by Tampa Police Detective, Hector Jimenez. Luke told the computer guy the basics about his situation and what he needed. The guy explained what he required to help Luke out, and even guided him with directions over the phone as Luke manipulated copies of his computer data and files. The computer guy cautioned Luke not to use the original files just in case something unexpected happened. The computer guy then told Luke that the results would take a few hours because there were things he had to do to the files first to make everything compatible. Luke thanked the guy and said he would wait for him to call back when the computer searches were complete. Luke logged the call in the file and turned to his next task, the BOLO on Stanley Robbins' Honda, the quickest and easiest thing he had to do.

Luke hadn't received any more notices on the white Honda BOLO since the last one, but he wanted to check just to be sure. He called the officer that coordinates such things, and not surprising, no new sightings were reported. Luke dutifully recorded this call in his file.

Next, Luke glanced at the Property Records showing the previous owners of the Kemp home. Not Stanley Robbins. Another dead end.

The third task: figure out how to find and talk to Trevor Kemp. Luke fired up his computer again and began searching for businesses with the name "Trevor" and/or "Kemp". Within seconds, Trevor and

Nancy Kemp's address popped up on his screen. Not new information since Luke already knew Trevor operated out of his house, but it was additional confirmation. No other hits on Kemp. Several businesses with the name "Trevor" were listed, but none were related to the construction or building industry. Luke then decided to check with local home building and improvement organizations. The first five calls were fruitless. No Trevor Kemp listed as a member or involved with the organizations.

On the sixth call Luke was able to convince the nice lady on the other end that he needed to find out where some of Trevor Kemp's jobs might be. The young lady told Luke to check with the County Building Permit Office. All construction and major home improvement jobs required a permit specifying the work to be done and who was doing it. If Trevor was reputable and followed the rules he would apply for a permit to do major work. The owner of each property with the particular address was all on file. Luke thanked the lady and called the Pinellas County Building Permit Office. He was politely informed that it would be much easier if Luke could stop by in person. Luke thanked the man and grabbed his sport coat.

◻ ◻ ◻

Trevor Kemp had four current open permits on file scattered around the northern part of Pinellas County. Trevor could be at any of them—or none. Luke decided not to just chance a phone call to the job site because Trevor might find out and disappear. Luke would just go to the home that was the farthest away and take the rest in order as he worked his way back.

The first two consumed over an hour of Luke's time. Both were jobs to remodel a bathroom, and both homeowners said Trevor wasn't expected back for several days because he was waiting on specially ordered parts or materials.

The home owner on the third job site, Peter Holmes, was leery of the police and reluctant to talk to Luke. He sported menacing looking tattoos on both forearms. Diamond studs in both ear lobes. Big guy. Stocky build. Thin mustache. Long sideburns. Three day beard stubble. Luke figured he was a tough biker guy type. To stay on the cautious side, Luke was careful when he questioned the guy. Finally the homeowner let it slip that Trevor would be returning in less than an hour with a needed part to replace the garbage disposal under the kitchen sink. Luke thanked the man and left the job site.

Thirty-five minutes later Luke was sitting in his SUV under the shade of a large oak tree a half block away. He killed time by checking in to see if the computer guy had called with some results. He hadn't yet. The same disappointing news for Stanley's Honda BOLO.

Luke continued waiting for Trevor to show up by thinking about the case. That was nothing new since he thought about the case almost every waking hour. A smattering of cars and minivans wandered up and down the street with most eventually turning into a random driveway and disappearing into a garage. Not unusual activity for a typical middleclass neighborhood late in the afternoon.

Luke glanced up from his files and notes to spot a white car in his rear view mirror heading towards him from behind about two blocks away. Luke turned around to get a better look through his rear window. He could tell it was a Honda from the grill and general shape of the approaching car. But was it Stanley's Honda? Luke hadn't expected to spot Stanley's Honda here while looking for Trevor Kemp. Maybe his luck was changing.

Luke quickly pushed the files onto the passenger seat, grabbed and snapped his seat belt around himself, and started the engine. He was waiting for the Honda to pass and would follow it. Luke checked his outside mirror; the Honda was just finishing a three-point U-turn and speeding away. "Damn," snarled Luke as he threw the car into gear while jerking the steering wheel to the left. To his surprise, there was Peter Holmes jumping up and down in his yard, flailing his arms over his head, and pointing dramatically in Luke's direction. The Honda driver was obviously being tipped off by Peter Holmes.

"Son of a bitch," muttered Luke under his breath while making a mental note to do something about this blatant interference in police matters. Peter Holmes would be toast when Luke was finished with him. But, not right now.

Luke skillfully executed his own U-turn and sped off in pursuit of the Honda which was just turning left onto a side street three blocks away. Luke gunned the engine as he requested backup, but didn't expect much in the next five or so minutes.

Luke's SUV was equipped with the largest and most powerful engine available for that vehicle, so he wasn't concerned about being outrun by a small Honda. The problem was the maze of curved streets that snaked through the neighborhood. Luke's red and blue lights flashed on accompanied by the wailing siren. Luke squealed around the corner of the street where the Honda had turned, and Luke looked everywhere searching for the Honda. He screeched to a stop at the next intersection and snapped his head back and forth. No Honda. Tires squealed again as Luke lunged forward to the next intersection. Still no Honda.

All the while Luke kept wondering why Peter Holmes was warning Stanley Robbins. Luke had only mentioned Trevor Kemp to him; nothing about Stanley Robbins. He was now more convinced than ever that there is some connection between Stanley Robbins and Trevor Kemp—but what?

Luke switched off the lights and siren after about eight minutes when a St. Petersburg police car arrived to lend a hand. The backup officer's role is to assist and take directions from the requesting officer. Luke pulled alongside and they spoke for a few minutes through open side windows. Luke explained the situation and asked the officer to keep patrolling the area looking for the Honda. Luke had more important things to do.

Luke made his way back to the house where Trevor Kemp was supposed to be doing some contracting work. Peter Holmes had a lot of explaining to do.

Luke pulled into the long driveway and leaped out with eyes glued to the front of the house. Peter Holmes was no longer in the front yard. Luke pounded hard on the door shouting, "Peter Holmes. This is the St. Petersburg police. Open the door, sir."

No sounds from inside and the door remained closed. Luke tried again, "Mr. Holmes, I need to talk to you **now**." He waited for any response. Still none. "Mr. Holmes, if you don't open this door right now, I'll be forced to call in the SWAT Team and break it down." Luke knew he was making an empty threat—no warrant—and hoped Mr. Holmes didn't know any better.

Luke waited in silence with cell phone at the ready to call for a warrant. His gaze scanned the front of the house. Solid windowless door. One large bay window with heavy dark curtains hiding whatever was inside. Two smaller windows to his left with white blinds closing out all light. The lock clicked as the door opened an inch. Peter Holmes spoke through the crack in the door, "I already told you everything I know about Trevor Kemp."

Luke pushed the door farther open and stuck a foot inside preventing Holmes from shutting it, "No you didn't, Mr. Holmes."

"Yes, I did. I don't know anything else."

"Okay. Then why did you warn Stanley Robbins that I was looking for him?"

"What are you talking about? Who's Stanley Robbins?" Peter opened the door wider and faced Luke with a quizzical look.

"Stanley Robbins owns a white Honda. You signaled him when you saw me down the street." Luke pointed to his left.

"I waved to Trevor Kemp. I don't know a Stanley Robbins." The man was genuinely confused.

"You're telling me that Trevor Kemp was driving the Honda?"

"Yes, my contractor, Trevor Kemp."

"You're sure?"

"Sure, I'm sure. I've hired him a few times for other stuff. This job was the smallest I hired him to do for me. He's still working on the other things, too."

Luke wasn't so sure, "Mr. Holmes, would you accompany me to my car and look at a few pictures?"

"Uh, am I under arrest?"

"Not yet, Mr. Holmes," Luke swept his arm towards his car with his other hand jingled his handcuffs. Peter hung his head and marched outside with Luke following a step behind.

Luke reached inside and shuffled papers and photos while concealing his actions. Peter waited next to the open passenger-side door with his arms folded across his barrel chest. Luke finally had his photos and backed out of the car door.

Luke showed the composite sketch Megan helped create of the second, still unknown, man, "Do you know this man, Mr. Holmes?"

Peter took the sketch and looked at it carefully, then back to Luke, "Sorry, I've never seen him before." Peter handed the sketch back, "Anything else, Detective?" Peter was hoping he had performed his civic duty and was done with Luke.

"One more photo, Mr. Holmes," Luke handed Peter the small picture from Stanley Robbins driver's license.

"Why not? I'm always willing to cooperate with the police." Peter took one quick look at the photo. "Trevor Kemp," Peter handed the photo back matter-of-factly, as if everyone knew that.

Luke took the photo and studied it himself, "You're sure this is Trevor Kemp, not Stanley Robbins?"

Peter took it back, glanced down at it, and then handed it back again, "Trevor Kemp," he repeated, "I don't know anyone named Stanley Robbins. That guy in the photo is Trevor Kemp." Peter pointed emphatically at the small photo.

Luke was caught off guard. He looked back and forth between the photo and Peter trying to understand what all this meant. Finally, "Well, thank you for the identification."

"Always glad to help out the police," grinned Peter with fake sincerity.

"Just be more careful about not interfering with the police."

Peter's hands flew in the air, "Hey man, I never wanted to interfere."

Luke let that go. Peter had provided valuable new information. Luke now just had to figure out what it meant, and how it fit into his investigation, "Thanks again, Mr. Holmes."

Peter backed away as Luke tossed the photos into the SUV and closed the door before walking around to the driver's side.

Luke drove back to the police station half concentrating on the new developments and half on how to proceed. His theory needed revision and he knew Loo should be briefed. Maybe now Loo would authorize more officers to help him.

Luke was still debating how to proceed as he arrived at the station a few minutes before 5:00 p.m. As he walked to his desk Lakesha Johnson greeted him with a pink message slip. Handing it to Luke, she said, "He said it was important."

Luke glanced at the name, "Thanks, it is."

Making his way across the room, he knew Lakesha's offer to help should be accepted now that he had more information. Hopefully the next phone call would produce even more.

Luke flung his jacket across the back of his chair, snatched the phone, and dialed the number on the pink paper. Introductions and pleasantries were brief. The computer guy said, "I ran the files you provided and got some interesting results. Can you stop by so I can show you?"

Luke scribbled down the address and told the guy he'd be there in 15 minutes. On the way over he called Lacey on her cell. She was happy to hear from him. When he finally got around to asking her if she could come by the station later to review the case she agreed without hesitation. Her last session ended over an hour ago. Luke had firmed up his plan: he would get the new information from the computer guy, brainstorm with Lakesha and Lacey over the next few hours, then take everything to Loo and ask for more help.

Luke called Lakesha Johnson and gave her a very broad overview of the case. He told her to take the file from his desk and go through it while he was out. They would discuss it further when he got back.

Luke pulled into the parking lot of a strip mall and looked around for the particular business. He found a parking space directly in front and went inside. The guy he was talking to over the phone greeted him with a hardy handshake, and ushered him into a semi-dark room filled with humming machines, all with blinking lights. No one else was in the room, "Over here, detective," The guy pointed to a cluttered area. A very large computer monitor was perched in the center of the desk.

Luke got right to the point, "What did you find?"

"First, I checked all the fingerprints. Hundreds as you know. Same result you got. No matches in the system, because they weren't associated with any known person. But, when I compared the fingerprints with other cases I got several hits."

Luke was staring at the monitor as the guy typed instructions on the keyboard. Several lists popped up. Prints in four of the stolen vans in Pinellas county matched each other and two more stolen vans in Hillsborough. One in Manatee County also matched.

"So at least seven stolen vehicle cases involve the same person," Luke exclaimed as he kept staring.

"Maybe more. I also got partials on two others, but they aren't conclusive."

"Understood. What about other forensics?"

"DNA mostly. Couldn't identify an individual, but the same DNA showed up on six of the murder cases and two stolen vehicles."

Luke sat down. He now had evidence that proves connections between most, or all of his cases. Next, he had to connect the fingerprints to the DNA—and identify who they came from. That might be harder to do.

Chapter Twenty-One

Wednesday, Second Week in October
Police Station
St. Petersburg, FL
6:54 p.m.

Lacey was waiting for him when Luke got back from meeting with the computer guy. Luke had a thick red manila folder in his hand. They embraced and went into the large detective area. Luke strolled over to Lakesha with Lacey following close behind. Gesturing towards Lacey, then Lakesha, "Dr. Lacey Hirsch, this is Detective Lakesha Johnson."

Luke had called Lakesha again as he drove back, and asked her to help him out some more. Lakesha was again the only detective scheduled to work after 6:00 p.m., but another detective was sitting at his desk with his feet up and a cell phone stuck to his ear. Probably not working on a case.

The two ladies nodded at each other and shook hands. Both then looked at Luke waiting for him to continue. Luke held up the red folder, "I have strong evidence that connects these cases right here, and I need your help to get this investigation moving forward." Luke looked back and forth between Lacey and Lakesha, "Both of you. I need help from you both." Luke repeated himself, and seemed like a little boy pleading with his mother to go out and play with his buddies.

The ladies had never met each other before. They looked at each other then back to Luke. Lakesha spoke first, "Sure, Brasch. I'm game. Whatever you need. It's been slow here anyway." Lacey cocked her head in surprise at how Lakesha addressed Luke, but nodded her agreement as she said, "Whatever you need."

Lakesha handed the file she had reviewed to Luke. He nodded, handed it to Lacey, and headed for the conference room. The ladies followed. Luke tossed his folder on the large table. Lacey set hers down more gingerly as Luke trotted over to the white board that covered most of a side wall and picked up a black marker. The ladies sat down and watched, intrigued by the suspense.

"Here's what we know," Luke started writing in the upper left hand corner as he outlined the details, pausing occasionally in his animated narrative to write something else down. When he came to the dead teens, he asked Lacey to arrange the photos on the table in chronological order of their deaths. All three looked at and touched each, making sure they knew which ones had been identified and which ones not. Next, he asked Lakesha to read off the dates of the stolen vehicles. Luke wrote as Lakesha read the highlighted dates from the computer printouts from a week or so ago. The pattern was becoming obvious. There was indeed a stolen vehicle found in an adjacent county near a long bridge a day or two after each murder, but never in the same county as that murder. Luke picked up the red marker, drew a line between the date of each girl's death and the date the stolen vehicle was found. He picked up the blue marker and walked towards the table. He pushed the red folder towards Lacey and returned to the white board, "Lacey, please read the dates where the fingerprints matched other cases."

Luke was looking at Lacey poised to write on the white board. She opened the red folder and stared at the unfamiliar computer printouts. Lacey flipped pages while shaking her head, "What am I looking for? This makes no sense to me."

Luke put the marker down and went over to Lacey. Lakesha moved in closer. "Sorry, Lacey. I forgot the computer guy told me that these printouts are not the final report version." He flipped pages and pulled out a short list of what turned out to be column headings. "The columns are arranged in this order. He called this a column key," pointing to the column of names. Lacey looked back and forth between the column key and the computer printout, "Okay. Now I understand what I'm looking at." Lakesha leaned in closer still and counted with her finger as she too started to understand.

Lacey scanned the computer printout again while occasionally glancing at the column key. As Lacey read off the dates where fingerprints matched those in other stolen vehicles, Luke drew a big blue circle around the date on the white board. He used the green marker for the DNA matches in other crimes.

Satisfied, Luke stood back to survey his masterpiece. On one large whiteboard in living color was all the cases strongly suggesting that they, or at least most of the cases, were linked together, and probably committed by one or two people. Luke had identified multiple factors common to all the cases. Lakesha got up and slapped him on the back, "You did it, Brasch. I'm convinced. This shows how each case is related to the others," as she smiled in the direction of the white board.

Lacey followed with a hug and a peck on the cheek, and then asked, "So what's next?"

Luke pushed a chair between where the two ladies had been seated. The ladies returned to their seats and waited for Luke to lead. A glance at each lady then Luke slumped back in his chair, "That's what I need your help in figuring out."

Both ladies were now fully aware of everything Luke knew about all the cases. After a few seconds of awkward silence, Lacey leaned forward, "I think the most important factor is Stanley Robbins."

Lakesha jumped in, "We can't find Robbins, but we know where Trevor Kemp lives, and we know his job sites. I think we should track Kemp down."

Luke was watching each lady as she spoke, "Here's my theory." Four sparkling eyes moved to Luke.

"I think Stanley Robbins and Trevor Kemp are either identical twins or the same person."

Both ladies were already leaning towards that conclusion, but not quite. Lakesha offered, "Maybe they're just two guys that look a lot alike."

Luke shook his head, "Not likely. Too much of a coincidence. They're either closely related or the same person. They can't be look-a-likes. Too improbable."

Lacey piped up, "Let's look at this from another angle." Luke and Lakesha turned towards Lacey.

"First, it's unlikely that identical male twins have completely different names. Those that do were probably adopted into different families, and they rarely meet each other until much later in life—if ever. Such twins most often get separated at birth or when they're very young. Sometimes they don't even know the other twin exists. When they do, one twin, rarely both, often spends decades as an adult searching for their other twin. Some don't reconnect until they're in their 50's or 60's. The internet may make it easier now, but historically it's much later in life. It's also very unlikely that two people look so much alike that they could fool a wife of one of them. Then there's the matter of Stanley's diminished mental capacity. Could he even find a twin if there was one? He has enough mental ability to run a small business, but what else can he do intellectually? So, Luke's second option makes the most sense. If Stanley is Trevor, the same person, we have to wonder why he's using two names and concealing one of them from his own wife."

A lot to think about. Luke rubbed his chin in contemplation. "Good points, Lacey. Nancy Kemp did seem to recognize the picture of Stanley Robbins but denied doing so. She was definitely unnerved by seeing the picture we said was Stanley because maybe she knows him as Trevor Kemp—her husband."

Lacey leaned around Luke, "Lakesha, do you have any insights?"

"Well, what you both say makes sense, but I'm not comfortable ignoring any possibility."

Luke tried to clarify, "We're not ignoring anything, Johnson. We're just trying to prioritize and start with the option that has the best chance of being right."

Lakesha was still skeptical, "Why? Shouldn't we pursue all angles?"

"We just don't have the manpower right now. Until this evening, Lacey was the only person Loo let help me. And, I'm not looking forward to telling him about you helping out now."

Lakesha shot to her feet and smacked the table with her hand, "Then by God let's change his mind. Nine dead girls and Megan deserve better than this meager effort," as Lakesha made a circling motion with her finger. She wasn't ridiculing anything Luke and Lacey had already done, and they knew exactly what she meant.

Luke needed to calm Lakesha down a little so they could come up with a plan. He patted Lakesha on the shoulder and tried to push her back into her seat, "We agree with you, Johnson. Now we have something more concrete we can take to Loo. He was sympathetic before, but without more evidence he couldn't justify putting more guys on it—and gals," Luke quickly corrected his slip of the tongue as he nodded at the ladies. "Now we have more evidence."

Lacey jumped back in, "I think the next thing we should concentrate on is finding Stanley Robbins, alias Trevor Kemp. We can stake out the Kemp house and grab Trevor whenever he shows up, and put an end to this damn name mystery."

Luke looked at Lacey with renewed admiration. Even though that's what he was about to suggest he said, "Good idea. We can propose exactly that. But, first we'll just march up to the Kemp house and ask to see him."

Lakesha countered, "Then we can determine if any of the fingerprints or DNA comes from Stanley or Trevor, whoever the hell he is."

Lacey was back in the fray, "Then we can make Stanley tell us who this other character is."

Luke kept swiveling his head between the ladies as each spoke. Finally, "I can release the composite to our media folks and get the public involved," Luke held up the composite.

Lakesha asked Luke, "What's your take on getting help from Hillsborough and Manatee?"

"I think it's pretty good now. We've got unsolved murders in all three counties with a clear connection between many of them. Loo shouldn't have much trouble getting them on board, especially if our esteemed Chief of Police gets involved personally."

Luke and Lakesha both knew from experience that the St. Petersburg Police Chief often let his lower level minions do the dirty work. He preferred the politics and notoriety of the office, and was pretty good at snagging resources and support, even in these hard times. He loved big, important cases, and this one should peak his interest.

Luke stood up, "Okay, let's recap to make sure we haven't missed anything."

Lacey and Lakesha watched as Luke went over to the whiteboard and pointed to the names, dates, lines, and circles as he went through it all again. He wrote, "Stanley Robbins, Trevor Kemp, and stranger" in orange on the whiteboard. When he finished and gestured at the board, "Do we agree that this represents everything we know?" Both ladies nodded their agreement.

Luke snatched the red marker and started writing "DO NOT ERASE" in several blank spots on the whiteboard. Next he ripped out three blank pages from a pad of paper and boldly wrote "ROOM IN USE" on each. He handed the pages to Lakesha while pointing, "Could you hang these on the door and anywhere else to make sure this doesn't get lost?"

"Sure, Brasch. I'll close the door and tape it shut after we leave," as she took the papers and looked around for a tape dispenser.

Luke glanced at his watch. It was almost 8 p.m., "It's too late to brief Loo tonight. Lacey, are you free tomorrow morning?"

Lacey fished inside her purse for the smart phone she kept as a constant companion. She searched for a few seconds and looked up, "No sessions with clients until 11:00."

"Good, can you be here at 8:00 in the morning?"

"Sure."

Turning to Lakesha, Luke asked, "Johnson, when does your shift end?"

"Night shift all this month." Luke knew what that meant; Lacey didn't, but she kept quiet.

"Would you mind coming back at 8:00 tomorrow morning to join Lacey and me when we brief our lieutenant?"

"No, I don't mind, I'll be here. I want to be a part of this."

"Thanks, Johnson. I know how much of a problem this might be for you."

Luke clapped his hands together, "Now, let's make sure we have our theory correct. Nothing left out, and no way to shoot it down." The three comrades-in-arms spent the next 25 minutes discussing the overall theory each was now confident fit all the facts and evidence.

Finally Luke slumped back into his seat and set his pen down, "I think we're ready. Anything else?" Both ladies shook their heads.

"Fine, Lacey and I are going home." Directly to Lakesha, "Thanks, and you have a good night. See you in the morning"

Luke stood up, "We'll leave everything here for tomorrow." Lacey stood, slung the strap of her purse over her right shoulder, and headed for the door. Luke caught up with her halfway across the detective room, "We both missed dinner. How about a bite to eat?"

Lacey turned around with a smile, "My treat for the great job you're doing."

Luke looked up in disgust, "Argh," he grunted, "You never give up, do you?"

"No, I don't, Detective Lucas Brasch."

Lakesha watched the entire episode while beaming from ear to ear. Lacey slipped her arm under Luke's as they disappeared from the police station.

Chapter Twenty-Two

Thursday, Second Week in October
Police Station
St. Petersburg, FL
7:54 a.m.

Luke was seated at his desk holding a cell phone next to his ear as Lacey strolled over. He looked up with a smile and pointed to the phone. Lacey nodded and returned the smile, then took a seat in the chair next to his desk. Lacey looked around for Lakesha as she waited for Luke to finish his call, but didn't see her.

Luke finally slapped the phone shut and turned to Lacey, "Lakesha is preparing the conference room for our meeting with Lieutenant Thompson. You remember him, don't you?"

"Yes, I do." She didn't tell Luke that she felt uneasy around Nick. She thought he was leering at her the last time they met and it made her uncomfortable.

"He's coming out in about fifteen minutes. The three of us will make our presentation and ask for help."

"Just like last evening?"

"That's right. I'll start off like we did last night when we put the whole thing together. I'll lay out everything. After that Loo will start asking questions. He's a good listener and probably won't interrupt until we're done. If you or Lakesha have any input at any time just jump in. We're pretty loose around here when it comes to collaborating like this."

"I'm fine with that."

For a few moments Luke and Lacey stared into each other's eyes and were whisked away from all this nasty business. Luke broke the spell, "Thanks for taking me to dinner last night. God, I never thought I'd ever say that to a woman," as he covered his eyes with a hand.

Lacey giggled, "This isn't the dark ages, Luke. Women do ask men out on dates."

Just as Luke patted Lacey's hand, Loo stomped over, "Good morning, Dr. Hirsch." He stuck out a thick paw and Lacey stood up to shake his hand.

Lacey was still wearing only black, white, and gray, but her tailored black pantsuit and white and gray patterned silk blouse was less spectacular than some of her other outfits. Smiling at Nick, "Good morning, Lieutenant. Nice to see you again."

Turning to Luke, "Okay, Luke. Let's see what you've got."

Luke stood up and motioned towards the conference room, "We have everything in there, Loo."

Loo led the way as Lacey and Luke followed. When they stepped through the doorway Lakesha stood up, "Good morning, Loo." Nick frowned in annoyance; he wasn't aware of her involvement. Luke saw the look on Loo's face, and immediately stepped forward, "I asked Johnson to help Lacey and me work out the final details last night. The station was quiet so Johnson had nothing else to do." Lakesha nodded her confirmation.

Loo frowned again, but said nothing. Lacey remarked, "Lieutenant, Detective Johnson helped sort out details that only someone with her experience could have done. I'm grateful she had some free time to help us out."

Loo looked at Lakesha, then Lacey, and finally at Luke. He knew his detectives often unofficially helped each other and sensed this case would soon become much bigger than originally thought. Loo took a seat at the end of the table facing the colorful whiteboard, "Show me what you've got."

Lacey and Lakesha took seats closer to the whiteboard as Luke walked towards the whiteboard and picked up a black rod with a red tip. Over the next 45 minutes Luke and his trusty pointer waded through the details of the nine dead teens, the dumped vehicles,

Megan, Stanley, Trevor, the unidentified guy with Stanley, and how their theory fit all these facts.

Loo absorbed the presentation in silence as Luke plowed on in an amazingly competent manner. Finally, Luke said, "That's all of it, Loo."

Loo rocked slowly in his chair with arms folded across his chest. The three others waited in silence. Eventually Loo said, "Good job, Luke." He looked around at the ladies, "All of you, nice work. I'm on board."

All three smiled and nodded, "Thank you."

"So, what's the plan?" Loo was starting his questioning.

Luke sat down next to Lacey and took out his note pad. He then carefully explained how a team comprised of detectives from all three counties should be assembled. Each county could investigate cases in their respective jurisdictions and share information with the others.

"I agree. This is now at least a three county case. I'll call the Chief as soon as we're through and get him to twist some arms if needed. Anything in Pasco?"

Pasco County was on the northern border of both Pinellas and Hillsborough Counties, but there are no long bridges connecting them. "No, Loo. It doesn't look like they're involved. It's just the three counties surrounding Tampa Bay, because we only see incidences on all three big bridges and the Courtney Campbell Causeway. "

"All right. What else?"

"We need to nail down the Stanley Robbins—Trevor Kemp identification issue."

"How do you plan to do that?"

"The key is Nancy Kemp. We think she recognized the photo of Stanley Robbins, but she denied it. We'll go back to the Kemp home. If Trevor isn't there, I'll bring Nancy in here if we have to and get her to clear all this up. And, Peter Holmes identified the photo of Stanley Robbins as Trevor Kemp, so we know there's some connection between Stanley and Trevor."

Lacey spoke up, "Nancy Kemp is a perfect example of an old-style innocent homemaker. She is definitely conflicted about the Stanley—

Trevor relationship, whatever it is. Upon saying that, I caution whoever interviews her to be gentle. If she feels threatened we'll just have a sobbing, emotional wreck on our hands."

Loo turned to Luke, "Let Dr. Hirsch take the first shot at her—the Kemp home or here. What else?" The lieutenant was clearly in charge and expected obedience. He also recognizes situations for what they really are; titles and egos were not as important as results.

"We need to find Stanley Robbins' Honda. The BOLO alert spotted his car already, but we couldn't actually stop it and interrogate him."

"Bump the BOLO to a higher priority, and get more patrols into the area where he was already spotted. Put out an APB on him. Maybe that might turn up something. What else?"

"I think we should get the composite of the guy with Stanley Robbins to our media people."

"Good. Get whatever exposure you can. What else?"

Luke treaded carefully now and asked a question no one expected, "Loo and Johnson, do you remember any of these older cases from Pinellas? It seems to me that murders of teenage girls should have had more of an investigation than these files indicate," Luke picked up a handful of meager files for emphasis.

Nick leaned forward and looked at all three before speaking. He knew Lakesha would wait for him to speak first, "No, I don't remember any of them, just like I don't remember many other murders I'm not involved in personally. I was a detective just like you until 15 months ago and didn't oversee all the cases I do now. Luke, you said it yourself that these murders occurred over a five year period with no hint that they might be connected back then, and no real leads. After several months our normal onslaught of new cases forces us to put cases we can't pursue effectively on the back burner until new clues turn up. That's what you three have done—given us a good reason to take another look at new evidence. Now we'll reopen the investigations on all of them to catch these bastards." Lakesha was nodding in agreement.

Luke persisted, "Alarms didn't go off?"

"No. None. You have the reasons right there," Nick pointed to the array of reports and photos, "Remember, we only had the Pinellas cases to look at. There wasn't any indication that Hillsborough or Manatee was involved. Nothing indicated a similarity other than the young ages of the four girls from here and that they were homeless. We had maybe a dozen homicides to deal with at any one time, and there were no similarities in those murders. No pattern, Luke. Nothing to set off the alarm bells. Maybe we just weren't smart enough to connect the dots." Nick looked down and shook his head, sincerely apologetic.

Luke thanked him for his insight and candor, "One more thing Loo. I need Detective Johnson officially assigned to the team. Her years of experience would be helpful since what these guys are doing is pretty clever," Luke looked around almost in disbelief as he recapped his theory, "Dump a murdered teenage homeless girl in one county at one end of a big bridge and abandon the car at the other. And, use both ends of all the bridges to do it over a five year period. Luckily for these pedophiles no family reported any of these girls missing and no one claimed the body. Like those girls were disposable. As if they had no value to anyone. Also, there was no obvious time or location pattern as to when or where a girl gets murdered. Ten victims over five years, but nothing to get us more involved. These guys are deliberately screwing with us by using our poor inter-county law enforcement communication to their advantage. We need to turn that around." All eyes were on Luke and all agreed completely. Luke was preaching to the choir.

Nick stood up, "Done. Detective Johnson, I'll find someone else to finish out the graveyard shift this month. Luke, you'll head up the three-county team. Dr. Hirsch, thanks for your help so far, and I want you to stay on the team."

Nick walked hurriedly to the door, stopped, and turned around, "Good job, all of you. And Luke, I still can't find that folder we talked about. Now, get back to work." Nick's smile told it all; Loo wanted Luke to continue working full time on all these cases while ignoring the limited duty order from Luke's Doctor.

Luke looked at both Lakesha and Lacey with a broad smile of his own, "We did it, ladies. Thank you both." He hugged Lacey and turned towards Lakesha to shake her hand. She stood up and said,

"No you don't, Brasch," and grabbed him for a hearty bear hug. Luke surrendered and patted Lakesha on the back until she let him go.

Then they got down to work. Luke instructed Lakesha to secure the room again, "Once the team is named we'll need to go through all of this again," as he swept his arm around the room. "I doubt we'll know the names of the other team members until tomorrow morning. Once we do we can hold our kick-off meeting." Lakesha nodded and started putting up her signs again.

Turning to Lacey, "When is the earliest you can go with us to the Kemps?"

Lacey consulted her smart phone, "My last patient is at 1:00 p.m. Pick me up at 2:00." She shoved the phone into her purse and stood up, "Now, I've got to run back to the office."

"Certainly. Do what you've got to do. We'll be by at 2:00 this afternoon."

Lacey said goodbye, kissed Luke, and waved at Lakesha across the room. Luke then picked up his folder with the composite of the man with Stanley Robbins and went off to the Police Media Department.

Luke was back at his desk a half hour later, and started preparing for the detectives who might be assigned from Hillsborough and Manatee Counties. He also thought about how he would assign tasks for Lakesha and Lacey. Being a leader of a six to eight person Task Force was loaded with responsibilities Luke was not used to, but he was confident that he was up to the job.

When Lakesha marched over to report that she had secured the room, Luke assigned her to the BOLO and APB, "Follow up on the bumped up BOLO, and get out an APB on Stanley Robbins."

"What about Trevor Kemp. Shouldn't we put one out for him too?"

Luke nodded, "Yes, do that. If by some remote chance Stanley and Trevor are two people we need to talk to both of them. We haven't had any luck trying to find Trevor at his house or on the job sites he's supposed to be working."

◻ ◻ ◻

Luke and Lakesha leisurely strolled into Lacey's bright and modern office not far from downtown St. Petersburg. No one was in the waiting room. No receptionist desk either. A sign alerted them to press the buzzer for assistance, which they did. A frosted glass panel slid open as Lacey greeted them, "Hey guys, just give me a minute. I'll be right out."

A few minutes later Lacey appeared from the door that led to her offices. They chatted about how nice her office looked as Lacey ushered them outside. Lakesha relinquished the front seat to Lacey and settled into the back seat. More idle chatter as Luke drove towards the Kemp home.

They arrived just after 2:45 p.m. No car in the driveway and no sign of a white Honda on nearby streets or driveways. Luke actually cruised around the neighborhood looking for the Honda before pulling up at the Kemp home. When they arrived all three piled out and leisurely walked to the front door. Luke rang the bell and stepped back to where the ladies were standing. Nancy Kemp answered the door, took one look at Luke, and sneered, "What do you want now?"

Luke and Lakesha just stood motionless as Lacey responded calmly in a reassuring voice, "Mrs. Kemp, I'm Lacey Hirsch, and this is Detective Brasch and Johnson. We need to ask you a few more questions. It's very important that we speak to your husband and determine from him if he knows Stanley Robbins. This shouldn't take very long. I promise."

Nancy didn't budge from her position in the doorway, "I already told you Trevor doesn't know anyone named Stanley Robbins, and neither do I."

"I'm sorry, Mrs. Kemp, but we need to hear that from him."

"Trevor isn't here," she sneered as tightlipped as possible.

"Can you tell us where to find him?"

Arms hugging herself tightly, "No," she shot back.

Lacey looked at Luke skeptically, then back to Nancy, "You don't know, or you won't tell us?"

"I don't know where he is—and I wouldn't tell you if I did." Nancy Kemp glared menacingly at Lacey.

"When was the last time you saw him?"

"Early this morning when he went to work."

Lacey let out a slow breath. Getting information from Mrs. Kemp wasn't going to be easy, "Do you know which job site he's at?"

"No, I told you I didn't."

Lacey decided to move to another topic. "Mrs. Kemp, when we showed you a picture of the man we called Stanley Robbins you said that you didn't know him. Was that the truth?" Lacey was being as gentle as possible. Nancy's shoulders slumped and she slowly shook her head "No".

Luke and Lakesha looked at Lacey urging her to go on. "You know that person in the picture, don't you?"

Nancy nodded "Yes" just as slowly.

"How do you know Stanley Robbins, Mrs. Kemp?"

"I don't know anyone named Stanley Robbins," Nancy whimpered.

Luke, Lacey, and Lakesha looked at each other again quizzically, "Mrs. Kemp," Lacey persisted, "then how did you recognize the picture of Stanley Robbins?"

Nancy put her hands over her face and sobbed uncontrollably. Luke took that opportunity to push the door open and marched inside. Luke knew he might have to deal with this unauthorized entrance into the Kemp home at some future time, but didn't care at the moment. Lakesha and Lacey followed. If Nancy objected she didn't protest. Lakesha and Lacey helped Nancy to an overstuffed chair and slowly lowered her into it while Nancy kept her hands glued to her face. Lakesha offered to get Nancy some water. Nancy lowered one hand to point towards the kitchen and Lakesha went off in the indicated direction. About ten steps later Lakesha stopped short and stared at a wall of pictures, "Brasch, you need to see this."

Luke and Lacey turned their attention from Nancy to where Lakesha was gesturing. Both walked over to get a better look. Lakesha moved closer to the wall, "Third picture over." Luke and Lacey followed Lakesha's gaze. Lacey gasped and Luke moved in for confirmation. Staring back at them was what appeared to be a wedding picture of the Kemps. Stanley Robbins' was in a dark suit smiling back at them with

Nancy looking beautiful in a traditional white wedding gown holding a bouquet of pink flowers.

Luke carefully took the fancy framed picture off the wall. Nancy was still sobbing into her hands. Luke turned to Lakesha, "Please get Mrs. Kemp some water." Lakesha hustled into the kitchen in search of a glass, and found one in the dish drainer rack next to the sink. The refrigerator dispensed ice and cold water through the door, so she filled the glass and hurried back to Luke. Lacey and Luke were standing facing Nancy. Luke held the picture behind his back. He motioned for Lakesha to give the water to Nancy. Lakesha addressed Nancy while leaning over in a motherly manner, "Mrs. Kemp, here's some water. It'll make you feel better." Nancy took the glass with two trembling hands and whispered, "Thank you." She took a small sip and let out a huge long sigh.

Luke handed the picture to Lacey behind her back and motioned towards Nancy. Lacey knew exactly what Luke wanted her to do; confront Nancy with the wedding picture. Lacey walked over to Nancy with the picture still behind her back. Nancy was now looking at her feet. She looked like a sad pathetic puppy that had just been swatted with a rolled up newspaper and really didn't know what she did wrong to deserve it.

Nancy looked up as Lacey approached, but was still slumped over. "Mrs. Kemp, we saw this picture on your wall," Lacey produced the picture and held it low with both hands directly in front of Nancy, "I hope you don't mind that we removed it from the wall. I promise we'll put it back exactly as we found it."

Nancy sat up straighter as Lacey continued, "Is this you and your husband at your wedding?"

"Yes"

"And your husband is Trevor Kemp?"

"Yes"

"Mrs. Kemp, did you think the picture we showed you yesterday of the man we called Stanley Robbins was your husband, Trevor?"

"Yes"

Lacey motioned for Luke to come over, "Would you look at the two pictures side by side and tell me if they are the same person?"

Nancy started sobbing again, "I can't. I can't"

"Please, Mrs. Kemp. It's very important." Luke took out the small driver's license photo of Stanley and handed it to Lacey. Lakesha took a few steps closer as she trained her gaze on Nancy.

Lacey held out both pictures, "Mrs. Kemp, please look at these pictures." Nancy slowly raised her head and pointed to the driver's license photo, "Why do you keep calling him Stanley Robbins? That's my husband, Trevor."

Nancy immediately returned to a sad position with her head in her hands, and the sobbing started anew. Lacey dropped both of her arms to her sides and looked away in disbelief. Lakesha's jaw dropped two inches.

Luke took a deep breath and stepped closer, "One more question, Mrs. Kemp." Nancy looked up at him, "When do you expect your husband to come home today?"

Nancy wiped her face with a sleeve, "I don't know. He's usually home by 6:30, but sometimes he's earlier, sometimes later."

Nancy didn't know what was going on or why the police were looking for her husband, and she had no idea why they kept calling her husband Stanley Robbins. Then her mood changed from being upset to fear of what might happen next. Now Nancy started to show the hint of outrage at her husband. She correctly suspected that the police wouldn't go to this much effort unless something really bad had happened and her husband was smack dab in the middle of it. She whispered to herself, "I don't know who my husband is anymore." Tears flowed again.

Lacey backed away and replaced the wedding picture on its hook as Luke thanked Nancy for seeing them, "I'm sorry if we upset you but we had to ask those questions. We'll be going now. Thank you again for your time." Nancy remained seated as the trio left her home.

Luke, Lacey, and Lakesha sat in Luke's SUV three blocks away from the Kemp home discussing the ramifications of what they just experienced. All three were now convinced that there was a very high probability that Stanley Robbins is Trevor Kemp. One person, two names. Luke suspected that Stanley Robbins assumed the name of Trevor Kemp and not visa versa based on his conversations with Miss Frankie. Stanley had been coming around the shelter for years and it was unlikely Stanley had two names as a teenager. Turning around to Lakesha, "Could you change the BOLO and APB to say Stanley Robbins aka Trevor Kemp?"

"I'll call it in right now." Lakesha turned around to minimize the noise from her conversation.

Luke turned to Lacey, "Stanley won't be home for a few hours. I think it's a waste of our time to stick around sitting on our hands waiting for him to show."

Lacey thought for a few moments, "And, don't forget we've been here before trying to find him. If he calls his wife she might mention our visit. That could spook him to the point where he might never return. Plus, if Nancy begins to doubt the innocence of her husband she might forbid him from coming back to their house. Because of Stanley's lower intelligence, I suspect Nancy has a more dominant personality, but leaves Stanley alone to run his business. I'm guessing Nancy runs the house, but includes Stanley in the important decisions. All this has been a shock to Nancy. She's probably tougher than she seems."

"Do you think we can get anything more from Mrs. Kemp?"

"Probably not right now. She's very upset and quite confused. She seems to be a descent person and probably respects the rule of law and authority figures. Right now she's terribly conflicted; torn between doing what she knows in her soul is right, while feeling obligated to protect her husband. She may very well need professional help when all this is over."

"Okay. I won't hold my breath, but I'll ask for stepped up patrols in the neighborhood just in case. Maybe we'll get lucky." Luke flipped his cell phone open and punched in some numbers as Lacey watched.

Luke's cell jingled on the way back to Lacey's office, "Detective Brasch."

Nick Thompson was updating Luke on the status of Luke's new team, "Hillsborough was easy. They assigned two detectives. Manatee was harder, but the Chief came through. They finally agreed to assign two guys also. Don't know the names yet, but all four will be here tomorrow morning at 9:00 bright eyed and bushy tailed."

"Thanks, Loo," Luke smiled and nodded at Lacey and Lakesha as he closed the phone.

Lakesha heard snippets of the conversation and was antsy for more information, "What did he say?"

"Game on. Four additional detectives, two each from Hillsborough and Manatee. They're coming here at 9:00 tomorrow morning. We go through the whole thing again and work out a three-county strategy."

Lacey immediately rummaged through her purse for the trusty smart phone and found the correct screen, "I can reschedule my two early morning appointments. I'll be there, too."

◻ ◻ ◻

Luke was putting the finishing touches on his report covering the day's events. Records, reports, and logs had become more important in the past few years, and Luke agreed with that policy.

Luke grabbed his phone on the second ring. The media department was reporting in. The pleasant female voice informed Luke that the composite had been sent to the St. Petersburg Times newspaper reporter that handled police matters. The same for the Tampa Tribune in Hillsborough County and the Bradenton Herald in Manatee County. The three local networks plus Bay News 9 all said they would put a story together and show the sketch on air."

Luke asked, "You only gave them vague details about why we wanted to identify this guy, right?"

"Yes. I told them that we needed to identify him as part of an ongoing investigation. I didn't say anything about murders, dead teenage girls, or any of that. I didn't call him a suspect or even call him a person of interest. He was only someone we wanted to talk to, just like you instructed."

"Good. Thanks. When will the sketch run?"

"Newspapers, tomorrow. The TV stations said they could get it out tonight on the early evening or late news. Friday at the latest, depending on whether or not other news stories were more important for them to run. Bay News 9 will run it hourly during the day tomorrow. The others are a one or two-shot deal."

Luke and the lady chatted for a few more minutes and then hung up. Luke sat back and smiled to himself. He was pleased with the progress they were making, and could only imagine what might turn up next. Then back to waiting for results from Stanley aka Trevor's BOLO and APB and preparing for the detectives tomorrow. He still didn't have enough help to station officers at the Kemp home, but police cars drove by every half-hour or so. None had spotted Stanley aka Trevor or the Honda.

CHAPTER TWENTY-THREE

Friday, Second Week in October
Police Station
St. Petersburg, FL
7:42 a.m.

Luke felt good. The forming of this new task force was the most productive thing that had happened since Luke started working on this case almost two weeks ago. Luke had been at his desk for half an hour when Lakesha greeted him upon her arrival. They made small talk about how excited they were to be part of this team, and how they were hopeful to get the whole case wrapped up in a few weeks or so now that help had been promised.

Unfortunately, neither the BOLO nor the APB had produced anything, and the periodic patrols around the Kemp neighborhood last evening and through most of the night were equally unproductive. Stanley Robbins was still a ghost. Eventually they got serious about what they needed to do and could actually accomplish, "I'll get the room set up," Lakesha announced and left Luke alone.

Luke was cautiously optimistic that significant progress could finally be made. Within an hour the detectives from Manatee County arrived looking for Detective Brasch. An officer escorted them to Luke's desk. The lady was obviously more senior than her partner and did most of the talking. Paige McDermott was an imposing 5'-11" tall with high cheekbones on a triangular face. Her dark hair was swept up in a tight bun. The navy blue pant suit over a white high neck blouse and thin smile meant she was all business. Her police badge was pinned to her left lapel. Paige made the introductions. Keith Cooper was two inches shorter but weighed more than Paige. Most of the excess poundage was around his waist. His round face was clean shaven. A dark sport coat hung loosely on his bulky frame. They shook hands. Luke asked if they wanted coffee and led them into the break room. Paige took her coffee black with a little sugar. Keith poured in so much milk and sugar his cup looked tan rather than the rich black Luke and Paige preferred. Luke led them into the conference room and introduced Lakesha.

Lakesha was offering the detectives a seat at the big table when Lacey marched in with two other strangers in tow, "I arrived just as Detectives Ferguson and Sparks from Hillsborough County came in looking for you, so I brought them back here." Everyone turned towards the trio as Lacey started the second round of introductions, "This is Detective Beth Ferguson and Detective Morgan Sparks," as she pointed to each. Both ladies wore dark colored pant suits and tasteful coordinating blouses. Both were attractive, tall, and slender with long straight blond hair that hung below their shoulders. They could have been sisters. Luke and Lakesha approached with outstretched hands followed by the two Manatee detectives. Each introduced themselves in turn. Lacey introduced herself to the Manatee detectives already in the room.

Lakesha moved forward, "Can I offer you some coffee?"

Beth answered, "That would be great. Thanks." Lakesha waited while the detectives selected a place at the table and deposited their purses and papers. Then off to the break room while the others remained and chatted. Lacey noticed that only Lakesha Johnson and Detective Cooper were wearing wedding rings and chastised herself for being so petty.

Ten minutes later everyone was settled in, had sipped coffee, and were prepared to start the briefing. All eyes turned towards Luke. "Before we get into the details of why we're here, I'd like to get to know a little about each of you. Teammates work much better when they know each other. I'll start and then we'll just go around the table." Everyone looked at someone else then back to Luke.

After Luke spoke about his military experience and the last few years with the St. Petersburg Police he pointed to Lakesha. She told the group about her years with the department, and really sparkled when talking about her family. Next it was Lacey's turn. She spoke about her professional experience with the courts and kids in trouble, which was usually caused by family problems, "I've only been consulting with the St. Petersburg Police less than two weeks. In fact, it's this case that got me involved." Lacey then relinquished the floor to Beth who was sitting next to her.

Beth was brief and gave few details about her background, but passionately said, "When our Lieutenant told the Tampa detectives about this case and asked for two of us to assist you guys, Morgan and I immediately volunteered. We've both worked teen violence and murders before, and we both detest the scumbags that prey on these defenseless little girls." Morgan said, "Yep. That's how we feel," as she looked around to see if anyone challenged their feelings. Luke asked, "Are you partners?" Morgan replied, "On and off the job." Everyone knew what that meant, but no one cared or said anything except Luke, "Good, then it'll be easy to work together from the Hillsborough angle."

Morgan responded, "We're looking forward to taking these bastards down."

The Manatee detectives took their turn and also said they too volunteered to be part of this team. When everyone was done, Luke slapped the table with both hands and pushed himself up out of his chair, "Thank you all. We'll make a good team. Let's get started," as he marched toward the whiteboard with his pointer aimed at the floor.

"Let me start with the basics, most of which you already know," Luke didn't like to appear that he was talking down to his team, but he also knew he had to get everyone thinking exactly the same way, aware of the surrounding circumstances, and clearly focused on the facts and mission, "We all know this, but it bears repeating and you'll see why in a few minutes. There are three big bridges connecting our three counties: The Sunshine Skyway, the Gandy, and the Howard Frankland, plus the Courtney Campbell Causeway. Four ways to cross Tampa Bay and get from Pinellas county to Hillsborough or Manatee. One end of all four roadways is in Pinellas County. The eastern end of two bridges and the causeway are in Hillsborough. The southern end of the Skyway is in Manatee. Law enforcement jurisdiction is primarily confined to each county. So when a crime is committed in one county there is rarely a need to talk to, or work with, law enforcement in an adjacent county. The guys who committed the nine murders counted on that. We never would have suspected anything had it not been for the last attack, Megan Fisher, the lone survivor of these ten cases."

Luke went on to outline Megan's case, and what he and Lacey discovered during their investigation into her identity. Luke pointed to Megan's name on the whiteboard for emphasis before he went on to explain about Stanley Robbins aka Trevor Kemp and the unidentified man with Stanley. Luke held up the composite. No one interrupted or asked questions. Some were taking notes. Everyone hung on Luke's presentation.

Next, Luke went through the five year timeline indentifying each murder, pointing to the appropriate date, showing a picture, reading the name if there was one, and pointing to the date and location of a dumped vehicle at the other end of the bridge from where the girl was found. The details of the cases from Hillsboro and Manatee counties were sent the day before so the detectives could review their own files before the meeting today and bring any additional information with them.

By 10:45 Luke had covered all the details, answered a few pointed questions relating to where Luke got his information and its validity. All were reasonable questions and ones Luke had expected, and had asked himself over the past two weeks. The answers soothed the concerns of the detectives, all of whom were familiar with the drudgery of verifying their own work and checking details.

Luke then went on to lay out his theory that linked all the cases in concise terms. Beth asked, "We still have three jurisdictions. How do you plan to coordinate all ten cases and the dumped vehicles?"

"Good question, thank you. That's why we have detectives from all three counties. We three," pointing to himself, Lacey, and Lakesha, "will continue investigating the Pinellas cases. Detectives McDermott and Cooper have Manatee, and you two," pointing to Beth and Morgan, "will work Hillsborough. All three jurisdictions are covered and each murder or vehicle case can be prosecuted in the county where it occurred, the county with the proper jurisdiction. Working as a team and sharing information will undoubtedly make each case easier to win in court. Each county is free to pursue their cases as they see fit. Only information needs to be shared, not arrests or convictions. But this will be a team effort."

Everyone looked around nodding in approval. Luke was making good sense. He fielded a few more questions before Morgan stood up, "I'd like a potty break if no one minds." Luke glanced at his watch, "Sorry. I lost track of time. Sure, let's take fifteen minutes."

Lacey stood, "I'll show you where the restrooms are," as she motioned for Morgan to follow her. Beth fell in behind while the others stood and stretched. Some headed back to the break room for coffee refills, or pulled out dollar bills to stuff into the vending machines. Luke sat down and finished his now cold coffee while he waited patiently for everyone to dribble back in.

Eventually everyone settled back into the chairs they vacated earlier. Several new cups of coffee, soft drink cans, water bottles, and candy wrappers were moved aside as they got back to work. Luke opened this session with a detailed examination of the Pinellas cases, focusing on what little forensics they had. Everyone present had something to say and an opinion to offer. No one was hostile or disrespectful, but the discussions about whether or not the cases were connected got heated. The fingerprint and DNA comparisons were somewhat inconclusive within Pinellas County, but were obvious across the bridges. What exactly did that mean? Luke conceded that all the cases he had identified may not be the work of the same people, but requested that the others withhold judgment until the investigation was over. He also noted that the connections were more obvious when all three counties were considered together. Four of the six agreed and the other two just sat there.

The detectives from Hillsborough had checked on their cases as soon as they were officially assigned to the team yesterday afternoon. They delved into their cases and ran into the same obstacle as Luke.

There was one new nugget of information: Beth and Morgan worked one of the dead teen cases in Hillsborough. They expanded on how little their investigation revealed at that time, and why that particular case went cold. Just like all the others, there just wasn't much to go on, and more promising, equally horrific cases needed their attention.

The Manatee detectives also researched their cases yesterday. There were fewer cases from Manatee and their overview took only fifteen minutes. Luke then gave an update on the BOLO and APB and told everyone about the media coverage he ordered.

By 12:30 Luke was running out of topics for discussion, decided to break for lunch, and offered to take everyone to a local restaurant courtesy of the St. Petersburg police department. Detective Ferguson declined his offer. Beth informed the group that she and Morgan were returning to Tampa to get started on their portion of the investigation. The detectives from Manatee also declined. They too, had a long drive back home and wanted to get started this afternoon.

Luke thanked everyone, "Welcome to the team, and I look forward to a successful outcome." All agreed and gathered up their files and papers. The newcomers shook hands with everyone else and departed leaving Luke, Lacey, and Lakesha alone in the conference room.

"How about the three of us get some lunch?" announced Luke as he marched towards his desk. Lacey and Lakesha accepted, "Sounds good, just give us a minute to get rid of all of this," Lacey held up her own files and papers. Lakesha nodded, "Five minutes, Brasch. I'll meet you both outside."

Luke asked Lakesha to pick a place to eat. "Something quick, easy, and cheap," was her response. They settled on a family-style restaurant that had been around for as long as anyone could remember. The food was good, the service friendly, and the bill reasonable. When the waitress stopped by to refill the half-empty glasses, Lacey whispered in her ear, "Could you please give me the check." The waitress set the bill down in front of Lacey, who snatched it with a smile, "My treat to celebrate the new team." Luke and Lakesha protested, but gave in without much of a struggle.

On the ride back to the station Lacey announced that she had to go back to her office for a few sessions, and to finish some reports for a judge who wanted them ASAP so he could adequately review them before the hearing on Monday.

"Not a problem. Thanks for being here this morning."

"My pleasure." Lacey kissed Luke on the cheek and patted Lakesha on the hand before heading to her car. Luke and Lakesha went inside the station.

It was mid afternoon when Luke checked again on the BOLO and APB. Still nothing. His phone rang just as Luke was rearranging some of his reports in the file. "Hello, is this the detective trying to identify the man in the photo? The one on the TV?" Luke sat up and grabbed a pen.

"Yes, Miss. I'm Detective Lucas Brasch. To whom am I speaking?"

A young female voice introduced herself as a counter agent for a car rental company at the Tampa International Airport. She said an operator routed her call to Luke, and went on to tell Luke that she saw the sketch on Bay News 9 a few minutes ago and recognized the man. She explained that she realized how important it was that she call and tell the authorities what she knew, "My shift starts at 5:00 p.m. all this week, so I decided to call from home before I leave for work."

Luke asked how she recognized the man in the sketch. The voice replied, "He rented cars three or four times from us, I think they were SUV's, but I can't be sure until I check our records." She quickly added before Luke could speak, "He seemed like a nice guy. Friendly and polite."

Luke was writing furiously, "That's good. We just need to talk to him. Do you remember his name, ma'am?"

"I'm not sure of that either without the records, but I am sure he rented vehicles from us before."

"Can you check your records for a name and address?"

"Yes, I can do that. But, I don't go in to work for a few hours."

Luke said, "Hold on a minute, please," as he shuffled papers. "If I send some officers to where you work could you talk to them?"

"I'd just have to clear it with my supervisor, but sure, I can talk to them. I might even be in charge, but I won't know until I check in," she answered proudly.

Luke thanked her and said that Detectives Ferguson and Sparks from the Tampa police department would be by to talk to her during her shift this evening.

"I'll be on the lookout for them, Detective."

"Thank you very much. I appreciate your coming forward."

Luke copied down the information the Tampa detectives would need to find her, thanked her again, and hung up. Luke called the Tampa police department and reached Beth Ferguson. He repeated the conversation he just had, and asked if they could go over to the airport and interview the car rental agent about the composite. "Glad to, Detective. Could you fax over the info so we get it right?"

"I'll type it out so you can read it—my hand scratching is terrible—and send it off in ten or so minutes."

"Thanks. We'll let you know what we find out."

Luke was not surprised that the teamwork was working so well so quickly. He always knew it would.

Chapter Twenty-Four

Friday, Second Week in October
Tampa International Airport
Tampa, FL
6:09 p.m.

A pimple faced kid with a mop of red hair stood behind the rental car counter wearing the lime-green uniform provided by the company. He killed time people-watching while waiting for the next customer to walk up. Then there they were; two Barbie Dolls headed his way. He stood up taller, smoothed some wrinkles in his shirt, and pretended to be busy as they got closer.

"Welcome ladies. Whatever you need, I'm your man." Pimple face sported a silly grin and obviously thought he was God's gift to women The detectives had seen this dozens of times before and got a kick out of playing around with jerks like this.

Detective Beth Ferguson leaned on the counter giving him a peek down her blouse. When she produced her badge pimple face froze. His grin disappeared as his gaze moved from her cleavage to her badge, back to her cleavage again, then to Beth's face, "Uh, what can I do for you, officer?"

Beth and Morgan were bi-sexual and they knew exactly what they looked like. Their model-like looks came in handy when used to their advantage, especially against twerps like this guy. Morgan saw what was going on and turned slightly sideways. She pulled her shoulders back, stuck out her chest and winked at him. The poor guy almost jumped out of his skin as he ogled her impressive bust. There were two of them messing with his hormones now.

"Is Ms. Connie Gleason here?" Beth cooed seductively as their feminine charms disarmed and confused the poor guy. He'd never seen police officers that looked and acted like these women. "Uh, yes. She's in the back," he stammered.

Beth batted her eye latches, "Could you please ask her to come out and talk to us?"

Without answering he took a last quick, parting glance at Beth's chest, turned on his heel, and disappeared through a doorway, never to be seen by these detectives again. A few moments later Connie Gleason appeared wearing a similar green uniform, but hers was tighter around her chest and she wore a short skirt instead of long pants. "I'm Connie Gleason." Her name tag confirmed it, but the detectives would need to see more positive identification.

The fun was over; it was all business now. The detectives showed their badges, "I'm Detective Beth Ferguson and this is Detective Morgan Sparks from the Tampa Police Department. Detective Lucas Brasch asked us to talk to you. Is there some place we could speak in private? And could you show us a driver's license, please?"

Connie leaned forward and looked in both directions before pointing to her left at a deserted area with a few benches at the end of the long underground baggage claim area. "Down there, but I need to get someone to cover for me first." She stuck her head through the doorway and informed whoever was back there that she was taking a break. To the detectives, "I'll meet you over there," pointing in the other direction. The detectives leaned back and saw the unmarked door, probably the only way in and out of their little world. Beth and Morgan went over and waited a few moments for Connie to emerge holding her wallet and a handful of papers. She opened the wallet clumsily and showed her ID. Beth took it, read the name, glanced at the photo, and was satisfied.. Connie shoved the wallet into a pocket after Beth handed it back.

The three ladies walked the few hundred paces in silence as they made their way through several small groups of travelers milling around. Police badges had been returned to purses. No need to unnecessarily heighten the jittery nerves of already uneasy travelers in a crowded airport.

After secluding themselves in the seating area, Beth and Morgan made a quick visual sweep of the surrounding area before saying anything. Connie watched with interest. Once Beth returned her gaze to Connie, Morgan took a few steps back and basically stood guard as the other two talked in private. Beth opened the interview with, "Thank you for talking to us, Ms. Gleason."

Connie smiled, "My pleasure, officer."

Beth produced the artist sketch and held it out for Connie to inspect, "Is this the man you recognized?"

Without hesitation, "Yes, that's him."

"How do you recognize this person?"

"Like I said over the telephone to Detective Brasch, he's rented vehicles from us several times. I personally rented to him twice and I was at the counter at least one other time when someone else helped him."

"I suspect you get many repeat customers renting cars and vans. What made this man stand out, Ms. Gleason?"

"He was always so nice. Even when we messed up his order, he just laughed it off and waited for us to fix the problem. Few other customers remain calm and patient when we screw up." Beth immediately wondered if this was their guy, but pressed on.

"All right," Beth returned the picture to the file and scribbled a few notes on a pad. "Did you find the paperwork for his car rentals?"

Connie handed the papers to Beth, "These are the originals so you can't keep them. My boss may get upset with me if he finds out I even let you look at them without some kind of court order or something. I don't want to lose my job."

"That's okay, Ms. Gleason. We'll just copy down the information we need. The District Attorney may subpoena them later, but don't worry about that right now." Beth took the five Rental Agreements and handed three to Morgan. Both officers began writing down important information: name, dates, vehicle info, mileage, and anything else of interest.

When they both finished Beth collected the Rental Agreements and handed them back to Connie, "Thank you again. Is your boss here? Will you get in trouble for talking to us?"

"Oh, no. He's off today. Actually, I'm in charge for this shift," she said with a grin.

"If you think of anything else, please call me." Beth handed Connie a business card, which she slipped into the pocket with her wallet.

◻ ◻ ◻

It was after 8:00 p.m. when Beth and Morgan got back to their police station. They wanted to write their formal police report while their thoughts were fresh in their minds. More work would be needed to prove this apparently nice guy was a murderer, and there was no illusion that this mystery man would be found any time soon. All they could do was report their findings to Luke if he was still in his office. He wasn't, so they left a cryptic message, "Detective Morgan Sparks here. Detective Ferguson is completing our report and will fax it over when we're done. We met with Connie Gleason who confirmed the identity of our mystery man. She claimed he was a nice guy and showed us five rental agreements spanning several years. Details to follow in our report. We can subpoena the agreements if needed. We plan to follow up Monday morning. Oh, by the way, the guy's name on all five agreements is Mitchell Harrington, from Charlotte, NC. We'll check back in on Monday afternoon when we know more. Have a nice weekend."

Saturday, Second Week in October
Luke's condo
St. Petersburg, FL
8:27 p.m.

Luke had spent a lazy day trying to wind down by doing nothing of importance—some laundry, eating simple meals thrown together from leftovers, watching a college football game on TV, and taking a much needed nap. Other than periodically checking on the Stanley Robbins' BOLO and APB he didn't think much about the case. No sightings anywhere in the Kemp neighborhood. A few other fleeting thoughts were all he allowed himself.

He didn't check his messages at the police station, so he was unaware of the developments at the Tampa Airport the night before. He didn't bother to check his office voicemail because he didn't expect any messages. All the detectives on the new team had his cell phone number. If they needed to contact him, they could. The expanded team was in place, the composite had been sent to the media, so all he needed to do was wait patiently until new leads developed.

Lonely was not a feeling Luke liked. He fought his impulse to call Lacey since mid-afternoon and finally relented. Luke clicked off the TV and tossed the remote onto the coffee table before picking up the phone. Lacey checked the Caller ID out of habit before picking up. Obviously happy to hear his voice, "Hi, Luke. I was just thinking about you."

"Good evening, Lacey. I've been thinking about you, too."

They chatted for about fifteen minutes, purposely avoiding the case. In mid sentence Lacey's call waiting tone announced a new call, "Sorry, Luke, but someone at the police station is calling me. Hold on a minute." Luke's phone went silent.

Lacey switched to the incoming call, "Good evening Dr. Hirsch. This is the Desk Sergeant at the St. Pete police station. A Mrs. Nancy Kemp called about ten minutes ago asking for you."

"Did she say what she wanted?"

"No, ma'am. She only wanted to talk to you. I told Mrs. Kemp that you weren't in and that I would forward the message. She said it was important so I called you right away. Sorry it took so long to find your phone number."

"Probably because I'm new to the police department. Don't fret about it, Sergeant. Anyway, did Mrs. Kemp leave a number?"

"Yes," He read it from his notes and Lacey copied it down.

"Thank you, Sergeant." They bid each other a good evening and Lacey switched back to Luke.

"Luke, I just got the strangest call." Lacey went on to replay the conversation, "I'm not a cop. She should have asked for you."

"Give her a call and find out why she wants to talk to you rather than me," was Luke's immediate sensible response, "Maybe she's had a change of heart and is willing to cooperate with us. Maybe she just feels more comfortable talking to another woman."

"It's kind of late, Luke. I don't want to upset her more than she already is."

"Call her and set up a meeting face to face. Call me back if you want me there with you."

"I don't know, Luke. Police-style interrogations aren't what I'm used to in my practice."

"Lacey, just call her back and set up a meeting as soon as you can meet with her. You'll be fine on your own if you go by yourself," Luke's voice was stern. He was her boss during this investigation. Lacey didn't respond so Luke continued, "Lacey, unless you think meeting Mrs. Kemp is dangerous, you should do this alone. That's what she wants. She'll open up to you. Get her to trust you. We can't expect anything more right now. Just suck it up. You're a pro."

More hesitation. Finally, Lacey pumped up her courage, "Fine. I'll call her right now and let you know when and where we'll meet."

"Good girl," Luke didn't intend his comment to be sexist or demeaning, and Lacey didn't take it as such.

Lacey was now a little more confident, "I'll call you back in a few minutes when I have the details."

Luke finally realized he hadn't checked his voicemail all day. Maybe one of the team had called him to leave a message. He punched in the numbers and was surprised that he had any on a weekend. He had only one; tt was from Detective Morgan Sparks. Luke listened intently and then pushed the number to replay it again. He wanted to be sure he heard the guy's name correctly because it sounded so familiar. He jotted down the name and saved the voicemail message so he could replay it again if he wanted to. Luke's initial instinct was to rush to the police station to check his files, but he quickly realized that tomorrow, or even Monday, would be soon enough because he couldn't do anything about it now even if he was right. Luke clicked the TV back on as he waited for Lacey's return call.

❐ ❐ ❐

Lacey took a deep breath. She didn't relish making the call, but wasn't sure why. She'd made hundreds of calls to women who wanted to talk to her before. One more deep breath and she steeled herself while waiting for Mrs. Kemp to answer. Five rings later Nancy Kemp answered in a very soft voice, "Hello."

Lacey introduced herself without her title. Luke didn't identify her as a psychologist, so Lacey suspected Mrs. Kemp thought she was a female police officer, "I got your message, Mrs. Kemp. Are you all right?"

Nancy whined, "I don't know. I just had to talk to someone. You were so nice to me the other day."

"I'd be happy to talk to you, Mrs. Kemp. Now, or any time."

Softly again, "Thank you, Officer."

Lacey was uncomfortable with the charade; withholding the truth was the same as lying in her eyes. There was, however, a simple way around this tricky problem. "Please call me Lacey."

"I'd like that."

"May I call you Nancy?

"Yes, please do."

Lacey waited a few moments for Nancy to continue. She didn't, "Nancy, what did you want to talk to me about?"

"I don't know," Nancy repeated. "This was a stupid idea. My life is falling apart all around me," Nancy was almost incoherent as her voice trailed off.

"Nancy. Nancy, listen to me. Talking to me is not stupid. Talking about whatever troubles you will make you feel better. Please talk to me, Nancy."

"I don't know," Nancy repeated a third time. The whine was back.

Lacey was quick to recognize familiar symptoms, "Nancy, when was the last time you got some sleep?"

"I don't know," a fourth time. "I can't remember." Nancy was scarily repeating herself.

"You need to get some sleep, Nancy. Things might look better when your mind is rested."

"I've tried to sleep, but I wake up in an hour or so, and then can't go back to sleep."

Lacey resisted telling her to take a sleeping pill because she couldn't be sure Nancy wouldn't just swallow a handful in her mixed up state. Lacey didn't think Nancy was suicidal, but why take any chances? "Do you have any milk in the house?"

"I think so."

"Warm some up in a pan or the microwave and drink a big glassful. That will help you get to sleep."

"I'll try that, Lacey. Thanks."

"We can talk tomorrow morning after you've rested. Will your husband be at home around 11:00, Nancy?"

"I don't know," Nancy was really whining again.

"Why not, Nancy? Why don't you know?"

"That's what I wanted to talk to you about. He's gone, Lacey. I don't know where he is, or if I'll ever see him again." The whining changed to whimpering punctuated by gasping.

This revelation startled Lacey, but she settled down in a few moments, "You drink some warm milk, get some sleep, and I'll drop by tomorrow morning around 11:00. Would that be okay, Nancy?"

"Yes, I'd like that. And, 11:00 is fine. I'll try the milk right now, Lacey. See you tomorrow." No goodbye and the line went dead.

Lacey immediately called Luke back. They exchanged greetings again before Lacey relayed a summary of her conversation with Nancy Kemp. When Lacey tossed the bombshell about Stanley being missing, Luke could only mutter, "Shit." He knew that was the reason the BOLO and APB hadn't turned up anything. But, was he really gone or just hiding out? They talked some more about Lacey's impressions of the conversation, and the details of the upcoming meeting tomorrow, as well as what Luke hoped to find out. Luke agreed that meeting Nancy tomorrow made more sense than trying to get anything out of her right now. Lacey told Luke that she felt strongly that Nancy would open up only to her, and if Luke or anyone else, went with her Nancy might not say anything of value. "She might even refuse to say anything at all," Lacey emphasized.

Luke readily accepted Lacey's opinion, but was very concerned about her being alone in the Kemp home. What if Stanley came back? What if he was still there and Nancy was putting on an act? What if all this was a trap to get an unsuspecting woman alone? Finally Luke decided on a course of action, "I'll go with you and stay outside in the car unless you get into trouble. I'll give you a remote signaling device you can use to alert me if you feel threatened in any way."

"I don't share your concerns for my safety, but I'm not trained to be a law enforcement officer suspicious of everyone and everything."

"Damn straight," chided Luke.

Lacey laughed before continuing, "I do appreciate your concern for my safety, Luke. Thank you." They made plans to meet at 9:00 tomorrow morning after Lacey offered to make breakfast. They would spend some leisure time together, then Luke would show Lacey how to use the signaling device and drive to the Kemp home together.

Chapter Twenty-Five

Sunday, Third Week in October
Lacey's Condo
Treasure Island, FL
8:54 a.m.

Luke was a few minutes early. Lacey didn't mind as she opened the door with a smile and a warm embrace. She wrapped one arm around his waist as they strolled casually towards the dining room area. Lacey joked as she glanced back at her front door, "That's not the door I hoped you'd be coming through, Luke." He stopped and turned to look at her. Lacey cocked her head toward her master bedroom door and smiled again. Luke laughed and resumed walking towards the table, "Are we ready for that, Lacey?"

"I think so. Don't you?"

"Let's not complicate our lives."

Lacey pulled away in a huff, "Letting nature take its course is not a complication."

"You know what I mean, Lacey." The chill returned.

"The case. It's always the case."

"For now, yes, it is about the case."

Lacey shook her head slowly, almost sadly, "Fine, Luke. Let's concentrate only on the case—after we eat breakfast. Will you please help me in the kitchen?"

Luke exhaled loudly. He knew he was upsetting Lacey and hated being put in that predicament, "Certainly. What can I do to help?" He hung his jacket on the back of a chair and followed Lacey into the kitchen fully prepared to be ordered around, but Lacey was easy on him. Nothing difficult, just putting pancakes on a platter and filling juice glasses and coffee mugs. The table was already set for two.

Luke and Lacey ate in an uneasy silence. They only spoke if the conversation was about the breakfast. Both were uncomfortable. Whatever romantic relationship they might have thought they had seemed to be disintegrating before their eyes. Both knew what was happening. Both hated it. Luke couldn't help himself. Lacey wasn't sure if she could do anything about it, but she had to at least try.

Being good friends—maybe something more—kept forcing itself into the crevices of their brains. Lacey put her fork down and covered Luke's hand with hers. Luke stopped eating and gazed into her eyes. With a weak smile and in a soft voice Lacey plunged in, "Luke, I know we need to be going in a few minutes, but we do have to talk." Lacey waited for a response that didn't come, "About us," she finally said squeezing his hand gently.

Luke slumped down into his chair, but wouldn't let go of her hand, "I know."

"Can we talk now, Luke?"

"I'm really sorry, Lacey. We can **talk about us** all you want, but I can't **think about us** right now."

Lacey sat back and let go of his hand. Luke looked away. He was trying to hide the sorrow he felt about hurting her.

"Luke, look at me, please." Luke turned around.

Lacey pushed on, "Luke, you know that I care a great deal about you, and I think you feel the same way about me." Luke nodded his agreement slowly. Lacey continued gently, "I'm speaking as a woman, not as a psychologist. Do you believe me?"

"Yes," Luke smiled for the first time in an hour. He rarely thought about her being a psychologist. To him, she was all woman. Also a trusted colleague, but definitely a woman.

For the next ten minutes they cleared the air. Lacey did most of the talking, and spoke about how married couples successfully balance family pressures with professional stresses, and that she was confident that she and Luke could do the same even if they weren't married. Luke said little and kept his feelings bottled up. Lacey knew Luke and his background well enough to recognize his inner fears; previous failed relationships he refused to talk about shaped his unrealistic impressions about their relationship. Lacey correctly suspected Luke was afraid of a serious relationship with her because he mistakenly feared he would lose her, just as he had lost others. It was too painful for Luke to get close to another woman. Lacey just had to prove to Luke that she wasn't going anywhere. She wisely didn't lapse into her expert psychologist persona and steered the conversation back to something Luke was more comfortable with. Their relationship would have to wait.

Standing up, "We can finish this later when we have more time. Help me clean up before we leave."

Luke was somewhat relieved, grabbed a few plates, and followed Lacey into the kitchen. Lacey let Luke deposit his armload into the sink first, and then did the same with hers. As she turned around to return for more, Luke took her in his arms, squeezed their bodies close, and lifted her six inches off the floor as he kissed her more passionately than she could remember. Lacey wrapped her arms around Luke's neck as her toes dangled above the shiny white tile floor. She returned the passion until her body went limp and Luke slowly lowered her to the floor. Lacey thought wistfully to herself, "Why didn't he do that an hour ago?" To Luke she said in a dreamy voice, "We don't have time now. Mrs. Kemp is waiting for me." Luke loosened his hold on her, kissed her again, and laughed, "Damn. You're right. Let's not keep the lady waiting." Another involuntary mood swing.

❑ ❑ ❑

They were fifteen minutes early when Luke parked two blocks away from the Kemp home. Lacey was turning the keychain gadget over in her hand as she examined it carefully. The square black plastic device looked like a car door remote with three buttons arranged in a triangular configuration. Luke explained that all three buttons did the same thing—send a signal to the receiver Luke was now holding up for Lacey to inspect, "Press any button," Luke told her. Lacey tentatively poked at a button. The receiver beeped repeatedly and a red light blinked until Luke pressed a button on the machine to stop the light and sound show. "If you get into trouble or need me just press any button. This thing has a range of over 500 yards. I'll drop you off and park a few houses down. I won't be more than 50 yards away and can get to you in seconds."

"I don't think I'll need this. Nancy Kemp is just a sad lady who's been deceived by her pedophile husband. She's not dangerous," said Lacey as she looked hesitantly at the keychain object again.

"Humor me. Put it in your purse and promise to use it if you get scared or feel threatened."

"Why can't you just wire me up for sound like they do in all those TV cop shows?"

"Because those TV cop shows don't bother to tell us that they probably need a court order for such things. Just use the remote signaling device, Lacey," Luke was quite stern and Lacey relented.

"Fine. If you insist," said Lacey as she opened her purse and dropped it in.

Luke tugged his seatbelt across his chest and started the engine. Lacey refastened her own seatbelt before Luke drove towards the Kemp home, "Okay, Lacey. Here we go. Are you ready?" It was five minutes before 11 a.m.

Lacey made a face, but said, "Ready as I'll ever be," and stepped out onto the sidewalk in front of the Kemp home. No other human was in sight. A few cars were in the driveways of several nearby homes. No sign of Stanley's Honda. Nothing else moved, but an unseen dog barked in the distance.

Scary thoughts swirled in Lacey's head. Stanley isn't here, I hope. So this was just another interview. She'd been alone with hundreds of other women. No reason to be scared, right? After a long moment Lacey took a deep calming breath, threw her shoulders back, and marched up the sidewalk to ring the doorbell. No answer. Lacey pressed the doorbell again and stepped back. Luke watched and waited a few houses away. Just as Lacey started to turn and walk away, the door opened. Lacey turned around and Luke could tell the women were talking to each other. Mrs. Kemp stepped back and Lacey followed her inside. The door closed behind them. Luke glanced down at the receiver sitting on the passenger seat. The tiny green light confirmed it was working. Its silence and unlit red light indicated that no distress signal was being sent. Luke settled into his seat, glanced at the Kemp house again, and waited.

Nancy Kemp showed the obvious signs of a seriously conflicted woman. She was wearing a floor-length pink bathrobe wrapped and cinched so tightly Lacey couldn't tell if she had anything on underneath. Her hair was a tangled mess. No makeup. Lacey noticed the tremors when they shook hands. Weak grip. Palms clammy. Lacey was her familiar well dressed, perfectly groomed self. No exotic clothes, but the contrast was obvious, except to Nancy, who had trouble noticing anything around her.

Lacey knew she had to control the mood and tone of the conversation, "Let's sit down, Nancy." Nancy looked around as if her own living room was an alien dungeon and she didn't recognize anything. "Over there," Lacey finally said motioning towards the couch.

Lacey tried to be a calming influence, "How are you feeling, Nancy?"

The whining returned, "I don't know."

"Did you get any sleep last night?"

"A little, I guess."

This was going to be tough and Lacey knew it. She changed her approach, "Nancy, where is your husband?"

"Gone," Nancy looked down as she wrung her hands nervously in her lap. Her shoulders were pulled up to her neck as she scrunched her elbows to her sides like a kid afraid of monsters in the dark. Nancy was clearly frightened about something.

"Nancy, I need to take some notes. Do you mind if I record our conversation?" Lacey held up the palm-sized tape recorder she used in her practice.

"No, go ahead."

Lacey had already clicked on the recorder and set it down between them.

"Tell me about your husband, Nancy. Where did you meet him?"

They talked for about a half hour as Nancy spoke about her life with the man she only knew as Trevor Kemp. Nancy was now a little calmer and more open than Lacey had expected her to be. Eventually, Lacey got around to the case, "What do you know about Trevor's past before you met him?"

"Not much. He doesn't talk about his past."

"What about family? Did you ever meet any of them?

"Trevor spoke about his mom. She was ill when we got married and couldn't make it."

"Did you meet her later?"

"Trevor's been to see her. I never have," Nancy hesitated then added, "I'm okay with that."

Obvious signs of serious mother-son issues. No need to pursue that now. Lacey took a deep breath before attacking the next topic, "We think your husband is really Stanley Robbins and changed his name to Trevor Kemp a few years ago. Do you know why we're looking for Stanley Robbins?"

"No, you wouldn't tell me," Nancy looked away and Lacey waited for her to look back. When Nancy did turn around her expression had changed. Nancy was no longer a whimpering mess, "I think it's something very bad. Why else would the police be so involved?"

"It is something bad, Nancy."

"Does it involve other women?"

"In a way," Lacey had to be careful with her answers.

"I knew it," exclaimed Nancy with conviction.

"Did you suspect that Trevor did something wrong?"

"I didn't at first, but now I think I do."

Nancy and Lacey talked for another fifteen minutes about the little clues Nancy tried to ignore, but no longer could. Then Lacey took a leap of faith, "Nancy, will you tell all of this to my boss, Detective Brasch?"

Nancy glanced around, "I guess so. Where is he?"

"I'll summon him. He can be here in a few minutes."

❏ ❏ ❏

Luke's cell phone buzzed. He glanced at the emergency receiver, quickly determining that he could divert his attention. He flipped the phone open. It was Lacey, "Are you okay? Why didn't you signal me?"

"Everything's fine, Luke. I'm not in any danger," Lacey was laughing at Luke's insinuation that she needed help.

"What's going on in there, Lacey?" Luke growled angrily.

"Nancy and I are having a nice girl-to-girl chat. I've got it all on tape."

"What? You taped your interview with her?"

"Sure. I do that with all my patients. She okayed it. Got that on tape too," Lacey was giddy and proud of herself.

"Fine. We'll discuss that later. What did she tell you?"

"Lots of things," Lacey was playing with him. He didn't bite, "She wants to talk to you."

"She does?"

"Yes, but she doesn't know you're right outside the door. Nancy went to the bathroom when I called you. She can't hear me. Take your time before you knock on the door. I kind of told her you'd be here in a few minutes, not seconds. I don't want her to think we were tricking her."

Luke thought for a few seconds, "Okay, Lacey. I'll wait about five minutes. You sure you're all right?"

"I'm fine, Luke. She's confiding in me. Nancy and I are becoming friends. I think she's starting to trust me, which means she will probably trust you too."

❏ ❏ ❏

Nancy was no longer a whimpering human bag of nerves. She sat upright and listened intently as Lacey recapped their earlier conversation for Luke's benefit. Nancy had brushed her hair, and it looked like she had washed her face while in the bathroom. As Lacey spoke she would frequently ask Nancy, "Did I get that right, Nancy?" Each time, Nancy either answered in the affirmative or just nodded her agreement. Nancy neither added nor corrected anything. When Lacey sat back and said, "That's as far as we got, Luke." Nancy turned her attention to Luke and waited.

Luke had needed information and was grateful for all Lacey had accomplished so far. But now he had to find Stanley alias Trevor. "Mrs. Kemp," Luke didn't want or need to be Nancy's newest best friend, "Will you help us find your husband? We have to talk to him about our ongoing investigation."

Nancy steeled herself, "Yes. He lied to me. Our entire marriage is now just a great big joke. I don't even know who he is anymore."

Lacey reached out and patted Nancy's shoulder, "You're doing the right thing here, Nancy. How do we find him?"

Nancy unexpectedly broke down again and covered her face with her hands. Lacey motioned for Luke to slow down. Luke nodded and pointed to Lacey who correctly understood that she should take back control of the interview. Lacey gently pulled Nancy's hands down and softly asked again, "Nancy, we need your help. How can we find your husband?"

Through a torrent of tears, "Is Trevor really my husband? Can I be married to a person that doesn't exist?"

Lacey shook her head sadly, but continued to hold Nancy's hands, "Nancy, don't worry about that now. We can work on that problem after we find Trevor."

Nancy stole a glance at Luke before returning her attention to Lacey. After a deep sigh, "I don't know where he is. If I did I'd take you there myself." Hysteria was turning into anger and resentment at being deceived. Lacey's gentle approach and reasoned logic was working. There would be no more tears from Nancy. In a little more than an hour Lacey had transformed Nancy's view of her life as Mrs. Trevor Kemp. Nancy was no longer afraid of what might happen to her husband and their lives. Now she was angry that Trevor had made such a fool of her. Of them. Of their marriage. Nancy still didn't know exactly what Trevor had done yet, but she guessed it involved young girls. Nancy was willing, and more than ready to feed Trevor to the wolves.

Luke thought that this miraculous turnaround in Nancy Kemp's attitude towards her husband was due to Lacey's skills. They weren't entirely. Nancy Kemp had been noticing little things here and there for some time over the past year or so. At first Nancy tried to ignore the disturbing feelings because she didn't understand or trust her own instincts. Lacey did help her work through all the concerns over Trevor and his strange behavior, but Nancy would need more therapy sessions to help get her life back to something approaching normal.

"Do you ever call him when he's out?" Lacey was trying to think like Luke.

"No, he always calls me."

"How does he call you, Nancy?"

"A cell phone, I guess."

"Do you know the cell phone number, Nancy?"

"No, I'm sorry, I don't."

That was all Luke needed to hear. He stood up, "I'll be back in a few minutes," as he whipped out his own cell phone and headed outside to order a dump of the Kemp home phone records. Two minutes later he was back inside. Nancy was smiling for the first time. Lacey was standing with a big grin on her face.

"What's all this?" asked Luke.

Lacey answered nonchalantly, "Nothing. I just offered to take Nancy out for lunch tomorrow and she accepted. Want to join us?"

Chapter Twenty-Six

Monday, Third Week in October
Police Station
St. Petersburg, FL
9:12 a.m.

Luke was studying the phone records he'd ordered the day before. One phone number was prominent, and was clearly the most frequent number calling into the Kemp house by a factor of ten over a 60-day period. Most days it was the only number. That was probably Stanley's cell phone number. Lakesha was looking over his shoulder. Luke had filled her in about the developments over the weekend. Pointing at the repeated phone number she said, "We can't just call him. He'll rabbit if he thinks we're on to him, if he hasn't already."

"You're right, Johnson. Any other ideas?"

"Can we find him through his cell phone? Maybe he has a GPS tracker or something."

"We can try that. Check with his provider and see what they can do."

"I'm on it, Brasch," as Lakesha pulled out her notebook and jotted down the information she needed.

Tracking Stanley down would not be easy, especially considering the bad luck they've had so far. There was a better option. Luke decided that the quickest way to find Stanley was to lure him into going someplace where the police could surprise and arrest him when he showed up. A sting of sorts. Above all, Stanley would need money. Perhaps he could be lured to one of his jobs.

Then Luke remembered Peter Holmes, one of the homeowners that Stanley was doing work for. Luke flipped through his file for the phone number and address. It shouldn't be too hard to get Mr. Holmes to ask Stanley to come by when Luke and several other police officers would be waiting. But, first he had to get Peter Holmes to cooperate.

◻ ◻ ◻

Luke didn't want to spook Peter Holmes so he didn't call ahead. To Luke's surprise Peter was home and answered the knock more pleasantly than Luke expected. Peter even invited Luke in. He didn't want another public confrontation. Luke explained enough of the case to satisfy Peter and gain his support.

About an hour later Peter had somehow contacted Stanley Robbins, the man Peter knew as Trevor Kemp, and asked Stanley to come by later that day at around 4:30 p.m. to discuss the job Stanley was doing for Peter. Stanley was at first reluctant claiming he had other commitments. The clincher was Peter promising to pay Stanley the $1,500 he had been withholding on previous work until Stanley made more progress on this latest one. Of course, Luke made that suggestion to Peter. All that cooperation by Peter resulted from Luke promising to forget the incident outside Peter's house last week; a small price for Luke to pay if he could arrest Stanley.

Luke thanked Peter and told him that he should leave. The police didn't want or need him there. For his own safety Peter should make himself scarce for the rest of the afternoon. Peter didn't care enough to ask why and simply nodded. Actually he didn't really want to know anything about what seemed to him to be a very nasty police problem fraught with danger for any civilian caught in the middle.

◻ ◻ ◻

Lacey had made good on her promise to take Nancy to lunch. Luke had graciously declined to join them. Nancy was waiting as Lacey entered the cute, but small café in the heart of the downtown area. They weren't best buddies, but both ladies were pleasant to each other and enjoyed a tasty salad and small talk over the course of the hour. Then Nancy turned serious.

"When you arrest my husband," Nancy laughed at her own joke before changing her expression to serious again, "I want to be there to look him in the eye and tell that lying bastard what I think of him."

Lacey sensed that Nancy's anger was becoming almost hostile, and didn't know what to do or how to answer her because she had no idea how police procedures worked. In an attempt to calm Nancy down, Lacey simply said, "I'll have to check with Detective Brasch and get back to you on that." A smart response to a difficult request, and it soothed Nancy's hostility.

The ladies finished their ice teas and Lacey paid the bill. Both left the café and headed for their own cars. Lacey called Luke before she started the engine.

Luke listened carefully and quickly gave Lacey instructions, "Tell Nancy we can't let her be alone with Stanley. Maybe she can talk to him. I'll see what I can do."

"Can we let Nancy observe the interrogation? Maybe she can help us decide if Stanley is telling us the truth." Lacey was sure Nancy wanted to help put her husband away, and told Luke exactly that.

"Sure, we can have Nancy observe through a one way mirror. You can watch with her if you want."

"I think I will. Any idea when you might arrest Stanley?"

"I'm hoping for later this afternoon. When we have Stanley in custody, I'll call you and you can work it out with Mrs. Kemp."

"That works for me. I'll be waiting for your call, Luke." Both said their goodbyes. But, before they hung up Lacey told Luke to be careful and not get himself shot again. Luke chuckled at the phone as he replaced the receiver.

Luke went back to arranging for other officers to help with the arrest. The preparation and planning process could take a few hours. Luke figured Lakesha and four others in two more cars should do the trick.

Morgan called as Luke was updating his ongoing police report, "Hello Detective Brasch. Morgan Sparks here. How's the case going on your end?"

Luke recapped his activities and plans they were making to arrest Stanley later that day. "Good luck, and be safe," she cautioned in a somber tone. Morgan went on to explain that her partner, Beth Ferguson, was running down some disturbing leads uncovered by their investigation of the guy with Stanley, and that they had identified him as Mitchell Harrington. His contact information from the car rental company showed him being from North Carolina. Luke interrupted, "Hold on a second, Detective. I got your message and have been checking my notes. Give me a second to dig them out. That name showed up here, too." Morgan waited patiently as Luke shuffled papers.

"Here it is," said Luke as he picked up the phone and continued, "Our latest victim, Megan, said the name of the guy with Stanley was Mike or Mitch."

Morgan replied, "Could be the same guy. But, remember that the car rental gal said he was so nice. Maybe the Mitchell Harrington from the car rental company isn't our guy."

"That's possible, but he's the only lead we have. Have you tracked this Mitchell guy down?"

"Well, yes and no." Morgan explained in more detail about the positive identification of the sketch by Connie Gleason and continued with the bad news, "The North Carolina Department of Motor Vehicles has no Mitchell Harrington at the address I gave them. They also had no driver's license for anyone with the driver's license number Harrington used to rent his SUV's. Probably a fake."

"Yep, you're right. And not good news. We know the Mitchell Harrington we're looking for is not such a nice guy. We need to find out if your Mitchell Harrington is the one we're looking for. What are you two doing now?"

"We're confident of the photo ID and probably the name. We're not so confident about where he actually lives or, as you said, if he's our guy. With that said, we're trying other things, including reopening the cases from Hillsborough and giving them another good scrub."

Luke didn't press her further. He knew Morgan and Beth were pros. They know what they're doing and that more investigation would take time. "Okay. Keep me in the loop, and I'll update all of you about what happens this afternoon when we try to take Stanley Robbins into custody."

◻ ◻ ◻

They wanted to minimize drawing attention to themselves, so the three unmarked police vehicles intentionally arrived individually from different directions over a ten minute period and took up their pre-assigned positions. Only Luke's SUV with Lakesha in the passenger seat was on the street near Peter Holmes' house. The other two vehicles, each with two plain clothed St. Petersburg police officers inside, were strategically parked on nearby side streets. Those two vehicles had a clear view of any cars heading toward the Holmes property from either direction. They were the early warning perimeter. Stanley was expected in about twenty minutes, so the tactical team checked their radios and weapons one last time. None of the seasoned officers were particularly anxious about what was about to unfold, but nerves are understandably tense before a potentially dangerous operation such as this.

Every five minutes each early warning vehicle checked in with Luke, "Nothing yet." Conversation and communication was held to a minimum as they watched and waited.

At 4:23 p.m. Luke's radio squawked, "White compact car headed your way from the north. Can't see the driver." Luke was parked facing the South, so Lakesha turned around to check it out

"Got it, Brasch." Lakesha watched the car drive slowly toward them before turning into a driveway across the street a few houses down from Peter's. "False alarm. Just a neighbor," declared Lakesha as she turned around. Luke pressed the talk button, "Not our guy. Stay alert, folks." Everyone returned to their assignments.

At 4:48 p.m. Luke was getting impatient, and began wondering if Stanley would ever show. Finally, "Look alive everyone. White Honda, male driver, coming from the south."

Luke started his engine and knew the other two vehicles were ready to roll as well. Luke and Lakesha watched the Honda approach Peter's house, seemingly without a care in the world. Stanley must not have talked to his wife. More likely, Peter must have been very convincing to make Stanley think this was just another routine business call. The Honda turned into Peter's driveway and stopped halfway up. Lakesha shouted into the radio, "Let's go. Let's go," as Luke raced to block the driveway so Stanley couldn't back out. The other two police vehicles made a mad dash to the house with lights flashing and sirens wailing. Luke and Lakesha jumped out with guns drawn as the other two vehicles screeched to a stop. Four more officers with guns pointed at Stanley approached the Honda cautiously. Luke shouted, "Hands where I can see them, Stanley. Right now. Get 'em up." Startled, Stanley immediately complied and swung his head back and forth as his fingers scraped the roof of his Honda. Big guns were pointed at him from all directions. Stanley never had a problem with the police before, and was now scared out of his mind.

To everyone's relief Stanley was taken into custody without further incident. He was patted down, handcuffed, read his Miranda rights, and placed in the backseat of the third police vehicle. That was the one that had the safety protections designed for transporting violent criminals. All three vehicles caravanned towards the St. Petersburg Police Station. Luke was in the lead followed by the vehicle transporting Stanley. The last vehicle brought up the rear a few car-lengths behind. No lights or sirens, but they traveled at a brisk pace. Lakesha called the station to make arrangements for Stanley's arrival. Luke called Lacey with the news that the three-car caravan was less than ten minutes out, but it would probably be an hour or more before the interrogation would start.

Several burly uniformed police officers guided Stanley through the booking process. Stanley was frisked again. His Miranda rights were read to him again. He again reaffirmed his understanding of those rights, and refused the need for an attorney. Stanley maintained he hadn't done anything wrong. He was fingerprinted and standard DNA cheek swab samples taken. He was photographed behind his booking number, and all those details were laboriously logged into the respective databases.

While they waited for the booking process to proceed at what seemed like a snail's pace, Luke tasked Lakesha to rerun Stanley's now identified fingerprints and DNA against the samples from the cases. Lakesha knew that the fingerprints would take only a few hours, but the DNA comparisons could take a week or more. They had no choice but to let the process run its course in its own sweet time.

By 7:00 p.m. Stanley had been booked and was placed in a sparse interrogation room wearing an orange jailhouse jumpsuit. He was handcuffed, sitting motionless at a steel table. Shackles were around his waist and ankles. He'd been waiting alone for over half an hour. His head was lowered into his hands on the table in front of him. He was a very confused, scared, and sad little man.

Luke and Lakesha had met with Lieutenant Thompson and the assistant prosecutor to go over what had happened already and plot strategy. They wanted to be damn sure that no case involving Stanley would be thrown out of court because of some bonehead technicality that could have easily been avoided. The next step was the interrogation.

Luke walked into the 12 by15 foot drab interrogation room scowling, and tossed the folder onto the table. Lakesha followed close behind and took up a position leaning on the wall behind Luke. Her expression was almost evil; she looked like she just wanted to cut his nuts off and stuff them down his throat. The daggers streaming from her blazing eyes scared Stanley even more and he refused to look up at her. Stanley was really freaked out now. Luke sat motionless for several long minutes just staring at Stanley. That was another police tactic to unnerve and throw the suspect even more off his game. When Luke thought Stanley was about ready to jump out of his skin, he started in a flat uncaring voice and reread the Miranda rights from a small plastic card.

"You have the right to remain silent. Anything you say, can and will be used against you in a court of law. You have the right to speak to an attorney, and to have an attorney present during any questioning.

If you cannot afford an attorney, one will be provided for you at government expense."

Luke looked up, "Stanley, do you understand the Miranda rights I just read to you?" Stanley bobbed his head up and down. "Tell me out loud if you understand them, Stanley." Stanley said he did in a weak, almost child-like voice. "Do you waive your right to have an attorney present when we question you?" Stanley repeated that he hadn't done anything wrong and didn't need a lawyer. All this was being videotaped. The audio portion was piped through a speaker on the other side of the one-way mirror.

"Let's get started then," as Luke leaned forward and glared at Stanley, who instinctively leaned backwards as he tried to escape as far away from Luke as possible. "Stanley, we know about the disgusting things you did to all those little girls. We know you need help, so make it easy on yourself and tell us all about it." Lakesha stood motionless, arms folded across her ample chest, not blinking, just staring at Stanley as she held up the wall with her shoulder. This was no **good cop, bad cop** act. To Stanley it was pure **bad cop, worse cop**.

Stanley protested loudly. An unexpected response. "I didn't kill those girls. You're making a big mistake." Stanley's limited mental abilities made him think that the murders were the only criminal acts. Stanley tried to stand up but the chains held him down. Neither Luke nor Lakesha moved a muscle as Stanley struggled with his restraints. Finally Stanley settled down again.

Luke sat back, "Okay, Stanley. Let's start at the beginning. We know all about your little charade. How you tricked everyone into thinking you were Trevor Kemp. How long did you think you could keep that dumb idea going?" A blank stare from Stanley. "Is your real name Stanley Robbins?" Stanley didn't answer but nodded *yes* very slowly.

For the record, Luke repeated, "So your real name is Stanley Robbins, not Trevor Kemp."

Stanley nodded again.

Luke pressed on as he opened the folder, "Fine, Stanley. Let's go over what we have against you. You can help us understand why young girls were molested, raped, and murdered by you. This is the first dead girl." Stanley remained mute as Luke pushed a picture of a dead teenage girl in front of him.

Luke proceeded to show a picture of each of the dead girls in chronological order. He made a point of drawing out the date of the attack, each girl's name if one was known, her age and ethnicity, where she was found, if there was a sexual assault or not, how she was killed, whether or not the police had good forensics, and on and on. Stanley looked wide eyed back and forth between Luke and the photo Luke was currently holding inches from Stanley's face. Stanley was clearly frightened. His unblinking moist eyes were wide as saucers. His head shook violently, "I didn't do that," he excitedly continued to protest as Luke waved each picture in front of him. Lakesha watched motionless with no expression.

It took an exhausting fifty-five minutes to confront Stanley with all the girls. When Luke was done he smacked his palm loudly on the table startling Stanley, "Okay, Stanley. If you didn't rape and murder these girls, who did?"

Lacey and Nancy were watching with Lieutenant Nick Thompson and an assistant prosecutor through the one-way mirror. Several other detectives and uniformed police officers wandered in and out just to see the show for a few minutes. Stanley was crying now as he awkwardly tried to wipe away the tears with a sleeve in handcuffs.

Nancy was getting madder by the minute. Her fists clinched and unclenched. Her face was distorted with the intense anger and outright hatred she was feeling for the man who deceived her for so many years. Hearing the gory details of each incident just increased the intensity of her inner rage. If she could have gotten her hands on Stanley, she would have strangled him herself in a slow, very agonizing, and painful death. Lacey reached out and put her arm around Nancy's shoulder. Nancy would make a great witness at trial.

The complications of the Marital Privilege, where one spouse cannot be forced to testify against the other, could probably be overcome in this case. If the marriage was valid, Stanley would own the privilege, since he's the one being accused, and could keep Nancy from saying anything they discussed in private. There are exceptions to that rule, and the circumstance of their marriage is not a private communication. But, no one would have to force Nancy to testify if allowed to. And, it was quite possible that the marriage wasn't even legal in the first place. With no valid marriage, there would be no privilege to deal with. This complication would work itself out in time.

Loo knew they were building a very convincing case. The prosecutor did too, as he and Loo shared a brief smile. Any additional forensics they would turn up in the next few days would be icing on the cake.

Nancy Kemp turned to the prosecutor and asked, "What do you need me to do?"

The prosecutor glanced at Nick Thompson before answering, "Will you give us permission to search your home?"

"Absolutely, whatever you want." The prosecutor pulled out a small notepad, scribbled a few words indicating that Nancy did indeed authorize a search, and asked her to date and sign it. Nancy signed her name in a neat cursive much larger and bolder than the prosecutor's handwriting. She was making a statement like John Hancock did on the Declaration of Independence over two centuries ago. The prosecutor smiled after seeing the prominent signature. He handed the paper to Nick who would turn it over to Luke as soon as possible.

At 8:25 p.m. the prosecutor told Loo to interrupt the questioning to give Stanley a break and a sandwich, "Let's not get this thrown out because we didn't let him go to the bathroom, or starved the guy." Loo walked around, opened the door, and motioned for Luke to come out. Loo related the orders from the prosecutor. Luke nodded and went back in to tell Stanley they were taking a break and getting him something to eat. Luke and Lakesha exited without another word and walked around to join the others watching through the mirror. Other officers attended to Stanley and his bodily needs. Nick Thompson handed Luke the note Nancy signed authorizing the search of the Kemp home. Luke thanked Loo and pulled Lakesha aside. She would head up the search team tomorrow.

A half hour later Luke and Lakesha had re-entered the interrogation room and resumed their original positions, "Feeling better, Stanley?" Luke inquired. Stanley replied that he was.

Luke started where they had left off, "Stanley, if you didn't rape and murder these poor girls," as he waved a handful of photos at Stanley, "you were there. I know you were, and so do you. You weren't alone were you?" Stanley broke down again crying almost uncontrollably. This time he made no attempt to wipe the tears away. Luke didn't let up and raised his voice for the first time, "Who was with you, Stanley?"

Stanley moaned and repeatedly banged his forehead on the metal table before Luke and Lakesha could stop him. Lakesha got to him first, grabbed his shoulders, and yanked him back into a sitting position. Once Stanley was stabilized in the chair and didn't need Lakesha to hold him there, the officers relaxed a little. The last thing they needed was a prisoner killing, or seriously hurting himself while in their custody. Luke said sternly, "Settle down Stanley. We're not done yet."

Stanley looked up at him. He was now a completely broken man. No fight left in him. Luke returned to his seat and Lakesha went back to her position against the wall. Luke picked up the picture of Mitchell Harrington and held it in front of Stanley's face, "Do you know this man?"

Almost inaudibly Stanley mouthed, "Yes."

"What's his name, Stanley?"

A little louder, "Mitch Harrington."

Luke and Lakesha exchanged a knowing glance. Then Luke turned to the mirror holding up the picture so everyone could see that Stanley identified Mitchell Harrington. Next Luke methodically got Stanley to tell them how he knew Mitchell, the connection to Stanley's mother, how Mitch forced Stanley to find young girls for him, and what happened when the girls didn't cooperate. Stanley told them how he snuck some of the girls out of the shelter, and how most of them willingly traded sexual favors for a burger and fries. Lacey cringed as she watched intently through the mirror.

The most disturbing revelation was yet to come. Stanley estimated that for every girl that didn't cooperate there were four or five that did. That meant there were an additional forty to fifty girls that Stanley and Mitchell had abused over the years. Lacey did these mental calculation in her head, gasped, and her hand flew to her mouth. Many of those girls would never be identified or come forward on their own, and most would need professional help to get their lives in order. Sadly, many wouldn't get any help.

Stanley told them how he selected a different county each time. Stanley also admitted he didn't understand, but somehow Mitch knew that cops in different counties didn't talk to each other. The big long bridges were just easy to use when they needed to dump a body on one side and a car on the other. Stanley didn't comprehend how having different police departments on opposite ends of the bridges was the key to Mitchell Harrington's plan.

Over the next twenty minutes Luke tried unsuccessfully to get an address for Mitchell Harrington. Stanley didn't know where Mitch lived, not even which state he lived in. Stanley claimed that Mitch always called him on his cell phone. They had no other mode of long distance communication.

Luke moved on to Megan, holding up a head-shot of her, "Tell me about Megan Fisher. What did you and Mitch do to her?"

Stanley said that Megan was drugged with date rape drugs that they were using more frequently. She and Stanley had fooled around for about a half hour, but before Mitch was to take his turn another car drove up and interrupted him. Mitch just shoved Megan out and she fell against the metal railing. They just left her there. Stanley didn't know what happened to Megan after they drove away.

Luke surmised that the teens, Randy and Randi, were probably in the car Mitchell saw. Luke now suspected that the cuts on Megan's body were the result of that trauma. He could decide later if they needed more forensics from the pier.

By 10:30 p.m. Luke was done. Stanley had remembered the names of two more previously unidentified girls, and Luke didn't think Stanley would provide any additional information and saw no reason to continue the interrogation. The prosecutor thanked Nancy for coming down and for her assistance in the upcoming search of her home. He told her they would be in touch, and Nancy left for home. Her head was spinning with horrible images of her husband and Mitchell Harrington doing disgusting things with so many young girls. Luke,

Lakesha, Loo, the prosecutor, and Lacey retreated to the conference room to go over what they learned from Stanley. They all agreed that the most important thing now was finding Mitchell Harrington.

The Hillsboro County detectives had one lead, but the team needed more, if they could find any. At 11:15 p.m. the prosecutor asked, "Do we have Stanley's cell phone?"

Luke opened a folder and flipped pages. "Stanley had it when we took him into custody."

The prosecutor continued, "Great. I'll start the paperwork to use the cell phone logs to track down Harrington's number. You guys can take it from there."

Everyone nodded their agreement. Loo rose and clapped his hands together, "That should do it for now. Good job everyone." Files and papers were collected, individual goodbyes given, and the small group dispersed.

Luke reached out and restrained Lacey by her arm until the room cleared. "Let's get a late night snack." Lacey smiled, gave him a quick peck on the cheek, and the two of them strolled out together.

CHAPTER TWENTY-SEVEN

Tuesday, Third Week in October
Police Station
St. Petersburg, FL
10:24 am

Luke had shown up for work only a half hour late. No one noticed or cared. Detectives and police officers don't punch time clocks. Luke spent his first two hours organizing the newly confirmed information, and checking on the progress made by the Manatee County police as he brought them up to date on last night's developments. He had yet to get in touch with Beth or Morgan in Hillsborough with the updates, so Luke left a second message on Morgan's voicemail. The prosecutor called Luke moments later, "Detective Brasch, hi. All the paperwork is in place. I can drop everything off within the hour."

"Thanks. I'll get my team on it right away." Luke was making headway, but the going was slow—too many fits and starts. He had to find the Hillsborough cops within the next hour.

Luke trudged over to Lakesha and told her to go down to the evidence lookup and sign out Stanley's cell phone and get it ready for the police technicians to go over.

Within the hour the prosecutor was at Luke's desk with the necessary paperwork. Luke asked the prosecutor if officers in Hillsborough County would be authorized to work on the records obtained from Stanley's Pinellas County cell phone, and was assured they could do so legally since they were part of a multi-county task force. Before Luke could thank the prosecutor for his legal advice Luke's phone rang again. "Detective Beth Ferguson here. I got your message. How you doing, Detective Brasch?"

Perfect timing. Luke held up the phone and motioned for the prosecutor to listen in on the spare phone. "Detective Ferguson, I've got the prosecutor on the line with us. He has the paperwork to track down Harrington's cell. I'll fax them over to you and you'll have another way to find him. Harrington's cell phone area code is from Raleigh-Durham."

"Okay. Thanks. We're kind of at an impasse here anyway. He doesn't show up anywhere we've looked in North Carolina. We know folks move all over the country while keeping the original cell phone number, so area codes won't always do the trick. But, it's better than nothing."

"Well, maybe this will help anyway. Just keep me informed, Detective."

"I will. We should be able to track down the provider and get a billing address if nothing else."

◻ ◻ ◻

Detectives Beth Ferguson and Morgan Sparks huddled around Beth's desk going over their files together. Beth asked, "We've got Harrington's credit card info, don't we?"

Morgan looked through her notes. "I copied the same credit card number down from two rental receipt, but one didn't show a credit card. Must have been cash. I thought that was strange. I didn't think car rental companies take cash." Beth was looking through her notes, "Some do, I guess. One of mine was cash, too. Wait, here's the credit card number I copied down." Beth read off the number and Morgan confirmed hers was the same.

Beth closed the folder and said, "You track down the cell phone. I'll take the credit card." Morgan walked around to her desk and both ladies went to work.

Two and a half hours later Beth and Morgan had returned from separate lunches and huddled again to exchange information. Beth wanted at least one of them in the office as much as possible the next few days. Morgan went first, "I was able to track down the cell phone provider," as she glanced at her notes, "A company named Mobile First, a local small outfit in the Research Triangle Industrial Park area." Both ladies knew that meant Raleigh-Durham, NC. Continuing, "They were reluctant to talk to a Florida Cop until I told them that I would be happy to send a half-dozen local cops to talk to them. I also reminded the guy that their local cops like to use their lights and sirens. That must have pushed him over the edge," she chuckled before continuing, "He said a very naughty curse word, but caved in." Beth smiled at the image. "Anyway, Harrington's billing address changed about two years ago to Savannah, GA." Morgan held up the paper with the address.

Beth nodded in amazement as she pulled out her own notepad, "Same address, Morgan. Let's call Detective Brasch and see if he'll spring for a road trip."

Luke called the prosecutor and relayed the information Beth Ferguson told him. The prosecutor insisted on doing everything by the book. No road trips just yet. Instead he instructed Luke to be available to testify before a Grand Jury where he would seek to indict Stanley Robbins along with Mitchell Harrington for the rapes and murders, as well as an assortment of other crimes against minors. The prosecutor thought their case was one of the strongest he'd seen in years. He went on to say that he hoped to present this case to the Grand Jury on Thursday, and expected a True Bill, the Indictment, the same day. Friday at the latest, if Grand Jury deliberations dragged out. Then any members of the Task Force could work out arrangements for the Savannah Police to arrest Harrington, serve the Savannah police with an Extradition Order, and transport Harrington back here for trial. Luke thanked him and immediately notified all the other team members.

Wednesday, Third Week in October
The Kemp home
St. Petersburg, FL
11:09 a.m.

Lakesha waited at the front door with two forensic technicians. Nancy opened it with a smile dressed as if she was going to the mall. Lakesha greeted her warmly and asked to come in. Nancy stepped aside with a broad sweep of her arm towards the inside. "The office is over there. I'll help you search it if you want." Nancy pointed and the officers followed with their eyes.

Lakesha led the team inside, showed the Search Warrant she obtained just to be as careful as possible, and replied, "That's not necessary, Mrs. Kemp. You just stay out here, please." The three officers marched to the office and went to work.

An hour and a half later the officers started carrying out several bags and boxes of papers and Stanley's computer. Lakesha was the last to leave. She thanked Nancy again for her cooperation and added, "We'll be in touch."

◻ ◻ ◻

Luke and Lakesha would spend most of the next day or so going through all the papers, while computer experts would search through the computer files for any additional evidence that could tie Stanley to any of the crimes or to Mitchell Harrington.

The technicians reported their findings by the end of the day. Several hundred photographs of young girls were found. Kiddy porn, with over half so well done they had to have been shot by professionals. All were of pretty teenage girls posed in various provocative and seductive positions. All were nearly or completely naked. And, all were showing bare teenage breasts. A few were full-length frontal views. No sex acts, and none of the images were of Megan or any of the dead girls. No emails or files mentioned Mitchell Harrington. Stanley was definitely a pedophile, but no additional evidence linking Stanley to any of the murdered girls or Mitchell.

<u>Thursday, Third Week in October</u>
<u>Grand Jury Room</u>
<u>St. Petersburg, FL</u>
<u>3:06 p.m.</u>

The prosecutor had been hard at work all day preparing his case against Stanley Robbins and Mitchell Harrington to present to the sitting Grand Jury. It took longer than he had expected to lay out all the arguments for an indictment, and he had arranged for the two witnesses he needed, Luke and Lakesha. Grand Juries meet in secret and prosecutors only need to present enough believable evidence to justify taking the case to trial. Realistically, the prosecutor must show a reasonably high chance of proving their case with credible evidence—winning at trial. If the Grand Jury believes the evidence is compelling enough, they issue a True Bill. No defense is allowed. In fact, the suspect isn't even present, and need not be informed that he's the subject of a Grand Jury proceeding. The normal rules of evidence don't strictly apply as they would in every criminal trial, so there's no need for a judge to decide issues of law. No one can object to anything, except the Grand Jury members in the form of a question.

In a criminal trial the accuser, the government, must comply with appropriate constitutional obligations to protect everyone's' rights—including even the rights of the most heinous criminals or someone that many think is obviously guilty. This is because the Criminal Justice system in the United States presumes the defendant is innocent until proven guilty in a court of law. That's called the Presumption of Innocence rule.

The prosecutor methodically went through the basics of the case. Luke's sworn testimony and a few of the photos were all he needed. Lakesha was waiting her turn but would not be needed. Grand Jurors often ask questions similar to what a defense lawyer might do on cross examination. Those questions probe the validity of the prosecutor's evidence, arguments, and theories. Sometimes a Grand Juror will simply interrupt the prosecutor in mid sentence.

This Grand Jury asked only one question, "How could the police have failed to thoroughly investigate so many crimes for so long?" The prosecutor asked Luke to explain how the two defendants relied on the out-of-date technology used by the police departments in three counties. The suspects developed a strategy that kept those same police departments off guard. Luke concluded with, "I admit that we let these girls down in the past, but now we have the chance to make it right." Many Grand Jurors looked at each other and seemed to accept that explanation. Then the prosecutor asked, "Please tell the Grand Jury how you and your team made the connections between the nine murders and the other crimes we talked about earlier."

Luke went into a lengthy chronological dissertation of the police activity that spanned the last two-plus weeks, ending with arresting Stanley on suspicion of multiple murders, and the information gained from questioning him. "It wasn't until we started investigating the identity of Megan Fisher, the only survivor we know about, almost three weeks ago, that we uncovered anything that would relate to the other cases. We had no suspects from the older cases, and couldn't identify anyone from the limited forensics we were able to collect in those cases. The connection began with Stanley Robbins working at the girl's shelter and built from there. We now know that Stanley Robbins had assumed the alias of Trevor Kemp. Maybe Mitchell Harrington has another identity, but we don't know that yet. We have forensics implicating Stanley Robbins, and Stanley Robbins has confessed to these horrific acts. Stanley Robbins also told us that Mitchell Harrington was involved in every one of these cases." More nods and knowing looks from the Grand Jurors.

At 5:50 p.m. the prosecutor dismissed the Grand Jury members. They would return to their respective homes for the evening and start their deliberations at 9:00 tomorrow morning.

CHAPTER TWENTY-EIGHT

Friday, Third Week in October
Police Station
St. Petersburg, FL
11:44 am

The third week of the investigation was coming to an end, and Luke was basically wasting time while waiting for the prosecutor to call with the news that would allow him and his team to go after Harrington in Savannah. He tried to look busy but wasn't kidding anyone. Lakesha checked in periodically as did Loo. Luke drifted off into fantasies and daydreams as he rhythmically rocked while staring into space. He hated the waiting—the doing nothing part of this job.

The sound of his phone ringing snapped Luke back into reality and he snatched it up before the second ring. "Hello, Detective Brasch." It was the prosecutor with the good news; the True Bill was returned. Both Stanley Robbins and Mitchell Harrington were officially indicted on nine counts of murder and dozens of other counts involving lesser felonies. There's no statute of limitations on murder and certain sexual assaults on minors, so it didn't matter that some crimes were four or five years old. The prosecutor told Luke that the paperwork would be ready by Monday morning. He also reminded Luke that additional charges could be added as new evidence turned up, so keep looking under every rock.

Luke called the Manatee County detectives first. They were pleased to hear that both scumbags were finally going to pay for what they did. Paige McDermott informed Luke that some of the unidentified fingerprints left at their crime scenes, indeed now matched Stanley

Robbins, whose fingerprints weren't in the system until they arrested him. The other unidentified fingerprints would have to wait until they could get Mitchell Harrington's for a proper comparison.

When he called Beth Ferguson and told her that she could contact the Savannah Police on Monday, she kidded that she was disappointed that she and Morgan couldn't leave immediately for Savanna. Luke and Beth shared a laugh at Beth's fantasy. After they got back to business, Beth informed Luke that she and Morgan would work the Savannah angle on Monday after all the paperwork was completed.

Loo and Lakesha were next. Both agreed that the case was going very well, and it was only a matter of time before Harrington would also be behind bars, and then it would be up to the prosecutor to keep both Stanley and Mitchell there. They had no idea if any new surprises would jump up and bite them in the butt as they chased down Mitchell Harrington in Savannah. Hopefully it would go as smoothly as Stanley's arrest.

When Luke called Lacey she congratulated him for doing such a good job. Luke reminded her, "I couldn't have done it without you."

Lacey laughed, "Well, maybe that's true. So why don't we congratulate each other this weekend?" They made a date for Saturday afternoon, taking care not to plan anything specific after that. Gratefully the case would be over soon, and they could concentrate on their own personal lives without the stress of this horrific case as a constant companion. Both expected to unwind and just spend time with each other.

Saturday, Third Week in October
Lacey's Condo
Treasure Island, FL
3:27 p.m.

Lacey greeted Luke with a smile, a long tight hug, and a longer kiss. Lacey was dressed in the most casual outfit Luke had seen her in; grey slacks and white shirt. No necklaces or pins. Simple white sandals. He was also dressed casually prepared for a leisurely afternoon and evening with his girlfriend. Once inside with the door closed behind them, they held hands and made small talk. Neither mentioned the bedroom as Luke's hormones battled his feelings. After fifteen minutes, he was getting antsy and didn't trust his own willpower to not throw himself at Lacey right then and there. His head just wasn't into their relationship as fully as he thought it should be to go any farther, so he suggested they head out. Lacey seemed okay with leaving, but was actually hoping Luke would stay and let nature take its course, as she had suggested several times already. She was ready for their relationship to move to the next level, but knew she had to wait for Luke to catch up. Lacey was smart enough to just go with the flow, so she grabbed her purse and a black windbreaker as she sported a forced smile.

Luke drove leisurely towards the movie theater. Lacey had chosen a romantic comedy that started at 4:50. It wasn't academy award stuff, but the critics said it was a sappy, fun flick with stars they'd heard of. They held hands while waiting in line to buy their tickets. Once in the concession line, Lacey tucked her arm under Luke's and just hung on while suggesting they share a large popcorn and a cherry coke. Sharing simple things often leads to sharing more important ones. Besides, they could get free refills on the way out and share it all over again.

The theater was less than half full so finding seats was a breeze. They settled in and attacked the popcorn and soda for the few minutes of commercials by local vendors, doctors, and other purveyors of goods and services. Luke wondered if anyone attending the movie wanted, or used any of what was advertised. The lights slowly dimmed as the previews started. Luke and Lacey took turns with their opinions of each one. "Dumb", "That's cute", "Dumber", "Not another horror film", "Didn't know she still acted," and on and on until the almost endless parade of coming attractions mercifully ended. When the feature film started they quieted down.

Lacey really enjoyed the film. She grabbed Luke's arm or hand when a romantic scene popped up. Luke too, was having a good time. He patted her hand each time and turned to gave her a quick peck on the cheek. On the third time, Lacey turned to kiss him on the lips. He wanted to wrap his arm around her shoulder to pull her close, but the armrest and the large drink in the holder between their seats prevented any such advances. They went back to just holding hands and smooching every ten minutes or so.

◻ ◻ ◻

Dinner was at a fish restaurant on Madeira Beach. Luke wanted to sit outdoors on the deck and Lacey readily agreed. The view was facing east towards the inter-coastal waterway. Watching the yachts and sail boats drift by was always romantic. They ordered shrimp cocktails and iced tea. Neither was an expert on wines, so they simply avoided ordering any. Luke would occasionally order a beer, but not on a date. Lacey hated beer. They were taking their time and would order dinner later. Both Lacey and Luke were really in good moods, and neither thought about the case at all. They were just two lovebirds out for a good time.

Four young teenage girls strolled in with three sets of parents. Two girls were in shorts and two in slacks. All four wore brightly colored short sleeve tops. The girls were placed at the table next to Luke and Lacey. The parents were seated a few tables away. The girls acted like normal teenage girls. They joked and laughed, whispered into each other's ear, talked about music and clothes, and made faces about boys. Luke and Lacey tried not to look at them, but couldn't help but overhear their typical teenage girl chatter. The girls weren't loud or obnoxious, nor did they misbehave in any way. But, their just being there definitely threw a cold towel on Luke. Lacey noticed, and Luke's declining mood affected hers.

Lacey was the first to speak in over five minutes, almost whispering to Luke, "Why don't we just order?" By now, neither Luke nor Lacey was very hungry. Thoughts were wrenched back to the case just because of this chance encounter with very normal girls seated at the next table. They both ordered, but neither expected to finish, and they both planned on asking for take-home boxes.

Neither Luke nor Lacey spoke much during the meal. Neither could put the girls at the next table out of their minds. Lacey thought about how these beautiful young ladies had their whole lives ahead of them. It appeared that they all had nice loving families that did things together and loved each other. Why couldn't all families be like that?

Luke's imaginary glass was half empty. His mind headed the other way, and focused on the contrasts between normal teenage girls and the few unlucky ones that suffered abuse. He thought about how horrible the home lives of the dead, and other abused girls must have been. Life had to be absolutely unbearable for them. There was no other reason for running away to live on the streets or in a secret girl's shelter. Or, for trading sex for fast food.

Luke and Lacey finished eating in moods much less cheery than when they arrived. Both sensed the mood changes in the other and in themselves. For all practical purposes the pleasant evening was over.

Luke paid the check and they headed out, each with a white foam box. Lacey now had no expectations of anything happening romantically between them that night, and didn't want to upset Luke any further. "Why don't we just call it a night after you drop me off?"

"I'm really sorry, Lacey, but you're probably right. I won't be much fun to be around anyway." They drove back to Lacey's condo in silence. More silence on the elevator ride up. As Lacey was unlocking her door, she asked, "Will I see you tomorrow?"

Luke pulled her close, "I sure hope so." Lacey rose up on her tiptoes and kissed him.

Taking Luke by the hand, she led him inside, "Let's make plans."

They sat on the couch about a foot apart as Lacey tossed out several choices: breakfast out, lunch out, brunch out, lunch at Luke's condo, dinner out. "I've always wanted to say this," chuckled Luke, "Let's do lunch." Lacey giggled at his parody of rich Hollywood stereotypes.

"Okay. Your place, my place, or out?"

Luke thought for a few seconds making a big show of it. He put his hand on his chin and made a screwed up face. Finally, "My place. When should I come and get you? "

"You always drive. I'll drive myself to you this time. Is 11:30 too early?"

'No, it's not. That's fine. I'll be ready." Luke was already thinking about the stores he needed to get to early Sunday morning to pick up the things he needed.

Slowly their moods were getting better. Luke reached over, pulled Lacey closer, and planted a big kiss. Lacey melted in his arms. Neither one had ever tried to touch the other in a sexual way, including all the dates in high school. Luke was a total gentleman back then. Even now he respected the ladies he dated, and wouldn't take advantage of them. He had only one prior sexual partner, another military officer, about six years ago when he was overseas. That relationship ended after five months when she was transferred to another military base. They both felt that a long distance affair couldn't work. Luke was as devastated then as he was when he and Lacey broke up in high school years earlier. Luke didn't kiss and tell, so Lacey had no idea about Luke's past sexual partners, nor did she tell him about hers. Neither ever brought up the subject.

Lacey didn't want to make the first move, but Luke hadn't done anything but kiss her and rub her back. Lacey wanted to give Luke a little nudge in the sexual direction, "Should I go change into something more comfortable?"

Luke pulled away and sighed, "What are we doing, Lacey? I want our relationship to be something special. I can't be what you want when my mind wanders so much. Maybe I should just go."

Dejected, "I guess you're right. I'll see you tomorrow at 11:30."

"Absolutely." Luke pulled her close again and kissed her, "And, I promise I'll be more enjoyable to be with."

"I'm counting on that." Lacey kissed him this time.

Luke got up and pulled Lacey to her feet. They ambled across the plush carpeting to the door and embraced again. This kiss was long and passionate. Lacey had no idea what it would take to get Luke to go farther romantically.

After Luke was gone, Lacey got ready for bed, but laid awake with wild thoughts about Luke never making any advances. She thought, "How can he be so passionate at times, and then turn so cold so quickly?" She knew the answer before she asked herself the question; she and Luke probably couldn't move forward as a couple until Luke finally felt good about this case—or their relationship as a couple. The only thing she could do was to help get Mitchell Harrington arrested and extradited. Maybe then Luke would know that some kind of justice and closure could be had for the abused girls. That problem had not changed, and Lacey was only kidding herself if she thought it had. Luke was almost single minded, just too focused, with a deep sense of commitment to his job. Lacey actually admired that quality in Luke and smiled in the darkness. She didn't know anyone else who felt so strongly about **doing the right thing**. Lacey vowed then and there to never try and change him. Luke cared more about others than anyone Lacey knew.

<u>Sunday, Third Week in October</u>
<u>Luke's Condo</u>
<u>Pinellas Park, FL</u>
<u>11:18 a.m.</u>

Luke had been up for several hours. He'd showered, shaved, and had already been to the bagel and grocery store. The table was mostly set and he was waiting impatiently for Lacey. Luke jumped up and rushed to the door at the sound of a soft knock. Lacey was standing there as beautiful and inviting as ever. "Welcome. Come in," as he pulled her inside and closed the door. Before she could even drop her purse, Luke grabbed her, lifted her up, and gave her a long kiss. Lacey returned the kiss, and wrapped both arms around his neck. Eventually Luke put her back on the floor, and took both of her hands in his, "Lacey, I have to apologize to you. I haven't been treating you very well, and I'm sorry."

Lacey kissed him again, "Luke, there's nothing to apologize for. You have a lot on your mind, and I understand that. Just remember that I'm here for you whenever, and however, you need me. They embraced again for a long minute.

Lacey broke the hold, "I'm hungry. I'll help you," Lacey led him into the kitchen and they busied themselves with getting breakfast ready. When the rest of the table was set, the platters of bagels and other tasty items brought out, juice and coffee poured, they sat down together and enjoyed the meal. They ate slowly and chatted incessantly, often reminiscing about **the good old days** of high school. Their hands touched at every opportunity.

An hour later they were done eating, and Luke rose to clear the dishes. "I'll help you clean up," stated Lacey as she pushed her chair away and picked up some items. They strolled back and forth a few times until everything was in the kitchen. Then all the leftovers were put in plastic baggies and containers. They loaded the dishwasher and wiped down the countertops together.

Luke turned to face Lacey. He placed his hands on her hips, and she plopped hers on his shoulders, "What should we do for the rest of the afternoon?" asked Luke with a grin.

Lacey immediately thought that maybe Luke had reassessed their relationship and was ready to move forward. Lacey was in heaven, her head swimming, but she knew they should go slowly. "We can go for a drive. We can stay here and watch TV or a movie," she pointed to the shelf of DVD's in the living room, "or we can just sit and talk. What do you want to do?" Lacey mentally crossed her fingers hoping for the reply she wanted.

"Last night didn't turn out very well. That was my fault, so I guess I'll have to try a little harder. But, let's not force anything. I don't want to jinx whatever we've got going between us." Luke was obviously sincere.

Lacey cooed, "And, what are you going to do to try harder?"

This time it was Luke kicking himself as he thought, "I've got a wonderful, very desirable woman in my arms, and I can't get up the courage to do anything about it. What the hell is wrong with me?"

Luke hadn't replied and Lacey sensed something was wrong—again. "Let's stay here and watch a movie," as she led him to the couch. "Sit down and I'll find something." Luke's taste in DVD's leaned towards action, adventure, and suspense themes. None of those were the least bit romantic. "Got anything else? I don't want to watch guts and blood stuff."

"I'll check the TV listings and see what they have." Luke flipped on the flat screen and pressed the button for the interactive TV listings. He remembered seeing some commercials about movies on the Hallmark channel this weekend. Luke pushed buttons until he found what he was looking for, a romantic comedy starting in about a half hour. "How about this?" Lacey quickly read the description, agreed, and settled on the couch next to him.

Lacey kicked off her flats and snuggled up against Luke. Luke wrapped an arm around her to pull her closer while he flipped channels with his free hand. He was killing time while waiting for the movie to start, but didn't find anything to watch for more than a minute or two. At 4:00 Luke flipped back to the Hallmark Channel, tossed the remote onto the coffee table, and leaned back allowing Lacey to snuggle even closer. They watched the romantic movie in silence, and neither wanted to change their position. They were both very comfortable, physically and emotionally. Almost serene.

Neither Luke nor Lacey slept much the night before, and both were close to exhaustion. Lacey was the first to drop off. Luke realized she was sleeping a few minutes later and repositioned her a little so she would be more comfortable resting against his chest. He held her loosely in his arms and was out like a light himself about ten minutes later.

◻ ◻ ◻

Luke woke up before Lacey. It was dark outside. The clock said it was 9:47 p.m. He carefully wiggled out from under Lacey, and gently lowered her to a sleeping position with her billowing hair spread out on the couch pillow under her head. After a few minutes Luke decided it would be best if he not wake her up, so he just covered her with a blanket, tucked it in around her, kissed her gently on the forehead, and retreated to his bedroom.

Lacey woke up around midnight and looked around in the dark until her eyes adjusted. For a few seconds she couldn't figure out where she was. Finally, she remembered, got up, visited the hall bathroom, and eventually wandered towards Luke's bedroom and stopped at the open doorway. The small nightlight provided enough illumination for Lacey to see Luke sleeping on his side in the queen-sized bed. He was shirtless with the blanket pulled halfway up his bare chest. She tiptoed over and peeked under the blanket. He was wearing gym shorts. Lacey smiled to herself and stripped down to her underwear before climbing under the covers beside him. Luke made a few restless sounds but didn't wake up. Lacey snuggled next to him, and closed her eyes as she flipped a leg over his thigh. Sleep returned quickly.

◻ ◻ ◻

Luke woke up first at 6:09 a.m. Monday morning. They had rolled apart during the night, and Luke had yet to realize Lacey was still there in his condo, much less in his bed. He spread his arms to stretch and poked something next to him. Startled, he turned around to see a massive volume of hair spread out on a pillow. The covers were up to her neck. Then he remembered Lacey, but didn't remember getting into bed with her. Instinctively, he raised the covers a little to see if he was wearing anything. He was, and so was she.

Luke quickly regained his composure. He leaned over and tenderly kissed the head next to him as he gently shook a small shoulder. "Wake up, Sunshine. Time to rise and shine."

Lacey moaned as she shook the sleep from her head before propping herself up on her elbows. The covers slipped to her waist as she turned to face Luke and smiled, "Good morning. What time is it?" He told her, she flopped back onto the bed, and yanked the covers over her head. "I've got a 9:00 counseling session at the office." Lacey snickered as she peeked out impishly from under the covers, "But, I've got time for round two."

"Round two? Was there a round one?" Luke was sure he would have remembered if they'd been intimate.

"Well, I had a good time. Didn't you?" Lacey cocked her head, smiled broadly, and batted her eyes.

Luke was confused, so he changed the subject, "I've got to get to the station early too."

Lacey tossed the covers off revealing her perfect figure with all the right places covered by skimpy, black lace underwear. Luke gawked as Lacey got out of bed and strolled uninhibited to his bathroom. She slipped off her bra as she approached his side of the bed. "You don't mind if I use your shower, do you?" Lacey giggled as she tossed the bra at Luke and stepped out of her panties.

Luke was really enjoying the show. His hormones spiked watching Lacey fiddle with the shower knobs until she was satisfied. Luke was sitting on the side of the bed, and leaned sideways to watch her disappear behind the shower curtain. Within seconds, Lacey giggled again as she stuck her head out and motioned with her finger for Luke to come over, "Come in, the waters fine."

It took Luke less than four seconds to shed his gym shorts and reach the shower. Round two was what they each needed and wanted. Both made their respective early morning appointments on time—but, just barely on time.

Chapter Twenty-Nine

Monday, Fourth Week in October
Police Station
Tampa, FL
10:49 a.m.

Beth Ferguson's annoyance level was rising rapidly. She'd made five phone calls to the Savannah Police department, left seven messages with various officers, and had been put on hold twice, only to be disconnected each time. She had yet to reach a live person that could actually help her. She would try again in two minutes.

Morgan approached, "Any luck yet?"

"Nope. I hope the locals there get better service than I'm getting."

"They have 911 for emergencies. That's all most folks care about." Morgan's remark didn't make Beth laugh. Instead, Beth just made a face and ignored her partner.

As Beth was reaching for the phone to try again, it rang, "Good morning. This is Detective Beth Ferguson. What can I do for you?"

"This is Carter Walsh, Chief of the Savannah police department. I understand you want us to arrest Mitchell Harrington for some crimes he allegedly committed in the Tampa Bay area."

"Yes, sir. That's correct. After you arrest him, we'll file an extradition order to bring him back here to stand trial." Beth pointed to the receiver so Morgan would know the call was important as she mouthed "Savannah".

"Detective, I personally know a Mitchell Harrington. He's engaged to my ex-wife. While that upsets me, I find it hard to believe he's your man. The Mitchell Harrington I know coaches my daughter's softball team. By the way, my daughter hates me because my ex-wife convinced her to detest me. Damn shame. So I have a huge conflict, Detective. I'd love to get Harrington out of my ex-wife and daughter's life, but if I do I'll bring down the wrath of God on myself. So, I'll need a lot more before I order an arrest of a guy I, and a dozen other parents, trust with our daughters. I need to be damn sure that the Mitchell Harrington ruining my life is the one you're looking for."

"Wow, that's a lot of information," thought Beth, as she quickly realized there might be a problem brewing. She knew the paperwork was very specific. It included the composite, his last known address, other personal information, and some of the details of the cases against him. "No disrespect, Chief, but have you seen the Indictment and the other paperwork we sent up there?" Beth knew that a Chief of Police is often just briefed about most cases, and does not always see all the evidence in detail.

"None taken. And no, my sergeant just barged into my office yelling about you guys wanting us to arrest Mitchell on a felony warrant from Florida. His daughter plays on the same team as my daughter. I called you to clear all this up myself."

"If you look at the file I'm sure you'll be convinced. It's all there, sir."

"I'll call you back in half an hour, Detective." The line went dead before Beth could thank him.

◻ ◻ ◻

It was almost noon before Chief Walsh called back. "I've looked over the file, Detective, and I'm still not entirely convinced. Your evidence indicates Mitchell Harrington *may* have committed these crimes, but I just can't believe that. The sketch could be him, but maybe not. Stanley Robbins implicated a Mitchell Harrington, but is he believable? What else do you have?"

"Maybe my partner and I should come up there with the entire file, sir."

"Are you and your partner the only detectives working this case?"

"No, sir. We're the team from one county. There are four other detectives from two more adjacent counties and a police consultant on the task force. And of course, there are the prosecutors."

Chief Walsh was first and foremost a cop. All credible accusations had to be taken seriously, even when those accusations implicated family and friends. "I have to do this right, Detective. I'll drive down later today and we can all get together at one time in the morning. That way I can assess every point of view." Before Beth could reply, "I still can't believe the Mitchell Harrington I know could do those things you're accusing him of, but I'll keep an open mind."

Beth was disappointed she and Morgan weren't taking a trip up there, but she skillfully hid her feelings. "That's fine, sir. I'll notify the rest of the team and set up the meeting for 8:30 tomorrow morning. We'll go over everything then and you can brief us about Mitchell Harrington. Any additional information about him would be most helpful."

Beth gave the Chief the address of the St. Petersburg police station and suggested a few inexpensive hotels. Chief Walsh said he should be able to drive to St. Petersburg by 10:00 that evening, and would go directly to the hotel.

<u>Tuesday, Fourth Week in October</u>
<u>Police Station</u>
<u>St. Petersburg, FL</u>
<u>8:39 am</u>

Lacey was the last of the St. Pete contingent to arrive. She was more than ready to put Harrington behind bars and get rid of this case. She gladly cleared her office schedule and was prepared to be here most of the morning. The six police detectives and Lacey were chatting amongst themselves when an officer knocked on the open door, "Detective Brasch, Chief Walsh is here."

Luke stood up and extended his hand, "Welcome to St. Petersburg, Chief Walsh. I'm Lucas Brasch, but Luke is fine. I hope you found your way around our city."

"Nice to meet you, Luke, and I had no problems at all. Call me Carter."

Carter Walsh was tall and thin, and quite handsome for a man in his late 50's. Carter was clean shaven and sported a full head of salt and pepper hair. His bright sparkling gray eyes seemed to take in everything around him. He was in full uniform and carrying a brown briefcase. Lieutenant Thompson saw the Chief as he came in and walked over to introduce himself. They chatted for a few moments, ignoring everyone else in the room until Loo excused himself and went back to his office.

Luke made the introductions of the team, and Lakesha offered to get a cup of coffee for Carter, who respectfully declined. Everyone took a seat and Luke started, "Here's what we have." Luke went through the whiteboard dissertation again. He used the same photos as before, and generally gave the identical explanation he used to convince Loo. Carter asked a few questions, but Luke fielded them expertly; he'd been through this so many times, he could answer questions in his sleep. At 10:30 Luke suggested a break.

A few ladies headed for the restroom to freshen up. The rest headed for the break room for more coffee and whatever the vending machines would provide. The Chief just tagged along to be friendly. The ladies soon dribbled into the break room for refills and chit-chat with the guys. At 10:50 they all reassembled in the conference room.

Everyone settled into the same seats as before, searched for pens, reopened files, and waited for Luke to restart the meeting. Luke leaned forward and addressed Carter directly, "That's all we have, Carter. Stanley Robbins is in custody and has implicated Mitchell Harrington as the driving force—and the killer. The prosecutor thinks it's a good case, and that we've identified the right man, a Mitchell Harrington living in Savannah. So, what can you tell us about *your* Mitchell Harrington?"

Carter bent down and picked up his briefcase, set it in front of him, and took out some loose papers. "This is the Mitchell Harrington I know. I have some background information," holding the papers out in front of him as he continued, "Mitchell moved to Savannah about 20 or so months ago from North Carolina. He quickly got involved in the community. Girls' softball coach, active in the church, and he helped in local political campaigns. He met my ex-wife—we were divorced six years ago—and they became engaged about four months ago. Both my ex-wife and daughter adore him. In spite of my personal feelings about him, Mitchell Harrington is a model citizen. I wish there were more like him. You know, folks that get involved in their communities in a positive way."

Beth asked, "Anything criminal in his background that you know of? We have a Visa charge card number, but his Credit Report is pretty skimpy. We can't find a Social Security number, which is weird, or any tax forms filed in his name. Nothing came back on a criminal check."

"I wanted to run him, but had no reason to. You don't run criminal background checks on your model citizens, do you?"

Paige McDermott answered, "No, we don't, but we do investigate multiple murders regardless of who the suspect might be."

Carter looked directly at her and replied, "Fair enough." He looked back at the others, "I've kept an open mind, and am honestly leaning towards your point of view. Let's keep going, and maybe you can knock me off the fence." Carter smiled and looked around at the small group.

Everyone had a short laugh, even though this was serious business and nothing to laugh about.

Keith Cooper asked, "When are Harrington and your ex-wife getting married?"

"In mid-December, I think. He met my ex-wife at church. They dated for a few months, and one day at softball practice Mitchell announced they were engaged and planning to tie the knot. They seem to be happy, and so does my daughter. Mitchell spends much more time with both of them than I was ever able to."

Lakesha asked, "How does he earn money? What does he do for a living?"

Carter looked at her, "He runs a website. Some kind of **Friends** thing where kids send messages back and forth to each other. Lots of links to stuff kids care about. Music, on-line stores, and such. They sign up, but I'm not sure if there's a fee or not. I've never been on his site, so I don't know anything else about it."

Beth was the most computer literate of the group, "Do you know the URL, the name of the website?"

Carter looked around a little sheepishly "SavannahTeens, I think," as he flipped open his cell phone, "Should I call someone to check?"

Beth said, "Not necessary. We can search for it easily enough."

Lacey was immediately skeptical. She sensed this would probably turn out badly.

Luke opened the laptop they kept in the conference room and turned it on. Beth wrote down what could be the URL as Carter repeated it out loud. Luke was staring at the screen waiting for it to settle down. After taking what seemed like forever to boot up, he clicked on the internet ICON.

The computer was connected to a projector focused on a side wall. The group, minus Lacey, turned to watch the projected images. Luke typed in the web name and waited for the search agent to confirm the mystery website and clicked on it. Lacey remained seated looking the other way, but listened to the chatter. Luke navigated around looking at the computer monitor. The others watched the action on the wall. "Just like you said, Carter, what teenage girls might want from an internet site."

Morgan pointed, "You can join to post and see photos and chat with other girls."

Beth said, "I'll join," and went for her purse.

Luke whipped out his wallet, "Don't bother. This one's on the St. Pete police's dime." Luke entered some minimal information, created a User Name and Password, and paid the $29 for an annual membership. The group was in and Luke started navigating again.

Luke was commenting as he checked out different aspects of the site, "Here's where we can set up our own personal page and post a picture," as he moved on to another ICON, "Let's check out other members." Luke navigated to a half-dozen individual girl's pages. Each one had what looked like a mini-biography, a photo, and other innocent types of information, like favorite song, BFF, for **best friend forever,** and similar types of information.

Paige pointed to a small nondescript ICON at the extreme left edge of the page, "What's that?"

Luke clicked on the ICON and a window opened announcing, "For our Special Members ONLY". Luke tentatively clicked on the ICON at the bottom of that window, and a new window opened, this time with a blinking message, "You are not a Special Member. To become a Special Member, set up your account now." Beth poked Luke in the back, "Go for it," she urged.

Luke extracted his credit card again, paid an additional $49, was immediately thanked for his **Special Membership**, and asked if he wanted to see the **Special Features** offered only to **Special Members**. Luke looked around at the group before clicking on the heart-shaped ICON, "Here goes."

Morgan gasped, "What the hell is this?" The larger than life images appeared on the wall-screen.

The site was well designed, colorful, and pleasing to look at, if you enjoyed leering at pictures of naked, or nearly naked, teenage girls smiling and waving back at you. Luke scrolled slowly through the hundreds of pictures until Carter shouted and pointed, "Stop. That's my daughter," and collapsed into a nearby chair. The others looked back at the wall to see a 15 or 16 year old attractive girl lying on a rug, propped up on her elbows sporting a huge broad smile. She was partially covered in a pink bed sheet—apparently totally naked. Her bare left breast was clearly visible under her hands as her palms held up her chin. The top of her bare butt was peeking out from under the sheet. Her right leg was bent, foot pointed at the ceiling. It was actually a good picture, well composed, and was good enough for a men's magazine, but no one cared about any of that.

Beth whispered, but not softly enough, "I see her…," she stammered, "her…, " she couldn't get the words out," as she pointed to the image on the wall. After a deep breath Beth blurted out, "This is child porn. How can he get away with doing this?"

Morgan asked very slowly, "We know Mitchell's been to Tampa Bay lots of times. Has he gone anywhere else?" They turned to Carter.

Carter took a long deep breath to calm is startled nerves and looked around before answering. He knew what his answer would mean, "I knew about some of his trips here. He told us he had clients to see and needed a backup coach for a few days." Carter took another long breath and exhaled loudly, "He did the same when he went to Memphis and Houston. Maybe Atlantic City too, but I don't remember."

Lacey's senses were right on the money, and she was sick to her stomach. In disgust she sneered, "You all know what this means. The police in every city Mitchell traveled to must be alerted. If there are other victims out there…" Her voice trailed off.

Lacey couldn't control her rage any longer, jumped up, flung her pen across the room, and rushed out with her hands covering her face. She'd heard enough and was sickened by this disgusting pervert. Lakesha bolted out close behind, "I'll just see if she's okay."

Luke killed the projection on the wall out of respect for the Chief. Morgan went over to a clearly shaken Carter Walsh, "Can I get you some water?"

"Yes, thank you," looking up sadly, "This is such a shock. I'm sure my ex-wife doesn't know anything about this either. If she did, she would have said something. She hates this garbage more than I do. We would never let our child pose like that. I don't know when or how she did it." Morgan left the room to fetch a bottle of water.

Lacey and Lakesha returned ten minutes later. Lacey had dried her eyes, applied fresh makeup, and forced a weak smile. Lakesha was behind her shaking her head back and forth to indicate things weren't going as well as Lacey wanted them to believe. Carter was the only one not looking at Lacey and Lakesha. Finally he pushed himself up and lumbered over to the group. All seven faces turned to watch as Carter thrust his arms in the air, "You win. Humpty Dumpty has crash landed on your side of the wall and will never be the same again."

Luke walked over to the table and found the papers he needed. Handing them to Carter with one hand, he plopped the other on Carter's shoulder. "Why don't you sign these here and we can make copies before you leave." Carter pulled a pen from his pocket and scribbled his name in the places Luke indicated.

Lacey sat down with a sigh, "Thank you, Chief. And, I'm truly sorry about your daughter. For the record, I don't think for one minute that you or your ex-wife are bad parents." Lacey paused to take a deep breath because what she was going to say next would sting like ice pellets in a snow blizzard. "Your daughter probably knows that the website is public and that you might have seen it. The picture is obviously posed and possibly taken by a second person. Posing for such pictures is not the same as posting them on the internet. That means that she either is proud of showing her body to you and the whole world, or more likely, she doesn't know her picture is posted there. Maybe a girlfriend took the picture just for fun, and Harrington somehow found it. Or, Mitch Harrington conned your daughter into doing something she otherwise wouldn't. Regardless of how it started, it's not your fault, but your daughter will need both of you for support to get through what's to come." Lacey went on to explain that photos posted on the web never go away, even if the site is shut down. Carter's daughter may be haunted by this picture for the rest of her life. Thankfully, she will soon be an adult; more mature, and better able to cope if the revealing photo resurfaces somewhere else. Hopefully, there aren't any others out there in the vast cyberspace. Lacey planned on reporting this site within the hour, and would get it off the web as soon as possible.

"Thank you, Doctor. I appreciate your insight. I know how hard it is dealing with dysfunctional families and their screwed up kids, and not get emotionally involved. I couldn't stand doing that when I was a beat cop, and dislike it even more now." Carter was walking over to Lacey as he continued, "I'm sure my daughter will need help. Maybe the whole family. Could you recommend someone in Savannah?"

"It would be my pleasure, Chief. I'll get back to you with a few names in a day or two."

Chief Walsh sat down at the table, opened his files, glanced back at the others, and said without emotion, "What are all of you waiting for? We need to make plans about how to take Mitchell Harrington into custody under your Florida felony warrant and get him extradited back here to you."

Chapter Thirty

Wednesday, Fourth Week in October
Police Station
Savannah, GA
9:33 a.m.

Chief Carter Walsh had selected his team, a Sergeant, two detectives, and four police officers. All were reassigned to this team less than a hour ago. When the team arrived he started the briefing with, "This will be as much of a shock to you as it was to me when I first heard about it yesterday." He paused and surveyed the others, "There's strong evidence that Mitchell Harrington, the coach of our daughter's softball team," pointing to himself and the sergeant, "is a child molester and a child killer."

The room erupted as everyone talked at once. A few leaped to their feet. All of them knew Harrington personally, or at least knew of him. Everyone knew that the Chief's ex-wife was engaged to Harrington, and had to wonder if there was some underlying personal motives for going after Harrington. No one ever suspected Harrington of doing anything criminal, much less child molestation and murder.

The Chief raised his hands to regain order, "Settle down. I need to tell you about the evidence we have," then added as if he were psychic, "My personal life has nothing to do with my willingness to pursue Mr. Harrington as a suspect in this case. In fact, I'm sure my ex-wife and daughter will hate me even more when they find out about the arrest." Those that were standing took their seats. Some continued the quizzical looks at each other.

Carter continued with the most important piece of information, "As police officers, we must respect and honor valid Court Orders and Felony Warrants from other jurisdictions, even out-of-state ones." Carter waved the Indictment and other court papers, "This is an Indictment issued by the Florida Courts in Pinellas County. The St. Petersburg police, along with officers from the two surrounding counties that border Tampa Bay, investigated the murders of nine teenage girls that occurred over the past five years. That Investigation led to a man named Stanley Robbins, a St. Petersburg resident who helped Mitchell Harrington find the girls. Mr. Robbins implicated Mitchell, Harrington, and the investigation led the Task Force to the conclusion that Stanley Robbins and Mitchell Harrington probably killed those nine girls. There may be others, and the Task Force is already looking into that possibility. It is up to us to arrest Mitchell Harrington because we have jurisdiction." Carter held up the Felony Warrant that authorized the arrest. "We will start the extradition process as soon as he's in custody." He held up the extradition package and looked around.

Carter passed the file to the officer next to him, "I was in St. Petersburg yesterday, and I've received a complete briefing from the Tampa Bay Task Force. They convinced me that Mitchell Harrington has been living a double life as a model citizen here and a killer down there. Look at the file yourselves if you have doubts. I'll be back in thirty minutes to discuss assignments."

Carter stood and left the room. The officer with the file opened it and thumbed through the pictures. Several others watched. After ten minutes of shuffling papers and photos they came across the report that implicated Mitchell Harrington. A second officer, the lone woman, picked it up and began reading out load. The others listened intently. When she got to the third and last page, she gasped, covered her mouth with a hand, and dropped the papers. The first officer looked at her with surprise, then picked them up and scanned the last page quickly. "Listen to this," as he read aloud the report about Harrington's website and the picture of Carter's daughter, but the picture was not included. He closed the file and pointed to the person closest to the door, "Get the Chief. Tell him we're ready for our assignments."

❏ ❏ ❏

They decided that the entire team—minus the Chief—would participate in the arrest. One detective made a few innocent sounding phone calls to get a feel for Mitchell's schedule that day. Fortunately, Mitchell and the Chief's ex-wife had not moved in together, so they could avoid getting her and her daughter involved when the arrest went down. Arresting Harrington at his home posed the least risk of involving bystanders since there would be few other people around. But, the arrest could still be dangerous.

The detective found out that Harrington should be at home for about a half hour sometime between 4:00 and 5:00 p.m. The seven person team divided themselves into three unmarked cars. Harrington lived in a rented house situated in the middle of a very long residential block, making it easier to cut off escape routes once he neared his home. One of the cars, the lead detective's vehicle, acted as a lookout watching for Harrington to come home. The other two cars were out of sight several blocks away waiting for the signal.

Mitchell Harrington drove up at 4:10 p.m., stepped out, slung his sport coat over his shoulder, and headed to his front door. He looked like a million other guys coming home to their loving families. Absolutely nothing about him looked sinister. The spotter made the call and the other two cars drove up a few seconds after Mitchell went inside and closed the door. No light or sirens, so he was totally oblivious to the activity on the street. Two of the officers remained in their car parked at the curb as backup if things didn't go as planned. The lead detective rang the bell as the other four stood nervously a few feet away.

Harrington opened the door with a smile, "Good afternoon, officers. What can I do for you gentlemen?"

All five officers knew Mitchell on sight so they didn't ask for identification. "Mr. Harrington, we're here on official police business. We have a Florida Felony Warrant for your arrest"

Mitch looked surprised, "You do? What am I being arrested for, Detective?"

"Maybe we should go inside."

"That's not necessary," declared Mitch emphatically as he stepped outside and shut the door behind him. He looked at each officer daring them to do something about it.

"All right, Mr. Harrington. We'll do this out here." The detective took out the Felony Warrant and started reading out loud. All eyes were on the detective as Mitchell seized his opportunity. He took a big step backwards towards the street, reached into his pocket, and pulled out a pistol. He frantically waved it at the officers shouting, "Don't move a muscle or I'll kill you." He started backing away slowly.

The officers had made a critical mistake because they knew Mitchell Harrington. They were only seconds from frisking him and placing him in handcuffs, but had talked instead of acted. They would have quickly found the gun had they tried to look.

The lead Detective shouted back, "Mitch, don't be stupid. There are five of us. Even if you shoot one or two of us the others will put ten bullets in your heart."

The detective started for his gun and Mitchell fired a shot in his direction, missing by a foot. "I told you not to move," he barked. The detective froze and raised his hands. The other four did the same. Mitchell couldn't, but the officers near Harrington could see the two backup officers approaching on their tiptoes with guns pointed at Mitchell. Harrington had yet to realize there were more officers behind him. Mitchell kept backing up towards his car as he kept his eyes glued on the officers standing motionless at his front door. He yanked open the car door and started to slide in, gun still waving menacingly at the first five officers.

The two backup officers were working their way toward Mitch from behind as Mitchell started the engine and put his car in gear. He yanked the wheel to the right, spun the car around on the lawn, and aimed it at the two police cars blocking the driveway. Dirt and grass flew everywhere. As Mitch roared past the two police cars, he shot at the tires of one, and was aiming at the other. All seven officers sprinted towards the speeding car, but the two backup officers on the other side were closer. Mitch finally spotted them and sneered as he leveled his gun at the head of one of the backup officers. Just as Mitch pulled the trigger, his car lurched and the bullet whizzed by harmlessly. The two backup detectives dropped to a crouch and started firing into Mitch's car. The other five officers emptied the 11-shot magazines of their semi-automatic weapons within seconds. Mitch's car side-swiped one tree and slammed head first into a second. No window glass in Mitch's car was left intact. If the bullets hadn't shattered them, the impact with the trees did.

The officers quickly reinserted fresh magazines as they gingerly approached the mangled car. All guns were aimed at Mitchell. An unrecognizable bloody mass resembling a head was tilted back against the headrest. A bloody arm dangled outside of the car still holding a gun. The lead Detective snatched Mitchell's gun and tossed it aside. No sound or movement from the body in the car.

"Call for an ambulance, and get some more officers out here," ordered the lead detective.

◻ ◻ ◻

Several neighbors were peeking out of windows and doors; some had gathered a few houses away. None had ever experienced a dramatic police take-down first-hand. All were curious about the gun fire racket and crashing car that shattered the serenity of their quiet, peaceful neighborhood.

EMS arrived and confirmed Harrington's demise. Guns were holstered, and the officers shifted into crime scene control mode. Other officers secured the scene and threw a blanket over Mitchell's car to prevent gawkers from seeing the gruesome sight of a bloody dead man. Chief Walsh arrived fifteen minutes after being notified of the failed arrest and took control. Standard procedure was followed exactly; there would be a review of the incident to ensure that the officers acted appropriately under the circumstances. The officers' weapons would be locked up for later examination. Forensics was collected, including bullets not lodged in Harrington. Pictures of everything and everyone involved were taken. At least 20 bullets penetrated the metal car doors and slammed into Harrington. All seven officers would be placed on temporary desk duty until the review was completed. Formal statements would be taken and transcribed within 24 hours; standard procedure after an officer-involved shooting.

A week later, the officers were cleared to return to normal duties and their weapons returned to them. The final report, a 15-page official document, detailed the events as described by the initial seven officers. It concluded, "All seven Savannah police department officers acted professionally within the guidelines established by this office."

The only negative in the report—if it was a negative—was a statement made by the officer nearly killed by Harrington when the officer was asked "Why did you shoot Mr. Harrington 11 times?" His quick response was, "I ran out of bullets," but immediately changed his answer to, "My semi-automatic pistol fired the entire magazine in about two seconds when I squeezed the trigger. I wasn't counting the shots. I was responding to an eminently dangerous situation with deadly force to defend myself and those around me." Both statements were included for completeness. The relatively short report included extensive references to photos and other forensics which were attached, making the final report file quite bulky. The actual Review Board Report was over an inch thick. It would be filed away never to be read again, which further buried the unanswered questions about why Harrington wasn't immediately frisked, and the actual firing rate of the semi-automatic weapons used to kill him. In reality, no one cared.

The Savannah police officers received commendations from the St. Petersburg police department for **_going above and beyond the call of duty_**.

The Chief's ex-wife wouldn't even discuss Mitchell Harrington's dark side for almost a week after he was killed. She even forbade her daughter from speaking to her father, and loudly blamed the Chief for Mitchell's death—and ruining her life again. After five days of ranting and raving, wild hysteria, and growing signs of a mental breakdown, the ex-wife's brother couldn't ignore the obvious any longer. He approached the Chief, and after explaining the dire situation, obtained copies of photos, the Indictment, and other damning paperwork. Armed with newspaper accounts from the Savannah newspapers and the materials the Chief gave him, the brother barged in on his sister, physically restrained her, and made her listen to him, and look at the evidence against Mitchell.

The ex-wife just wailed uncontrollably for hours as her brother hammered away. Finally, the ex-wife agreed to counseling and would take her daughter along. It would take over six months for the ex-wife and the daughter to stop blaming the Chief for Mitchell's death, but that was as far as the ex-wife was willing to go. The daughter made better progress, and agreed to start speaking with her father and go on unsupervised visits with him. During the second visit, the daughter admitted that she and her girlfriend took naked pictures of each other—just for fun. She never posed for Mitchell or anyone else, and was devastated when she found out after Mitchell's death that some of those pictures wound up on Mitch's website. The Chief comforted his daughter and speculated that Mitchell had probably stolen the pictures from her home computer.

The Chief and his daughter were slowly, but steadily rebuilding their relationship, and the Chief's daughter was getting comfortable with the therapist Lacey had recommended.

Chapter Thirty-One

Tuesday, First week in November
Bradenton Police Station
Manatee County, FL

Armed with forensics that actually had a name attached, the fingerprints taken from Stanley Robbins when he was arrested and Mitchell Harrington by the Medical Examiner's office in Savannah, detectives Paige McDermott and Keith Cooper were busy re-examining their two earlier cold teenage girl death cases. One had been cold for almost four years. They retrieved the old forensics, fingerprints, and some trace DNA. No matches then, but now Harrington's prints were a positive match, and his DNA profile was a preliminary match. Full DNA results would take up to another three weeks. New reports were generated, and other cases were examined to see if there might be some connection to Robbins or Harrington. The process would take weeks to complete even with the two additional officers assigned to help them. The renewed scrutiny would uncover another cold case where a teen didn't die, but she had told her father that she was molested by a man she didn't know. Forensics from that three year old case now pointed to Stanley Robbins. At the time of the incident, the police investigating the case had no way to implicate Robbins. Now they do.

The two girls had been identified, and the tedious task of tracking down their relatives had begun. It would take three weeks to find one of the dead girl's family in Alabama, and another two weeks to find relatives of the other identified dead girl in the Dallas, TX area. Neither family asked to have the girl's casket returned. Maybe it was the $1,500 charge for the exhumation and transport. Maybe not. Quite sad either way. Two cases finally closed.

The third girl was alive a few years ago. Neither she nor her family could be found after three months of serious searching, but her case might be prosecuted anyway. The perpetrator had been identified, but the victim could not be found. The prosecutor was looking into adding this case to the others where Stanley Robbins was the defendant if enough solid forensic evidence could be accumulated.

On Wednesday, the Manatee County detectives were planning to attend a briefing hurriedly called by Luke to clean up some loose ends, and to be recognized at a press conference called by the St. Petersburg Chief of Police and the Pinellas County prosecutors. Actually, the entire Task Force was invited and would be present.

Tuesday, First week in November
Tampa Police Station
Hillsborough County, FL

The same identifying forensic evidence from Robbins and Harrington was sent to the Tampa Police department. Detectives Beth Ferguson and Morgan Sparks were reexamining the three unsolved teenage death cases from the Tampa area. Two of those cases had enough forensics to implicate both Stanley Robbins and Mitchell Harrington. In the third case, the forensics actually cleared both Robbins and Harrington, dumping that case back into the abyss of Tampa Cold Cases. Two cases closed, and one again cold.

Two other rape cases were uncovered that implicated both Stanley Robbins and Mitchell Harrington. A third sexual assault case implicated Harrington, and a fourth had compelling, but not definitive forensics implicating Stanley Robbins. Additional officers were assigned to assist in these cases which included finding and notifying families. The Tampa police had better luck than the Manatee County officers. All these families lived in Florida, and were thankful that they could finally visit their child's grave and say their goodbyes. One family tearfully asked to have the casket of their daughter exhumed and reburied in a cemetery closer to their home.

<u>Tuesday, First week in November</u>
<u>St. Petersburg Police Station</u>
<u>Pinellas County, FL</u>

Luke and Lakesha had four cases where either Stanley Robbins or Mitchell Harrington—or both—were prime suspects based on the fingerprints and DNA collected from Robbins and Harrington. Plus, Luke had the lead in coordinating the investigation into where Harrington might have traveled. The authorities in each of those locations had to be notified, files had to be sent, and forensics provided so the unsuspecting police departments would have something to use as a comparison. Lakesha was assigned the lead in tracking down the families. One girl was still unidentified, but she was a victim of Robbins and Harrington. Robbins and Harrington were cleared in the rape and death of one of the identified girls, but Lakesha kept that case and tracked down her family in Alabama.

Lakesha budgeted some of her time to writing reports and attending press conferences with Luke and the other team members. By Wednesday Lakesha, on Luke's orders, was up to her elbows with contacting the police departments in three other states, providing information, and asuring everyone that she and Luke were doing everything they could to contact potential communities that may have been at risk from Harrington's forays outside of North Carolina and Georgia.

□ □ □

The Pinellas County prosecutors spent several days trying to determine if any Federal Laws were violated, which would drag the Federal Courts and US Prosecutors into the mix. It was unlikely that any one individual case rose to the level of a Federal crime. The key question then became whether or not the suspects crossed state lines in commission of a felony. While Mitchell Harrington did travel between states, these crimes were committed in Florida, and were within the sole jurisdiction of the Florida state authorities. The same was true for any crimes that may have been committed in other states. Those states would have jurisdiction over crimes committed within their state borders. No Federal jurisdiction for the sexual assaults, sexual battery, attempted murders, or the actual murders. Maybe the Feds could claim that Harrington crossed state lines with the intent of committing a crime. They were looking into that, but Harrington was dead. Who would they prosecute?

There was no evidence that Stanley Robbins was involved in any crimes committed by Mitchell Harrington in other states. The Feds were actively reviewing all the evidence hoping to find something they could charge Stanley Robbins with. Eventually they would give up on Stanley and leave him to the states for prosecution. Harrington was dead, so no criminal charges could be brought against him even though he was positively identified as the perpetrator.

Wednesday, First week in November
St. Petersburg Police Station
Pinellas County, FL
3:30 p.m.

Reporters from all the local TV Stations, the major Tampa Bay area newspapers, a few smaller weekly newspapers and monthly magazines, and three out-of-state news crews had gathered outside of the St. Petersburg police station for the scheduled press conference. The six detectives from Hillsborough, Manatee, and Pinellas County, plus Lacey and Lieutenant Nick Thompson, were standing behind the St. Petersburg Chief of Police on a portable stage set up in front of the station. The Pinellas County prosecutor and two assistant prosecutors were standing next to the Chief at the podium. Cameras and microphones were aimed in their direction. Reporters were waiting impatiently with tape recorders; some with old fashioned pens and pads of paper. An assortment of spectators swelled the assembled crowd to almost 100 people. This was an important event worthy of such public attention. At least the press release sent out by the Chief of Police's Media Coordinator said it was.

When all was ready the Chief stepped closer to the podium, looked behind him at the smiling Task Force, nodded curtly to someone in the front row, and then adjusted the microphone before he started speaking. The Chief identified himself, spelled his name for the record, and proceeded to identify everyone on the makeshift stage. He then launched into a broad overview of the events, the crimes, and suspected crimes over the last five years. He rambled on about the superb cooperation between the three police departments in the counties surrounding Tampa Bay, and the good police work by the Savannah police department. He identified Stanley Robbins as the only surviving suspect, and explained about how Stanley assumed the name of Trevor Kemp. Mitchell Harrington was identified with careful mention of his home state of Georgia, with frequent trips to the Tampa Bay area. It was as if the Chief felt it was important to tell everyone that a despicable child killer like Mitchell Harrington wasn't actually a Floridian. He just occasionally **came to Florida** to rape and murder young Florida girls. The Chief made a point of mentioning that Stanley Robbins had assumed an alternate identity, that Mitchell Harrington was also living a double life, and both had been doing so for many years.

The Chief wisely did not talk about the girls' shelters and simply said, "Most of the victimized girls were either runaways or lived on the streets."

After ten minutes or so the crowd was getting restless. All of what was being said by the Chief could have easily been obtained in a private interview, from written reports, or by reading already published articles. The Chief sensed the uneasiness and realized that he had milked this political stunt long enough. "I'd like to introduce Lieutenant Nick Thompson." The Chief motioned for Nick to step to the podium. "I'll let the Lieutenant get into more of the details."

This was a surprise to Nick, who looked around in a startled daze. After a moment's hesitation Loo stepped to the microphone. The Chief yielded his position while patting Nick on the back. Nick smiled, loosened his tie, and took in a huge breath trying to organize the details of the case flying around in his mottled brain. He was stalling for time to collect his thoughts. Finally, "My name is Lieutenant Nick Thompson. I'm in charge of the fine detectives," pointing to Luke and Lakesha, "that were so instrumental in first recognizing, then pursuing, and finally solving this case. They were assisted by our consultant, Dr. Lacey Hirsch," Loo motioned towards Lacey. Now, as ready as he would ever be, he dove into the details. Ten minutes later, he yielded the microphone to the lead prosecuting attorney, the only other person who cared about their political future and craved the limelight as much as the Chief of Police. In fact, he suggested the Chief call the press conference.

The prosecuting attorney proceeded to lay out the legal intricacies of related crimes committed in multiple counties. He explained the Florida Felony Murder law, where every defendant involved in the commission of a felony can be charged with, and convicted of, a murder committed entirely by someone else involved in that same, or ongoing felony. That meant that Stanley Robbins can be charged with, and convicted of the murders committed solely by Mitchell Harrington. Stanley, of course, would be charged with any crimes he, himself committed. Stanley could also be charged with, and convicted of conspiracy in the various rape and assault charges, because Stanley knew, or should have known, what Mitchell Harrington's intent really was when Stanley sought out the young girls at Harrington's insistence.

The prosecutor touched on such other legal issues, such as: will all the assault and murder cases be tried as one big case or individually? Which county will hold the first set of trials with Stanley Robbins as the sole living defendant? Which county would go next? Should the order be based on the number of cases in each county, the dates of the criminal acts, or something else, and other complex legal problems? His answer was, "My office will release more information about the legal process once every issue has been thoroughly researched and evaluated. The prosecutors in the counties affected will collaborate to resolve any conflicts. I assure the citizens of Pinellas County, and the entire state of Florida, that the prosecution of Stanley Robbins will fully comply with Florida State laws and all constitutional requirements," implying that they would be very careful to not let Stanley Robbins escape conviction because of some obscure legal technicality. They would seek the death penalty if Robbins was convicted and his mental condition allowed. At the very least, Stanley Robbins would never see freedom again. He will be sentenced, at a minimum to a life sentence for each dead girl to be served sequentially. Stanley would die in prison if he wasn't executed.

Fifteen minutes after he started, the prosecutor concluded his remarks by thanking the St. Petersburg police for a "job well done," and the assembled crowd for their indulgence. He then asked for questions. Several reporters raised their hands and asked questions that were mostly expansions on what had already been said. No real new information was provided by anyone that answered the dozen or so questions.

By 4:30 p.m. the crowd was dispersing. The law enforcement and legal professionals started returning to their respective jobs after handshakes and back slaps as everyone congratulated each other.

Luke hadn't seen Lacey since early Monday morning, except briefly this afternoon at the police station, and apologized profusely over the phone late on Wednesday night, "I've been slammed with my day job and I'm behind in my school work." He went on to lament about missing classes and not finishing school assignments. Lieutenant Thompson had to call his professor and plead on Luke's behalf for more time to submit a required research paper. The professor understood the unusual circumstances and gave Luke until Thursday, tomorrow, to turn it in. Unfortunately Thursday was also the scheduled date for the midterm exam. Luke was so stressed he was on the verge of pulling his hair out.

Lacey was sympathetic, "Don't worry about it Luke. We'll go out over the weekend. Just concentrate on your studies, finish your papers, and do well on the midterm. Keep your eye on the prize—graduation in six months."

"You're right," Luke let out a sigh, "But, I do want to spend some private time with you."

"I want to see and be with you too, Luke."

After a few seconds of hesitation, "My mom called to tell me she's going to Friday night services at the Temple, and wants me to go with her. How about joining us? We can spend the rest of the evening together after services are over." Luke was very upbeat now.

Lacey quickly answered, "I haven't been to services since the High Holidays last September. I'd like to go with you both. I'll come by your condo on Friday evening and we'll go to services from there. We can even pick up your mom on the way. After we take her back home we can spend as much time together as we want." Lacey was hoping for a long leisurely weekend at Luke's condo, and said so.

Luke had other thoughts. "I was hoping we could spend time together at your condo. Your place is much nicer than mine, Lacey."

Lacey thought to herself, "It doesn't matter which bed we use."

Silence for several long agonizing seconds, and then Luke had an idea, "Why don't we make this easy on both of us?"

"I'm all for that. What do you have in mind?"

"When you come to my condo dressed for services, bring some extra clothes and an overnight bag that you can leave here."

Lacey was giddy, "A pajama party after services? That sounds like fun."

"Hopefully the most fun you and I have had together so far. And, at some time over the weekend, I'll bring a few things to your condo. That's only fair, don't you think?"

Lacey laughed and Luke joined in. Luke finally said, "It's getting late and I've got to finish my paper and start cramming for the exam tomorrow night."

"Sure, Luke. Get back to work. I'll see you on Friday at your condo—with my suitcase."

"I'll be waiting with bells on." Luke paused and then said, "By the way, Lacey, I guess I was out of it for round one, and we didn't have much time for round two. Maybe we'll have more time for round three, if you're up for it."

"I'm more than up for it, Luke. And, then round four. Round five. Round…," Lacey giggled and then said, "Good luck on your exam. I'll see you on Friday. Good night, Luke."

Author Notes

The characters and events in *Secrets of the Bridges* are fictional; totally a product of my imagination. Any resemblance to actual people, living or dead, is purely coincidental. Of course, the Tampa Bay area in Florida is real, as are descriptions of some of the locations, roadways, and landmarks. All of the names of businesses, hospitals, or law enforcement organizations are made up.

Three bridges and one causeway connect Pinellas County to either Hillsborough or Manatee County. The Howard Frankland (often incorrectly referred to as the Howard Franklin Bridge), the Gandy, and the Courtney Campbell Causeway all run east and west between Hillsborough County and Pinellas County. The Sunshine Skyway runs north and south between Pinellas County and Manatee County. All four roadways are over five miles long and carry thousands of locals, travelers, and vacationers back and forth between the three counties every day.

I honor, and have the greatest respect for all the law enforcement agencies and departments, as well as the dedicated individuals who work in law enforcement in the Tampa Bay area, and everywhere else in the United States. In no way should *Secrets of the Bridges* be thought of as an indictment of what they do, or don't do. The story required the depiction of events that, to some, may look upon the Tampa Bay law enforcement agencies as "being inadequate". That is not my intent! *Secrets of the Bridges* is a story about how dedicated police officers can bring about justice, even when the odds are stacked against them, and huge obstacles block their progress. To me, the men and women in law enforcement are all heroes.

The problem of pedophiles living in our communities is a difficult one to solve. Some professionals feel that pedophiles can somehow be rehabilitated, and deserve to be reintroduced into society (with appropriate monitoring by local authorities) after serving their prison sentences. Other professionals disagree. It is true that many pedophiles don't return to old habits, but many do. The reason for both behaviors is not well understood by professionals. This debate will rage on for years to come. I have no illusions about **Secrets of the Bridges** resolving anything. It was never intended to do so. **Secrets of the Bridges** is only a made-up story for my readers' enjoyment. If a meaningful debate ensues, that's a welcomed added benefit.

Would you like to see your manuscript become a book?

If you are interested in becoming a PublishAmerica author, please submit your manuscript for possible publication to us at:

acquisitions@publishamerica.com

You may also mail in your manuscript to:

**PublishAmerica
PO Box 151
Frederick, MD 21705**

www.publishamerica.com

CPSIA information can be obtained at www.ICGtesting.com
Printed in the USA
LVOW090136280911

248128LV00002B/6/P